CRUST NO ONE

WINNIE ARCHER

WHEELER PUBLISHING
A part of Gale, a Cengage Company

Farmington Hills, Mich • San Francisco • New York • Waterville, Maine
Meriden, Conn • Mason, Ohio • Chicago

GALE
A Cengage Company

**LIBRARY OF CONGRESS CIP DATA ON FILE.
CATALOGUING IN PUBLICATION FOR THIS BOOK
IS AVAILABLE FROM THE LIBRARY OF CONGRESS**

ISBN-13: 978-1-4328-5278-8 (softcover)

Published in 2018 by arrangement with Kensington Books, an imprint of Kensington Publishing Corp.

Printed in Mexico
1 2 3 4 5 6 7 22 21 20 19 18

Dedicated to my two grandmothers,
Winnie Conrath Bourbon
and LaVerne Massie Sears,
who continue to fill my heart with
love and inspiration.

And to Elizabeth Petty, my
great-great-grandmother and
Bertha Archer Massie;
you continue to live on.

CHAPTER 1

My favorite places in my hometown of Santa Sofia were located in three different areas. The first was the charming Tudor house I'd recently purchased. The moment I'd stepped foot into the foyer, it had felt like home. I still had to pinch myself. I owned it! I'd moved to Austin for college, had gotten married, started a photography business, and then ended up divorced. The very unexpected loss of my mother had brought me back home. I felt as if I'd been wrung out, but my quaint, coastal central California town had breathed new life into my body. Into my soul.

The second was my parents' house. Pacific Grove Street would always be home to me. My brother Billy was two years younger than me. Growing up, we'd alternated between being best friends and staunch enemies, depending on the day and our moods. Now we were adults, Billy was serious with my best friend (and the deputy sheriff) Emmaline Davis, and we leaned on each other for support. Luckily, we had both finally started to heal and were moving on with our lives, helping our dad do the same.

I still couldn't believe it, but the place where I felt most at home was Yeast of Eden. I hadn't grown up as a foodie or baker, although I was perfectly capable of adding eggs, oil, and water into a box mix of some sweet treat, ending up with something tasty. I'd come to realize that it wasn't so much the bread shop itself that I connected to; it was Olaya Solis. She was the owner, had taken me in when I didn't even know I needed to be taken in, and had become like an aunt. While I worked to build up my photography business, I helped out at the bread shop, both with baking and at the front counter. Every day, I met new and interesting people. The locals of our little beach town were eclectic and some were downright fascinating. The tourists came from all over. There was never a dull day in Santa Sofia.

At the moment, I stood behind the counter, boxing up a dozen chocolate croissants. The rich, flakey dough of the pastries scattered as I placed them into the white square box. A mother, her two towheaded children hugged up next to her, was next in line. She ordered three baguettes and three scones, one lemon and the others cinnamon chip. One of the kids looked through the cases, her eyes wide. I could almost read her mind: So many treats to choose from! Should she ask for something else?

"Oh!" she explained, pointing to the back corner of the glass-fronted case. "Mama, look!"

The girl's mother looked down to her, one finger to her lips. She had her wallet in her hand, a twenty-dollar bill at the ready.

"But Mama, look! A skeleton!"

The girl's little sister pressed her tiny hands against the glass, her nose pressed up against it. "Where?" she said. "Where is the skeleton?"

I grinned, looking down into the case and spotting the target of their attention. I leaned over the glass to talk to the girls. "It's called a sugar skull."

Olaya loved seeing the sweet smiles of the kids who came into Yeast of Eden. The sugar-skull cookies were like Easter eggs — hidden treasures tucked away where children could find them and exclaim with excitement. She made a single batch every other day, taking the time to decorate them like the traditional Day of the Dead skulls.

She had it down to a science, able to complete the decorating of twelve cookies in about twenty minutes. She hid them in the displays of bread, tucked between scones, or anywhere else she could think of. When a bright-eyed child discovered one, he or she was treated to the cookie. I was convinced that Olaya had as much fun watching the surprised and elated expressions on the children's faces when they discovered a cookie as much as the kids who actually found them.

I reached for the pop-up box dispenser and pulled out a square of the dry wax tissue paper we used to take items from the cases, using it to retrieve the sugar-skull cookie the little girl had spotted. Once again, I leaned over the top of the glass. "Good job spotting it!" I said, handing it to her. "Maybe you'll share it with your sister?"

She looked to her mother for affirmation that she could take the cookie from me. "Can I?" she asked.

Her mother smiled and nodded. "What do you say?" she prompted.

The blond-headed girl looked up, gave me a toothless grin, and said, "Tank you." The gap in her teeth made the *th* come out as *t*.

I couldn't help but smile in delight. I could see why Olaya took the time to make the cookies. It was worth every extra minute it took to make a child happy. "You're very welcome, sweetie," I said.

She took the cookie, her chubby hands clutching it like a treasured prize and tried to break it in half. Her mom helped her and the little girl offered one half to her younger sister. They each took a bite, the crumbs falling onto their matching red jackets.

As I finished bagging the scones and collecting payment, laughter erupted from one of the bistro tables by the window. Four women were seated around the table, each donning fun hats adorned with flowers, ribbon, and a small bird. Once I'd realized they were blackbirds, I couldn't help but smile.

The Blackbird Ladies. They'd been called that since the dawn of time. Or at least since I'd seen them gathering for an every-other-day croissant at Yeast of Eden and had given them the moniker. They wore hats adorned with silk daisies, carnations, and roses.

Without thinking, I dubbed them the Blackbird Ladies. It was perfect. I'd tried it out in my head and then said it aloud, rolling the syllables around in my mouth. It described them to a T. Not only because of the little birds perched on each of their hats, but because the women were each so unique. So original. So utterly precious.

My favorite octogenarian, Penny Branford, was one of the four. Once everyone was served, I rounded the counter and approached the table. "What's with the hats?" I asked her as the other three women sipped their percolated coffees and nibbled on their breads.

She patted the wide rim of the one resting on her head. "Do you like it?"

My lips curled up into an amused smile. "I love it."

"Ivy, these three are my oldest friends in the world," Mrs. Branford said. She nodded toward the woman next to her. "Janice and I went to elementary school together." Janice, quite proper and sitting with her back stick-straight, dipped her head slightly in greeting. "Ivy? Quite an unusual name, isn't it?"

I shrugged, but my grin grew. "My mother liked plants."

Mrs. Branford swept her arm toward the next woman. "I taught school with Alice," she said, "and Mabel . . . ah, Mabel. She was the shoulder I cried on once upon a time."

I loved a lot of things about Penelope Branford, but what I adored most about her was her honesty. I knew that if I had my skirt tucked up in my underwear, she'd yank it free. If I asked her if I had spinach in my teeth, she'd hand me a toothpick and hold up a mirror for me. And if she had something to tell me, she wouldn't hold back. Plus, she was detail oriented. It was her years as a teacher, I think. She was a dot-every-i-and-cross-every-t sort of person.

She was *my* kind of person.

Which meant these women probably were my kind of people, too.

"I can't imagine you needing a shoulder to cry on," I said, curiosity getting the better of me. I didn't want to dredge up old memories, but we'd already gone there once, and she'd opened the door again.

She shrugged, almost nonchalantly, but I saw a flash of emotion in her eyes. "Almost losing your soul mate can bring a torrent of tears," she said.

I swallowed hard. I knew about the almost-affair her deceased husband had nearly succumbed to . . . with my other favorite woman in the world, Olaya Solis. Olaya had been the almost-mistress and the two women had been at odds ever since.

At least until I stepped in and somehow helped them begin to mend their fences. Because, as I'd predicted, they were basically the same person.

To the point where they'd loved the

same man.

The Blackbird Ladies. They were here now, sitting at the little bistro table by the window. They'd sashayed into the bread shop in their orthopedic sneakers, velour sweat suits, and embellished hats.

"We've heard quite a bit about you, Ivy," the woman named Mabel said. "Photographer, baker, part-time Nancy Drew."

I laughed. "I'll cop to the photography and the sleuthing. That just kind of happened. But the baking? I'm a complete novice."

Olaya Solis swept into the dining area of the bread shop, the skirt of her caftan dusting the floor. She brushed her short, iron-gray hair back from her forehead. Even with a rogue curl falling over her forehead, she was statuesque, looking a bit like an Aztec queen, but, oddly, she was incredibly warm and approachable at the same time. A genuine smile spread on her face. "Hardly a novice." She cocked her head slightly as she looked at me. "Do not sell yourself short, *mi'ja.*" To the other women, she said, "Beinvenidos, mis amigas. Everything is delicious?"

Mrs. Branford nodded, a flash of a twinkle in her eyes. "My dear Olaya, so good to see you."

Olaya shook her head in a barely perceptible way and scoffed. "You say that as if you are not here every day of the week, Penelope."

"Stop baking and we'll stop coming," she said.

"That, of course, will not happen. Now, do you need anything? A croissant? Cinnamon raisin bread?"

Janice, the most refined of the group, slathered strawberry preserves on her sweet bread. "My blueberry muffins can't compete, you know," she said with a wink at Olaya. "I tried. For years, we got together at my house, but when you and Penelope buried the hatchet — so to speak — that, as they say, was that. Who can pass up the best baked bread in Santa Sofia?"

"Certainly not me." Mabel Peabody, the most flamboyant of the four women, took a bite of her chocolate croissant. "I've gained close to eight pounds since we started meeting here. Eight well-earned, much enjoyed pounds."

The petite Alice Ryder looked Mabel up and down, and then raised her neatly shaped eyebrows. "With that tunic and — what are those? Culottes? A skirt?"

Mabel's forehead scrunched. "Wide-legged pants," she answered.

"Well, with those wide-legged pants and that tunic, you have room to add a few more," she said.

I thought for a moment that Mabel hadn't heard the hint of snark in Alice's tone, but then she leveled a look at Alice, smiled, and said, "Why do you think I wear them?"

Alice met her gaze. I waited, wondering what would happen next. For dear friends, the sparring was a little unexpected. But then Alice smiled back.

Mrs. Branford fluttered her hand in front of her. "It's impossible to compete with Olaya," she said. They all agreed and then their conversation shifted from bread and muffins to the television show of the day, to decorating. "Michael and I are having a gazebo built in the backyard," Alice said. She looked pointedly at Mabel. "Once it's done, we can start meeting there — with plenty of Olaya's breads, of course, so wear your expandable waistband pants."

Mabel scoffed. "You better believe I will."

"Well, of course," Janice said, pulling a few flakes and a soft tuft from her croissant and delicately placing them in her mouth. "No backyard could possibly be perfect without Olaya's breads. No offense, Alice, but baking has never been your strength."

I watched the dynamics of the women

with fascination. They were sparring, flinging their verbal jabs as if they'd been choreographed and they were each playing their roles expertly. Alice turned toward Janice, paused dramatically, and then cracked a smile. "None taken. I never claimed to be a baker." She fluttered her hand, gesturing to herself. "If I were, I'd outgain Mabel."

Mabel held out a plate, half of a scone and a good spattering of crumbs on it. "It's never too late to start."

Mrs. Branford tapped her cane on the floor and the women all turned to look at her. She took the scone from Mabel's plate. "Now, now. We can't waste a perfectly wonderful scone on Alice, can we? She'd never appreciate it the way we do."

And then she took a healthy bite.

Mabel, Janice, and Alice all looked at Mrs. Branford for a long beat, looked at each other, and burst out laughing.

"You are so right," Alice said, her smile reaching all the way to her eyes.

"Is Michael building it?" Mrs. Branford asked and then took a bite of her own butter-slathered bread.

Alice cocked her head. "What?"

But Mrs. Branford's cheeks were puffed with her bread and she couldn't answer.

17

Janice answered for her. "Your gazebo."

"Michael?" Alice blurted. "Ha! He can barely build a fire."

"Good thing we don't need to build many fires in Santa Sofia," Mabel said, dramatically dabbing a paper napkin against her lips. The women all nodded in agreement.

Alice turned to Janice. "Your handyman did a good job on Richie's patio cover, right?"

"Oh. You mean Collin?" Janice's face clouded for a moment, but then it cleared again. "He did, yes. A great job, in fact, but —"

"No, don't tell me he's too busy. There are a few things that can ruin a marriage. Moving, remodeling, infidelity, deceit — and in our case, Michael trying to build something," Alice said with a laugh, but I got the distinct feeling she wasn't really joking. "Your handyman might just save ours."

But Janice shook her head. "Another handyman might have to do that. He moved to the East Coast. I saw him off myself. I've missed him. He was quite good at building things."

"That's too bad," Alice said, her disappointment evident.

Janice patted the air with her palms facedown. "Settle down, Alice. I can get some names for you. I bet another one of Richie's tenants could probably do it."

The conversation was interrupted when the door to Yeast of Eden opened, the bell chimed, and a man, probably in his late sixties, ambled in. He walked slowly and with a slight limp, but he had a good build and he held his head high. The one thing that made me do a double take was his handlebar mustache. It was big and bold and . . . well, you just didn't see a mustache like that everyday. He looked weathered and haggard, but every one of the Blackbird Ladies instantly perked up, preening in their hats.

Once again, I looked on in fascination as they fawned over him. Mabel was the first to speak, tucking a strand of her vibrant red hair behind her ear. "Why, if it isn't Mustache Hank. You are a sight for sore eyes."

I raised my eyebrows at Olaya. "Mustache Hank?" I whispered.

She nodded. "He is our local produce man. That is what people have called him for as long as I have been here."

Which was a long time. Olaya hadn't been born and raised in Santa Sofia, but it was most definitely her home and had been for decades.

It wasn't hard to know why the man in front of us was called Mustache Hank. That salt-and-pepper thing attached to his upper lip looked like it belonged on Hercule Poirot, not the local purveyor of veggies and fruits. "The Blackbird Ladies certainly seem to like him."

This time Olaya lifted her eyebrows at me. "Blackbird Ladies?"

I pressed my fingers to my lips, hiding my smile. "It fits, don't you think?"

She let her eyes settle on each one of the four women before turning back to me. "Yes, I do think it does."

"How's that bum ankle of yours, Hank?" Janice asked.

"I can tell you when it's going to rain," he said lightly, but the grimace gave away the apparent pain he was in, one side of his mustache lifting oddly. He looked away and I thought he must be uncomfortable being the center of attention.

Mabel stood up from her seat and rested her wrinkled hand on Hank's forearm. "Here, Hank. Do you want to sit?"

Mrs. Branford used the rubber end of her cane to push the chair closer to him. "Take a load off," she said. She preened less than her three friends, but I still detected a glimmer of something mildly flirtatious. *Take a load off?* That was so *not* Penelope Branford.

20

And yet she'd said it, so maybe I was seeing a new side of her. As I watched the four women tumble over their words around Mustache Hank, I smiled to myself. Getting older — or just plain old — didn't mean your emotions shriveled up and died. These women definitely had libidos and poor Mustache Hank was the nucleus of their attention.

"You look pretty down in the dumps," Mabel said to Hank, concern on her face.

He shrugged and nodded his head. "Lost a friend."

The five women, including Olaya, frowned in sympathy. "That's never easy, is it?" said Janice. "Funeral?"

He shook his head. "No, no funeral," he said, but he didn't offer any more than that.

Olaya slipped behind the counter, returning thirty seconds later with a flakey chocolate croissant on a white ceramic plate. She set it on the table in front of Mustache Hank and laid her hand on his shoulder. "*Por usted,* Hank."

He nodded and smiled, but sadness emanated from him. I cataloged the things I observed about him. The mustache, of course. It hid a good part of his face, but defined him. A simple gold band on his ring finger. A trail of lines that showed the trials of his life.

He took a bite of his pastry and smiled. It lightened his face and softened the sadness in him. Olaya's baked goods had a tendency to help people deal with their woes. Whether she put in a dash of lavender, a sprinkle of anise, or a hint of lemon, her breads seemed to help the people who ate it.

"Thanks, Olaya."

Such a gentleman. I wondered what his story was. I left the Blackbird Ladies to their fawning and went behind the counter to help the other customers who'd come in and lined up. Olaya worked the register while I filled the orders. The Blackbird Ladies and Mustache Hank sat at their table, the women doing most of the talking. At one point, Alice actually stood behind Hank, leaned down, and whispered into his ear. I couldn't see his face, but he bowed his head slightly and I wondered if he'd smiled, or maybe even blushed.

I didn't have time to think about it anymore, however, because the bread shop buzzed with activity and I got wrapped up in the selling of bread. A half an hour later, Mrs. Branford sidled up to the counter and knocked on the glass. "I'll see you later, Ivy?"

"I'll stop by." I'd moved to my Tudor

house on Maple Street a few months back and now I lived just half a block from Mrs. Branford. The street was a hotbed of historic-committee conflict, but I loved it there. At thirty-six, I was finally a home-owner, but at the same time I was close to my father and brother and missed being in my family home.

"Stop by Baptista's first," she said.

I stopped myself from rolling my eyes at her. She was being Little Miss Matchmaker, and she wasn't subtle at all. Sure, Miguel Baptista and I still had chemistry. We'd spent half of high school together, after all. But then he'd up and left with hardly a backward glance, I'd gone to college in Texas, and we'd both moved on. I still didn't know what had happened that he'd left me so suddenly, and part of me would always care about him, but I also thought that maybe our time in the sun had passed. I put my hands on my hips. "And why would I do that, Mrs. Branford?"

She waggled her eyebrows suggestively. "He came by a bit ago. Said he has a *question* for you."

I couldn't imagine what kind of question Miguel might need to ask me. He and I were trying to be friendly since I'd been back — trying to let bygones be bygones —

but we hadn't gone out of our way to seek each other out. I usually saw him when my best friend and I headed to Baptista's for Mexican seafood, which had been about once a week lately. Baptista's was the best in town and I couldn't pass up *queso*. I couldn't help but wonder what kind of question Miguel might have for me. My curiosity was definitely piqued. "Maybe he wants to marry me," I said with a wink. Which, of course, was utterly ridiculous. I'd gone through the stages of grief after he'd left me — and town — so abruptly. I was in denial, and then unabashedly hurt. Finally the anger set in. I'd planned to spend my life with him, and suddenly he was gone. I thought I was long over it, accepting the change in my life plan long ago, but a pang of anger surfaced unexpectedly.

But Mrs. Branford didn't take it as the joke I'd intended. She nodded sagely and replied, "Oh, my dear, of that I have no doubt. It's just a matter of time."

I notched an eyebrow up. She was so wrong about that. But I let it go. She had nearly as much energy as me, but by anyone's standard, she was elderly. I'd seen her be forgetful; it stood to reason that she was also, at times, delusional. Of course, I really didn't believe that. She was of sound body and mind, but Miguel and I would never be together.

Like I said, bygones.

One by one, Olaya and I worked our way through the small crowd until everyone had been taken care of. The bread shop cleared out. The Blackbird Ladies had gone. There was no bell on the door to the bread shop, so I hadn't noticed them leave. Mustache Hank was gone, too. I hadn't gotten the feeling he had been keen on the company, but then again, what man didn't love the attention of a bevy of fawning women? In passing, I wondered what magic Olaya had baked into the bread she'd given Hank and if it would lift his spirits. I didn't know him, but I hoped so.

I spent the next half an hour restocking the display cases with fresh pastries and breads for the rest of the afternoon, cleaning the counters, and tidying the brochures, business cards, and general register area. The bread shop had become a second home for me, the place where I felt welcome, as if I'd been enveloped in an aromatic cocoon of yeasty baking bread.

As I looked around to see what else I could do, Olaya took the soft rag from my hand. "Go on," she said. "I will finish."

"I have yard work to do," I said, ignoring

the little grin playing on her lips. I grimaced, realizing that she'd heard Mrs. Branford telling me that Miguel had wanted to talk to me. "Flowers to plant. Weeds to pull."

"Ivy," she said, with a little lilt at the end of my name.

Before I could reply, the shop's phone rang. Olaya picked it up with a snappy, "Yeast of Eden!" The bell on the door tinkled and a customer came in as she listened for a moment. "*Por supuesto,* she is right here beside me," she said and handed the phone to me, a little sparkle in her eyes.

I, on the other hand, narrowed mine. Nobody called me here, which probably meant . . .

I took the handset from her and stepped away from the counter. "Hello?" I said into the phone.

"Hey, Ivy."

Just as I suspected. Miguel's voice was low and gravelly. It used to have a way of washing over me like a warm blanket. I took a deep breath and could almost smell the salt of the ocean and the seafood of Baptista's, but I pushed the thoughts away.

"Hey."

There was an awkward pause. After so many years, we didn't know what to say to each other anymore. "Settling into your new

26

house?" he finally asked.

Reference to my 1930 Tudor brought a smile to my lips. It had taken a good month before I'd gotten used to the fact that I was actually living in my dream house. The tree-lined street made my heart happy. "I am, slowly. I love the Galileo thermometer, by the way."

Miguel had gotten the hand-blown glass cylinder with the colorful vessels bobbing up and down inside from the custom glass shop on the pier. He'd left it on my new front porch on the day I moved in; now it stood sentry in the entryway on a vintage sideboard I'd found at a local antiques store in town. I was shedding my past, bit by bit, and in the process, I was discovering more about who I was.

And who I was, was my mother's daughter. Same curly, ginger hair. Same emerald eyes. Same moral compass. Same fiery spirit and insatiable curiosity. And same dogged determination. I'd wanted nothing more than to resettle in Santa Sofia after being gone for so many years, and now I had. More than that, I'd found a place in my town where I really belonged.

"I guess I still know you," he said, but his tone was off. Strained, somehow.

I paused, thinking about how to respond

to that. The fact was, he didn't know me anymore. "I'm not so sure about that."

Now *he* paused, a thread of tension forming between us. "Ivy, I —"

But I cut him off, thinking it was best to change the subject. "Mrs. Branford said you wanted to talk to me?"

He was silent and for a few seconds I wondered if he'd hung up. But then he spoke again, a shift in his tone, and he sounded more upbeat. "That woman is everywhere, isn't she?"

"Well, she is a Blackbird Lady —"

"A what?"

I pushed a loose strand of hair behind my ear as I explained. "Mabel Peabody, Janice Thompson, Alice Ryder, and Penny Branford."

"They named themselves the Blackbird Ladies?"

"They didn't," I said, clarifying. "*I* did. They wear these hats. Kind of like the Red Hat Society?"

"You mean those women who wear purple clothes and the red hats everywhere?" He sounded a bit puzzled by the idea.

"Yes, Miguel. Those women. Those spunky, stylish, sassy over fifty women who wear purple and red. That'll be me someday."

There was a pause, and then he said, "I can see that." I could hear a hint of a smile coming back into his voice. "So why blackbirds?"

"All their hats happen to have blackbirds on them. By accident or by design, I'm not sure. I just thought the name fit for their collective group."

"The Blackbird Ladies," he said, as if he were seeing how it sounded. Trying it out.

"Yes, the Blackbird Ladies," I said.

The tension from a moment ago dissipated as he laughed, the sound deep and rich. Against my will, I went a little tingly. The chemistry was still there, but so was the memory of him leaving me. No goodbye. No regretful glance in his rearview mirror. Just the back of his head as I stared at him driving away. Even after what felt like a lifetime, those feelings reared their ugly head. It was hard to forget that heartache.

"How's your grandmother?" I asked, pushing those emotions away.

"She's exactly the same as —" He stopped and I knew he was remembering something about our past, just as I had. "— as whenever you saw her last. I don't think she ages. She actually knows Mabel Peabody." He cleared his throat. "Of the Blackbird Ladies," he added.

I conjured up an image of Miguel's grandmother. From my recollection, she stood about five feet, was soft and stocky, and had thinning hair. She hadn't spoken a word of English, which made me wonder how she and Mabel Peabody were friends. "Does Mabel speak Spanish?"

"Interestingly enough, she does. Better than me, in fact."

As far as I knew, Miguel spoke fluently, so I didn't understand how Mabel Peabody could be better. Before I could ask that question, he answered: "She used to teach Spanish at the high school. If I'm remembering right, she got her degree in Spanish and then lived in Spain for a few years."

I leaned against the back counter, folding one arm across my chest, my fingers clasping the crook of the other arm. "But it was your first language," I said, that memory of his history coming back to me.

"But once Laura and I were in school and learned English, that's all we wanted to speak."

"But not to your parents," I said.

"Right, but everywhere else. I was gone too long. I lost a lot of it. My vocabulary and proficiency are pretty limited."

I guess that made sense. Not speaking anything but English, it was hard to get my head around Miguel's Spanish fluency compared to Mabel Peabody. "Mrs. Branford said you had a question for me," I said, getting back to my octogenarian friend's comment.

He took a beat before he spoke, and I wondered if he even remembered what he'd wanted to ask me. Or maybe he'd changed his mind. "I do have a question," he said, and then he launched into it. "I saw the brochure you did for Yeast of Eden. I'd like to hire you to take some pictures of Baptista's. For a new menu. And the website. I'm having it revamped. And maybe for some promotional material. I'm thinking about doing some direct-mail advertising."

I don't know what I'd been expecting, but it certainly hadn't been about a photography job. And I wasn't sure how I felt. Relieved? Disappointed? Maybe both. I exhaled, not realizing that I'd been holding my breath. "Oh. Yeah. Yes, of course," I said. "What kind of pictures are you wanting? Food? The building?"

"I'm not really sure, Ivy. I have some ideas, but —"

"I guess I could come by the restaurant —"

"No, don't do that!"

I felt my jaw drop. "What — ?"

31

"Not you, Ivy. God, sorry. There's a server here putting his fingers inside the clean glasses — Stop!" His voice was stern, but not cruel. "Blake, like this. No fingers where the beverage goes."

"Maybe we should talk lat—"

"No, sorry. Yes, yes, come over. Let's talk in person. I'll show you what I have in mind."

He was still distracted, but he was trying to focus on our phone call. "Sure," I said. "I'll stop by later."

"Anytime. I'm always here," he said, but then he covered the mouthpiece and said something, presumably to Blake again. He seemed to remember that I was on the line. "Okay?"

"Okay," I said, but after I hung up the phone, I regretted the promise, thinking it a bad idea — a very bad idea — to go and see Miguel Baptista.

CHAPTER 2

I put it off, and *later* turned out to be two days. I got wrapped up with Yeast of Eden and the upcoming Winter Wonderland Festival, and with some work my dad needed help with at the house. But the majority of my time had been spent helping my brother move in with the love of his life. Em and I had been friends for more than twenty years, and we'd known each other for longer than that. Our mothers had done playgroup together, but even back when both of us were knee-high to a grasshopper, Emmaline was tough. She played by the book, but all that meant was she'd become a master manipulator at an early age. I had never been able to hold onto a single pack of gum or candy bar — or Barbie doll, for that matter — until I was ten years old. I had been on the receiving end of her manipulation through elementary school, finally getting wise and turning the tables on her in junior high. I'd learned what to say, and when to say hold back.

We'd developed a mutual respect of each other, and from the age of twelve, we'd been inseparable. Things had changed since we'd grown up and gotten lives outside the school grounds, but we were more like sisters than friends, and now, with her and Billy finally together, it looked like we might be sisters for real.

Helping Em and Billy move in together was the best reason to have put other things on hold. Truth be told, I had also dallied a bit on purpose. I wasn't the type of woman to jump just because a man said *jump,* especially if that man was Miguel. I refused to do anything unless it was on my terms. And *my terms* meant I would stop by Baptista's when I had time.

My mother left an indelible mark on me, as all mothers do on their children. I grew up loving walks on the beach, collecting seashells, and reading mystery novels (Agatha, my sweet fawn pug, was named after the grande dame of mystery, after all). She also gave me my love of photography by gifting me with my first camera and sending me out for the afternoon. I took pictures of everything I saw. That was that. My fate was sealed, for better or for worse.

The one thing she did not impart on me was her cooking ability. She had had finesse in the kitchen, and she worked to the very end to get better and widen her skills, but I'd always been too busy to spend much time baking and creating stews and casseroles and things in Dutch ovens. That all changed after she died. The kitchen was the very place I found the most solace. I hadn't known it would be like that, but Olaya Solis, before I'd ever formally met her, had me all figured out. She'd become a surrogate mother to me, but no one could replace the real thing. I saw my mother everywhere and in everything. Most of all, at the ocean.

Now, as I parked my mom's car — my car — in the Baptista's parking lot, it was the beach that called to me. I slung my camera bag over my shoulder and started toward the restaurant, but abruptly stopped and redirected my footsteps toward the pier and the wooden steps that led down to the sand. The day was cool, a brisk breeze blowing in from the water.

A few people strolled along the shoreline, walking their dogs or playing with children in the surf. I did none of those things. My feet seemed to direct themselves; I ended up at a cluster of rocks and perched on the edge of the flat bolder that sat in front of the formation. I tilted my head back against the cool breeze and let my eyes flutter closed. This spot on the beach had been one of my mom's favorite places in Santa Sofia. Maybe in the world. At this moment, it almost felt as if she were here with me.

A mist of water kissed my cheeks and a shiver passed through me. The breeze seemed to call my name. I smiled to myself. Maybe she actually was. I grabbed my camera from my bag, walked along the shoreline, and took a few shots of the pier to capture the moment: the rocks off in the distance, the breaking waves, the seaweed strewn on the water-packed sand.

"Ivy!"

The light wind carried my name across the surf.

"Ivy!"

I turned toward the restaurant. It wasn't the wind calling my name. It was Miguel. He stood on the pier and waved.

I took a deep breath before turning my back on the ocean, letting the loss of my mother fade to a warm memory. I trudged up the beach toward the pier.

Miguel watched me, leaning in to give me a kiss on my cheek when I finally reached him. A shiver of — something — went down my spine. Which is not what I wanted to

36

feel. I wasn't in high school anymore, after all, but Miguel still seemed able to coax a schoolgirl quiver out of me.

I swallowed as I backed away, creating space between us. "Sorry it took me so long. The Winter Wonderland Festival. It takes a lot of planning."

He brushed away the apology. "Oh, yeah, I know. We have a booth. Soup. Tamales. Chips and salsa." He winked. "And *queso.*"

I couldn't help my smile, but deep down there was an ache in the pit of my stomach. I tried not to care, but I couldn't help myself. I wanted to ask him why he'd left all those years ago. I wanted to know. Or did I? Did I really need to dredge up our history? Maybe he simply hadn't loved me enough and couldn't see a life with me. If that was the case, did I really need to know that? Better to leave well enough alone. "So, you have some ideas for the brochure?" I said, getting down to business.

"I do," he said. His green eyes, set against his olive skin, suddenly seemed . . . I don't know — detached. I couldn't read his expression. It was as if the effort of being jovial had taken its toll and now he was done. He gestured with his arm, sweeping it in a circle toward the ocean. "I want a new menu. And I want a brochure to put at some of the local hotels, motels, and bed-and-breakfasts. Is that something you can do?"

"It depends. What do you want them to look like?"

"I want them to capture the setting. The ocean. The coast. Seafood. But all of it infused with Baptista's Mexican culture."

I gave a slow blink, my lips pressing together in contemplation. Or, if I was being honest, bafflement. Nothing like some high expectations. I had no idea how to capture all of that.

"It's a little vague," he said.

I nodded in agreement. "A little."

"I don't have much direction, Ivy. I just know we need to freshen things up. Not all that much has changed since my grandfather first opened the place, and that was in the fifties."

I reached back into my memories. "Didn't your parents remodel it when we were in high school?"

"The kitchen had an overhaul. They recovered the old Naugahyde booths and got new tables, but my folks never did much more than that. We can afford to make some changes now. My dad . . . he had life insurance, so . . ." He trailed off, swallowing. His father had died of a heart attack a few months before my mom had passed away. It was one thing we still had in common.

"So you want to remodel Baptista's, but we'll have to wait until the remodel is done to take pictures."

He shook his head. "I'm going to do the renovations in sections. I can't afford to have the place closed completely. But it's time. I'm going to start with the dining room on the right, then work my way to the left. I'll do the patio last. Too cold for that right now, anyway."

The wind had picked up, whipping strands of my curls across my face. Miguel reached out, pulling a piece of my hair free from my eyelashes. "That . . . um . . . sounds like a good plan," I said, just as someone called Miguel from the restaurant.

We both turned to see Mrs. Baptista, Miguel's mother, standing at the end of the pier just outside the restaurant. She waved her arms over her head. "Miguel! Ven aqui, mi'jo!"

"Todo esta bien?" he called.

I remembered enough Spanish to know she'd called for him to come to her and he'd asked if everything was okay. Her response was insistent.

"Ven, ven! Ahorita!"

Miguel and I locked eyes for a split second

before we both hurried toward the restaurant. Miguel, with his long stride, beat me there, but I wasn't far behind. "Que, Mama? Que es la problema?"

They spoke in Spanish, and while I could pick out some of the words, I didn't follow the thread of their conversation. Miguel translated for me a moment later. "Jason Rivera was here looking for his dad. He's worried about him. They were supposed to have dinner last night, but Hank didn't show. He missed a delivery and now Jason can't get ahold of him."

The name rang a bell. Rivera. Rivera? "Is his dad Hank? As in Mustache Hank?"

Miguel lowered his chin, but his eyebrows rose. "You know him?"

"No, not at all. I mean, I just met him a few days ago."

"Donde?" Mrs. Baptista asked at the same time Miguel said, "Where?"

"He came into the bread shop." Where else?

"He does love his bread," Miguel said.

"Why is his son looking for him here." I asked.

Mrs. Baptista frowned. "He say he no see him for days. I think he — he —" English was not her first language and she paused to think about how to say what she wanted to say. "He worry. No se. *Pero* Hank, he no come here."

She started to turn, but stopped and took my hand and gave it a gentle squeeze. "Good to see you, *mi'ja*. Miguel, he say you are back to Santa Sofia. To stay?"

"Bought a house and everything," I said with a smile.

"Your father, I know he is so happy you back with him."

Her English, while broken, was better than I remembered it being. "I think so. I hope so. It's been . . . rough."

She nodded, her own sorrow evident. "I know that. It does not get better fast."

"I was so sorry to hear about your husband," I said. Mrs. Baptista knew exactly what my father had been through losing his wife, because she'd been through her own loss.

"After what happ—" She stopped, searching for the words. "After Laura saw —"

"Mom." Miguel's tense voice cut her off.

"Laura?" I asked.

But Mrs. Baptista clamped her mouth shut, looked at Miguel, at me, and then shook her head. "Muy triste," she said. I recognized the word: *Sad.* Was she talking about our breakup so many years ago, or my mom? Either way, I nodded.

Mrs. Baptista gave my hand another squeeze before letting it go and turning to go back to the restaurant.

There was a moment of awkward silence between Miguel and me as she walked away. "Is Laura still in Santa Sofia?" I asked.

He looked at me, puzzled. "We took over the restaurant together," he said. "I thought you knew that."

"No, I don't think you mentioned it." Neither had Emmaline, but then why would either of them? Laura was three years younger than me. When she was in middle school, I'd been her brother's girlfriend, nothing more. I remembered her prank calling my house and hanging up, sticking childish warnings she'd written about me dating her brother into my backpack, hiding anything of mine when I'd been over at the Baptista house. I'd dismissed it as the antics of a jealous sister. We'd never been friends, but we were adults now and that was all in the past. "Is she here? I'd like to say hello."

He started walking up the pier toward the restaurant. I fell into step next to him. "She's out today," he said.

"Oh, well, another time."

He spoke, but kept his gaze straight ahead, his pace quickening. "I need to call Jason."

"You're worried about Hank," I said, feeling silly for stating the obvious. "Maybe he's just sick, or something."

But Miguel shook his head. "I don't think so. Jason told my mom that he's missed his stops for the last few days."

"Since Monday," I said.

"How did you know —"

"High school Spanish," I said with a little smile. "She said *lunes.*" Before he could comment on my rudimentary Spanish, I forged on. "Where else was he supposed to deliver to?"

Miguel stopped and turned to gaze toward the ocean. Something in his attitude had changed. He was tense. Almost coarse in his tone. He rattled off a few local eateries, and then paused. "Something doesn't feel right," he said after a minute, but he was just talking aloud more than he was speaking directly to me.

"What do you mean?"

He looked back to me. "In all the years I've known him, Hank has never missed a delivery."

"Never?" That was some crazy work ethic.

"Never."

"Is there a Mrs. Mustache Hank?" I asked, not meaning the question to sound as silly as it did.

"There's an ex–Mrs. Mustache Hank."

"Ah, divorced." That explained the fawning Blackbird Ladies. Hank was an eligible bachelor, although in a May-December romance, the Blackbird Ladies were December to Hank's May.

"He always said they both went into their marriage with the intent of going the distance."

"I had the same intent. Divorce wasn't an option." I shrugged with resignation. "It happened anyway."

He looked me in the eyes, his gaze intense. "I'm sure that was tough," he said, but I didn't sense any sympathy. In fact, it sounded slightly smug. Or had I imagined that?

I cleared my throat and got back on track. "So Mustache Hank was divorced."

"Yeah, it's pretty new," he said. "He actually stayed in the office at the restaurant for a few days when it happened."

"Then what?"

"Then he found a place to live."

I turned toward the parking lot, ready to head up the pier. "So let's go check it out."

Miguel shook his head. "We can't."

I was curious, and I knew myself. If I didn't find out where Mustache Hank was, I'd mull it over and over in my head and end up calling Miguel to get updates. It was better to just figure it out right now. "Of course we can. And we should."

"But we can't."

"Why can't we?" I asked, but then realization dawned. "Ohhh. You don't know where his new place is."

He grimaced. "I wish I did."

"He must be sick. That's the only explanation, right?"

Miguel seemed to consider, and then nodded. "Maybe." He took his cell phone from his back pocket, used his thumb to scroll, and held out the phone between us. He'd put it on speaker. A few seconds later, a man answered. "Jason? Hey. It's Miguel. Baptista. I heard you came by."

"Yeah," a voice said. "I'm looking for my dad." He repeated what he'd already told Miguel's mother, but there was something else. Something he wasn't saying.

Miguel picked up on it, too. "Is there more?" Miguel asked.

On the other end of the line, Jason sighed. "He owes my mom money."

Miguel's eyes looked toward the sky. I could tell he didn't want to get involved in an alimony dispute between his produce supplier and the guy's ex-wife. "I haven't seen him, Jason."

I didn't blame Miguel for not wanting to

45

stick his nose into someone else's business, but I wasn't sure I felt the same. Something about Mustache Hank had elicited my sympathies. He'd seemed melancholy. He'd put on a smile for the Blackbird Ladies, but there was something . . . a kind of sadness that permeated his being.

I looked at Miguel. He took my meaning, nodded, and said, "Jason, I have a friend here with me. She saw your dad."

"Hi, Jason," I said. "My name's Iv—"

Jason's voice shot out like a bullet through the speaker, cutting me off. "You've seen him?"

"Yes."

"Where?" he demanded. "Where'd you see him?"

I caught Miguel's gaze, raising my eyebrows. Jason was worked up. "I work at the bread shop in town. Yeast of Eden."

"He was there? At the bakery? When? What day?"

"It was Monday. He didn't stay long."

"So he's okay?" Jason asked, his voice calmer.

"I'd never met him before," I said, "but I think he seemed fine. Maybe a little sad, but like I said, I don't know him."

"And you're sure it was him?" Jason asked.

"According to the Blackbi—" I broke off,

rephrasing my answer. "According to some of the women who were in the shop. They called him Mustache Hank."

"And you said that was Monday?"

Instead of answering, Miguel said, "Jason, what's going on?"

Jason hesitated. "Look," he said after a few seconds. "I'm going to be straight with you. My dad hasn't been right since the divorce. And . . . I'm worried about him."

Miguel scrubbed his fingers through his hair. "What do you mean, Jason? What's going on?"

"He's just . . . he's not the same."

"Do you think he's depressed?" I asked. I'd gone through an array of emotions after my divorce, including depression. The marriage had been a bad decision on my part. I'd been lied to and cheated on, but despite all of that, I'd still felt as if I'd failed.

Jason sighed. "I don't know. Maybe?" He thought for a second. "Yeah. Yeah, I think he might be. He still loves my mom. The whole thing tore him up."

"Where's he staying?" Miguel asked.

He exhaled. "I don't know."

"He didn't tell you?" Miguel asked.

Jason scoffed. "He didn't tell me anything. He thought I sided with my mom with the divorce. Who knows, maybe I did. I don't know." His voice wavered. "But I wanted to see him. That's why we were going to have dinner last night. When he didn't show, I thought maybe he was still pissed at me, but then I heard that he missed a bunch of deliveries. Miguel, I'm worried about him and I don't know how to find him."

Neither of us had any answers for him. Miguel told him he'd keep an eye out, Jason thanked him, and then the line went dead.

CHAPTER 3

Miguel and I spent the better part of an hour walking around the restaurant, talking about what he wanted for his new menu and brochure, but I could tell his heart wasn't in it. We wandered out again onto the back dining deck overlooking the pier. His eyes were downcast and two vertical lines formed between them. "Miguel, we can do this another time," I said.

"It doesn't add up, you know?" he said, as if we'd been talking about Hank. The lines on his face deepened. "Something has to be wrong. Why wouldn't he tell Jason where he's staying?"

"Maybe he just needs space?" I suggested. "I mean, if he didn't want the divorce, maybe he just wants to escape for a little while." It was another thing I could relate to.

He stared out at the ocean. "Were you always so intuitive? I don't remember that

49

about you."

I shrugged, not wanting to think about our past again. "Am I?"

We stood side by side, each of us leaning against the railing of the pier. "The thing with your mom," he said. "You knew something was wrong and you figured it all out. Not even Em suspected. Did anyone believe you?"

"Did *you* believe me?" The wind whipped my hair around. I gathered it into a ponytail, holding it in one hand.

Before he answered, he ushered me away from the railing and closer to the exterior wall of the outdoor dining space to escape the breeze. "I don't know," he said honestly. "I think I wanted to, but it seemed so crazy."

He was right about that. Sometimes I still couldn't believe it. "When I stop to think about it, it still does," I said.

He leaned one shoulder against the wall and slid one hand into the pocket of his jeans. "This is going to sound crazy, too, but . . ."

I let my hair go. In our position by the wall, the spiral curls stayed in place. "But what?"

He wore his concern like a black eye, all brooding and bruised. "Something is wrong. This thing with Hank, it doesn't feel right."

50

I agreed. Hank hadn't wanted the divorce, and now he was staying God knows where, alone, and maybe feeling a little desperate. I hoped not *too* desperate.

"I could dig around a little," I suggested. "Maybe go see his ex-wife, see if I can figure out where he's staying."

He eyed me with curiosity. "You don't even know him. Why would you want to do that?"

I cocked my head and looked at him. "Why wouldn't I? If someone's in trouble and I can help, then I want to."

"Let's go." He grabbed my hand and started toward the parking lot.

I pulled back, yanking him to a stop. "Wait — now?"

"Yes, now."

I'd planned on digging around on my own. Or with Mrs. Branford. Traipsing around with Miguel had not been part of my plan, but we were both determined to make sure Hank was okay, so I went with him.

Before we drove off in Miguel's truck, he made a call to Jason Rivera to get his mother's address. A twenty-minute drive later and we were across town. "Where does Hank grow his produce?" I asked as Miguel searched for Mrs. Rivera's house in a sea of

51

cookie-cutter homes. I couldn't imagine a man who cultivated seeds and grew organic produce living in such a sterile, lifeless neighborhood.

"He's got a small farm just outside of town."

"So they used to live there?" I asked. "As a family?"

"For as long as I can remember," he said, his voice taking on a tinge of sadness. "Hank moved here for Brenda, but it wasn't enough to save their marriage, I guess. It's hard to understand how people who once loved each other, who got married and had a child together, turn so completely against each other."

I'd given that very thing a lot of thought over the years, especially after my divorce. It was a decision I never thought I'd make. Yet at the time, after the betrayal, there had been no other choice. "I think marriage and kids are a huge commitment," I said, "but things happen. Things you can't always predict."

He nodded, but thankfully didn't press me for information. "There it is," he said a minute later, parking his truck alongside the curb. The Rivera house itself was nondescript. One amid ten others just like it, each with the same siding, the same roofline, the same faux balconies and postage-stamp front lawns. Some people tried to make their spaces unique with a potted plant here, a hammock there, but overall, one house bled into the next, which bled into the next.

Our knock on the front door was answered by a tall, big-boned woman. Her hair was short, a nondescript brown, and parted in the middle. A thin strip of glistening gray ran like a stripe down the part. She was attractive, but in need of some hair coloring and an updated style, but I suspected her divorce had derailed her too much to deal with those things. "Yes?" she said, but before we could say anything, her expression changed from curiously cautious to recognition. "Oh, Miguel! What in the world? I haven't seen you in ages."

"Much too long," he agreed, and then he introduced me. "Brenda Rivera. Ivy Culpepper."

"Nice to meet you," I said. I would have held my hand out to shake, but that seemed so formal. A nod seemed the better choice.

"Come in, come in!" she said, flinging the door open and ushering us in.

I followed Mrs. Rivera in, Miguel following behind. She brought up the rear and closed the door. We waited and she led us to the small living room right off the entry-way. I looked around, taking in the details of the house. It was clean, but on the dingy side. Once upon a time, the walls had been white, but now they were dull and grayish. A yellow stain marked the wall on the left of the entry hallway where a piece of furniture had once been.

A series of photos hung on the wall, evenly spaced and lined up like soldiers marching down the hallway. I looked at them as we passed. They were school photos of a boy, presumably Jason, through the years. My study of photography had taught me to look for the uncommon details, so my eyes kept scanning the house: A stack of bills on the edge of the hall table. A half-burned three-wick candle. A stack of well-worn paperback novels.

I tried to form a picture of Brenda Rivera from her environment. All I came away with was that she seemed lonely. She spent her time reading, and maybe rereading, her favorite books. They were comfort for her. And she loved her son. There were no other family photos. No other mementos. Nothing of Hank. Just a chronicling of Jason Rivera's childhood.

I smiled my thanks as she led us to the living room on the right. Miguel and I sat side by side on the faded plaid upholstered couch. Magazines were strewn across the worn coffee table. A side table held a lamp with a battered lampshade. It looked to me like Mrs. Rivera had not won the furniture lottery in the divorce. I wondered if Mustache Hank had, either. Divorce was like that; it took its toll on both parties. *All* parties, if there were children involved.

"Thank you for inviting us in, Mrs. Rivera," I said.

She nodded and gave me a slight smile. "Baptista's has been one of Hank's clients forever. Maybe one of the first. Any friend of Miguel's is a friend of mine. The Baptistas have been good to us."

She didn't say her ex-husband's name with animosity, which struck me as unusual. To my knowledge, amicable divorces were rare. Maybe Mrs. Rivera had no hard feelings over the divorce. But then again, I knew better than to take everything at face value. People let you see what they want you to see. I took her sincerity with a grain of salt.

She offered us something to drink. "Water or soda," she said. "I'm afraid that's all I have." After we both declined, she straightened in her chair. "What brings you here, Miguel?"

He didn't mince words. "We're here about

Hank," he said.

I had wondered what approach Miguel might take with Mrs. Rivera. I knew he didn't want to alarm her, but on the other hand, we needed to find out if she'd seen her ex-husband. I needn't have worried, because she seemed to know right off what our concern was. "You talked to Jason, didn't you?"

Miguel nodded. "He came to the restaurant looking for Hank. Said he hasn't been able to get ahold of him."

She absently scratched her head. "I know Jason's been worried."

"You're not?" Miguel asked.

She tilted her head a fraction of an inch. "I've tried to let go of the worry since the divorce."

Miguel gave his head a single, skeptical shake. "I don't believe that." I stared at him, shocked at his bluntness. I tended to be direct, but I also had a little more tact than he was currently exhibiting. He kept on. "You were married for a lot of years, Mrs. Rivera, and now Hank is missing. You can't tell me you're not a little bit concerned."

"*Missing* is too strong a word, Miguel," she said, but her lower lip quivered slightly and her shoulders sagged a tiny bit. Her veneer was cracking. "He hasn't been himself since we finalized everything. He's just off somewhere. Probably drinking himself into a numb stupor."

The harshness of her statement took me by surprise. Miguel had known her, through Hank, for a long time. Obviously being with Mrs. Rivera was the way to go; he knew she'd be direct right back at him.

"Jason said he thinks Hank might be depressed?" Miguel's voice lifted slightly, leaving it as an open-ended question that he wanted Mrs. Rivera to either confirm or deny.

But this time, the bluntness didn't come. Without warning, her brown eyes teared up. She squeezed them shut for several seconds, her nostrils flared, and she drew in a deep breath. When she spoke, her voice quavered. "I spent too many years worrying about him, Miguel. Do you understand, that's why I left him? I had twenty-six years of anxiety. Would there be enough crops to supply his clients? Would he be able to keep up with the work? Would he collect the debts that were owed to him? What would he do if he couldn't pay his workers? Would he even come home each night? He worked his fingers to the bone and still, we barely scraped by most months. Every second of every day felt more stressful than the last. I couldn't take it anymore." She dropped her head, chin to her chest. A sob escaped as she repeated, "I couldn't take it."

I reached out and put my hand on hers, but I didn't have any comforting words. I'd been through divorce and I'd lost my mother. Nothing anyone said would have made that better. It was true what they said: Time would heal. I knew it was true, but me saying so wouldn't make Mrs. Rivera believe it. It had been months, but she still felt a loss. The loss of her marriage. The loss of twenty-six years together. The loss of the life she'd known and the man she'd loved. And now the man himself was incommunicado. I could see she'd been trying to act unaffected, but her emotions told a different story. She was hurting.

Miguel comforted her and then gave her a minute to compose herself. When she seemed under control again, he asked another question, more softly this time. "Is there any place we can look for him?"

She pulled her lower lip in, creating a tight line and wiping away the quiver that had been there moments before. "A few years ago I'd have said the Broken Horse, but he gave up drinking and took up bowling. But since the divorce? I have no idea. No idea where he's living. Nothing. He cut me off completely." She gave a hurt smile. "I guess I can't blame him, though, can I? I left him." She pressed her open palm against her chest. "*I* pulled the plug on our marriage, so of course he doesn't keep me informed about his comings and goings. I even asked him: 'Where are you staying?' I said, but he wouldn't tell me. Said I gave up the right to keep tabs on him. And you know what?" This time she gave a harsh laugh. "He's right. He doesn't have to tell me anything. But Jason? That's a different story. Jason is his son. He deserves to know, right?"

Miguel leaned forward and clasped his hands, propping his elbows on the table and folding his hands under his chin. "He's never missed a delivery, Mrs. Rivera. Never. I'm worried about him."

Her spine stiffened and she ran the backs of her hands over her eyes. "He's around," she said. "That's what I'm saying."

"I saw him a few days ago," I said. Not knowing the man, I didn't have any insight. All I could do is report what I saw. "But your son says no one has seen him since."

Her head snapped toward me and I thought for a second that she was going to bite my head off. But her expression softened. "Where was that?"

"At Yeast of Eden. The bread shop in town."

"I know it." She fell silent for a moment, and then asked, "Why was he there?"

The only answer I had for that was the obvious one. "For some bread, I suppose?"

Her control vanished. The look she gave me could have withered a rose. "Who was he with, I mean. Was he alone?"

I ignored her tone and agitation. Despite the divorce and everything she'd said about not being able to handle her husband anymore, she clearly still had emotions tied to him. I couldn't say if it was love, but it was hard to let go of your feelings after twenty-six years. I had only been married for a handful of years and there'd been plenty of pent-up emotions that still surfaced, and we'd long ago signed the divorce papers.

I thought back to the morning I'd seen Hank. "He came in alone, as far as I remember. He sat with a few friends."

She angled her head toward me. "If there's one thing I know about Hank, after so many years together, it's that he doesn't have friends. He's too busy to have friends."

Miguel stepped in. "Everybody has friends," he said.

"Female friends?" she asked, a hint of bitterness in her tone. I nodded, and she shook her head. "I knew it. He didn't have friends, but let me tell you something. For a while, I thought he was unfaithful. I really thought he was. But he swore —" She drew out the word, and then repeated it. "He swore it was in my head. Who was he with? Just tell me."

Miguel looked at me and I answered the question. "Mabel Peabody, Penny Branford, Alice Ryder, and Janice Thom—"

She slapped her palm against the table.

Miguel and I both jumped. "Mrs. Rivera," Miguel said, "are you okay?"

Her eyes grew as round as quarters and suddenly she looked a little bit unhinged. "Alice? He was with Alice?"

Mrs. Rivera seemed to have become a different person from the time we entered her house to now. The change sent a shiver down my spine. "And the others," I said, hoping to placate her.

She turned on me. "Don't fool yourself. It's *always* a woman. Hank and Alice, they were high-school sweethearts. Can you believe that? I wondered, you know. I walked in on him once when he was on the phone with her. He said it was nothing. A business deal. I should have known better. He was so distracted. I thought it was the business, but it was her. It had to be. Whenever he shows his face again, I'm going to . . ." She trailed off, clamping her mouth shut as if she remembered that they weren't married anymore and she couldn't do a thing about it. Instead, she muttered under her breath, "Unbelievable."

"Mrs. Rivera," I said, wanting to calm her down. "I don't think we should jump to any conclusions. It wasn't as if he was sitting only with Alice. In fact, I don't even know if they spoke to one another. Truthfully, he seemed kind of withdrawn."

She looked at me as I spoke, and she even dipped her head in a faint nod, but I got the distinct impression that she didn't really register what I'd said.

"Can I get you anything?" I asked, still wanting to calm her down. "Some water?"

She shook her head and I let it drop, but I secretly wished I had a loaf of Olaya's rosemary brioche, the bread that I always turned to when I felt nervous or on edge. I was convinced Olaya's bread had magical powers. She claimed it did, so who was I to question it? And Mrs. Rivera, from what I was seeing, could use a healthy slice of magic. Or two.

"Can you think of any place he might be?" Miguel asked tentatively. We'd come here to try to get information — something that could help us track down Mustache Hank. I could tell Miguel didn't want to upset her more, but he also wanted to get back to some semblance of a productive conversation.

"If he's anywhere," Mrs. Rivera said with a grimace, "I bet it's with Alice."

CHAPTER 4

Miguel and I walked shoulder to shoulder down the path to the sidewalk. I glanced over my shoulder and saw Mrs. Rivera still standing in the doorway. I lifted my hand in a little wave. She returned it, albeit a tad less enthusiastically. "I feel bad for her," I said to Miguel. "After so many years, it's got to be hard to be where she is."

Miguel nodded, but he was distracted and only offered an innocuous, "Yeah." He held the door to the truck open for me. "I'll take you back to the restaurant."

"Then what are you going to do?" I asked as he slid into the driver's side. He turned the ignition and pulled away from the curb.

He kept his eyes on the road, one hand on the steering wheel, the other elbow on the window frame, his fingers pressed to his forehead. "Go see Alice Ryder."

I spun toward him. "You are not."

Still, he looked straight ahead, his expression turning grim. "I am. If Brenda Rivera is right, she might know where Hank is."

I turned back to face front, crossed my legs, and folded my hands in my lap. "You'll just have to take me with you, then."

"It's okay. Don't you have to check on your dog, or something?"

I eyed him, trying to decide what his motive was. Was he giving me an out, or did he really want to do this alone? "Miguel," I snapped. "If you think you're just going to drop me off at Baptista's while you gallivant all over Santa Sofia —"

He turned to me, one eyebrow cocked. "Gallivant?"

"Yes, gallivant. You said it yourself: I solved that murder at Yeast of Eden. You run a restaurant. Who has the better track record?" He slowed the truck, flicking on the turn signal to head toward the beach.

"I didn't know we were keeping score," he said, one corner of his mouth quirking upward, the long dimples in his cheeks materializing.

I didn't, either, but I was invested now and that was my ace. "Miguel, I mean it. I'm coming with you."

"You don't have anything better to do today?"

Did I? I could go back to Yeast of Eden,

but Olaya didn't need me for another few hours. The Winter Wonderland Festival was just two days away, but we'd already prepped the ingredients for the bread shop's booth. We couldn't actually bake until the morning of the festival, so until then, nothing was pressing.

I could go home and plant the winter flowers I'd bought. The pots on my porch needed sprucing up. I could go visit with Mrs. Branford. That, in all honesty, was my favorite way to spend an afternoon. But right now, in this moment, I wanted to stay put in Miguel Baptista's truck. My motivation in my thirties was different than it had been when we were in high school. Now, more than anything, I wanted to find out what was happening with Hank. After talking to his ex-wife, hearing Jason describe him as depressed, and knowing about all the struggles he'd been through with his business, I understood why I'd sensed a sadness in him. Had he simply just run away from it all?

"As a matter of fact, I don't."

Miguel hesitated, but finally nodded, put on his turn signal, and headed south. He pushed a button on his steering wheel and said aloud, "Call Alice Ryder."

The automated voice replied: "Calling Alice Ryder."

"You have her number?" I asked as the car's phone system dialed.

"I've done catering for her."

Made sense. Baptista's was one of the most popular restaurants in Santa Sofia. A high-end Mexican seafood restaurant on the water. There was a lot to love. I imagined the restaurant's catering business was just as popular as the in-house dining.

A woman's voice came on the line. "Hello?"

Miguel greeted her, saying he was sorry to bother her. "I wanted to ask you something. Mind if I stop by?"

"What would you need to ask me?"

He tapped his fingers on the steering wheel as he drove. "I'm looking for Hank Rivera. I thought you might have seen him around."

On the other end of the line, Alice Ryder sighed, but I couldn't quite place the context. Aggravation? A love-torn breath? Nervousness? I couldn't be sure. "Why would *I* know where Hank Rivera is? Did you call his cell phone?"

"I have. No answer. I was just wondering if you've talked to him lately?"

She answered quickly. "No, not at all. Why would I?" she said again. She seemed a little too indignant, if you asked me.

"I haven't, either. I'm a little worried about him," he said. I noticed that his approach with Alice Ryder was different than the tack he'd taken with Brenda Rivera. He was more tentative with Alice, feeling her out so as not to spook her, I imagine. He paused for a second before speaking again, looking at me and putting his index finger against his lips. "Ms. Ryder, do you have a few minutes? I'm not far from your place."

The request clearly took her by surprise. "Oh. You mean right now?"

"It'll just take a minute."

She hesitated. I think she wanted to refuse, but couldn't think of a valid reason to. "Of course," she finally said. "Come on over."

Miguel ended the phone call and continued driving. A few minutes later we pulled into a suburban community. The streets were wide, the yards big, the flowers bright. It was nicer than Brenda Rivera's neighborhood, but at the same time it felt a little sterile. The houses were all similar, with stone facades and stucco. There were different elevations, the stucco on each house was painted a different color, and the roofs alternated between two different types of material. I could understand why it was an appealing place to live, but there was nothing unique about any of the houses and being here made me appreciate life on Maple Street and my Tudor house even more.

We traveled through the neighborhood, turning left, then right, then right again. The neighborhood kept going and going. It was much larger than it looked.

Finally, Miguel pulled up in front of a modest house. Interestingly, the neighborhood did not have traditional sidewalks. Instead, a stone runoff ditch circled the entire community, river rock lining it and giving the entire area less of a tract-home feel and more of an upscale sensibility.

The stucco of Alice Ryder's house was painted neutral beige. The rock facade and the roof were equally neutral, but darker. The front yard was a good size. Not so big that it would be daunting to care for, but not miniscule, either. I gazed at the big-leaf maple tree. The branches were bare, but in the summer, it would shade the house.

Miguel and I walked up the meandering path toward the front door. It was made of real wood and looked custom. What I had surmised, so far, was that Alice Ryder had good taste and had a fair amount of money. I wondered if the inside of the house would match the outside.

Miguel raised his knuckles to the door to knock, but before he could make contact, it opened. Alice Ryder greeted us with a forced smile, looking from Miguel to me and back. "You really were in the neighborhood, weren't you?" she said, trying to sound light and amused, but coming off more as accusatory. I hadn't really spoken to her before so I hadn't registered the accent, but now I heard it clearly. She was Southern. The drawl was slight, but it was distinct and definitely there.

"We were," Miguel said with his own disarming smile. "We are."

Mrs. Ryder looked as put together as she had the first time I'd seen her, at Yeast of Eden. She was about as tall as me, but she wore pointy-toed heels that gave her another few inches. It was the middle of the afternoon on a Thursday and she was at home, but she looked like she should be at a high-powered job or out hobnobbing with the who's who of Santa Sofia. If there *was* a who's who, which I'm thinking there actually wasn't. Our little coastal town wasn't anywhere close to city life in Los Angeles or San Francisco, with politicians and celebrities and money. Santa Sofia was more like a getaway from all of that.

And yet here was Alice Ryder looking as if

she was ready to go to a fund-raising luncheon at the country club.

Miguel and I stood there awkwardly. Was she going to invite us in? "As I said on the phone," Miguel started, "I'm looking for Hank Rivera. We talked with Mrs. Rivera a little while ago and —"

"They're divorced," she interrupted.

"They are," Miguel agreed. "But their son is worried. He hasn't seen his dad in a few days and can't get ahold of him."

Alice looked at me more closely. "You're from the bread shop, aren't you? Didn't I see you there the other day?"

"Yes, you did. I'm Ivy Culpepper." This time a formal handshake felt right, so I held my hand out. She took it in hers. I'd half expected a firm power grip, but she fooled me and we ended up in a weak clasp, which I quickly disengaged.

She turned back to Miguel with a sour look on her perfectly made-up face. "I haven't seen Hank Rivera for a few days. I am afraid I simply cannot help you. Frankly, I'm not sure why you thought I could."

As if on cue, a man appeared behind her. He was a silver fox. Tanned skin, tall and lean, and a full head of shimmering silver hair. "Everything okay?" he asked, placing his hand protectively on her shoulder.

She smiled up at him, her demeanor softening. For his benefit, I gathered, which was interesting. Was she hiding something? "Fine, darling. Do you remember Miguel Baptista?"

Miguel held out his hand and the man took it. *Theirs* was a firm handshake. They disengaged and Miguel introduced me.

"Michael Ryder," the man said. "Good to meet you both. Something we can help you with?"

"No, darling, it's fine. They're looking for the produce man. I gather he was last seen at the bread shop a few days ago. I'd been there with the girls, you know."

Michael looked up sharply. "You mean Mustache Hank?"

I'd been feeling like a dolt, just standing here and not taking an active role in the conversation, but now I inserted myself. "Do you know him?"

"Sure. We went to high school together," he said. "Alice dated him for a while back then, for what —" He looked at his wife — "a few months, right?"

Alice smiled, but her lips were tight. "Right."

"I actually went out with Brenda," Michael said with a chuckle. "Ironic that Hank and I dated Alice and Brenda back then, but ended up with the opposite woman. We laugh about that sometimes, don't we, honey?"

She just nodded.

I was interested in the unspoken dynamics between Alice and Michael, but Miguel just forged ahead. "Like I said, we talked to Hank's wife —"

"Ex-wife," Alice interjected.

Her husband nodded. "Yes, that was sad. I always thought Brenda and Hank could survive anything, you know? There are people like that. They just seem to be thick-skinned. Tough. You can throw things at them, but they'll manage to fend it all off. Me? I take the blows and it wears me down. I mean, how could it not? Alice and I, we've had our share of —"

He broke off suddenly, looking down at his wife, and I wondered if she'd thrust her elbow back slightly, poking him in the ribs to get his attention, or perhaps she'd pressed her stiletto heel down on his shoe. Or maybe she'd pushed her back up against him slightly, just enough to let him know what she was thinking. People who'd been married for a long time had the gift of silent communication. I'd witnessed it over and over with my parents. A nudge here, a look there, a raised eyebrow or a scowl.

I hadn't noticed a signal, but the way Michael Ryder had stopped abruptly, and now looked at her, and then at me and Miguel, was a clear sign. She'd aborted whatever it was he'd been about to say, redirecting it somehow. Michael responded by making a slight course correction. "We all have our fair share of troubles, you know? I guess Brenda and Hank didn't quite handle theirs. At least not like we thought they would."

He'd opened the door, though, and I was ready to walk through. "What kind of troubles did they have?"

He glanced down at his wife as if looking for permission before speaking. She was stony-faced. I read Michael's face as he weighed his options: Go forth and say what he'd planned to, retreat altogether, or temper his comments to satisfy my question *and* his wife's dictates. The lines around his eyes deepened as he fought the grimace surfacing. He'd opened a can of worms, and he was clearly realizing that he had to put the lid back on it, and quickly.

His face relaxed and he grinned at Miguel, man-to-man. "Oh, you know, the type of troubles we all have, right?"

Miguel went along with it. "Right."

A light bulb seemed to go off over Michael's head. "God, bad manners: Would you folks like to come in?"

Alice had taken a backseat while her husband dug himself out of the hole he'd made, but now she piped up again, jumping in before we could say anything. "We don't need to disrupt their day, darling. They were just stopping by for a minute. Miguel has a restaurant to run, and Ms. Culpepper has . . ."

She looked at me as she trailed off, leaving the space for me to fill in just what I needed to take care of. "I actually need to get back to the bread shop. We have the Winter Wonderland Festival this weekend. Lots of baking to do."

"Right, of course," Michael said. "Maybe we'll see you there. Alice's home-decorating company has a booth."

I perked up. "I just bought a house recently. It's an old Tudor. It's in wonderful shape. The woman I bought it from had done some pretty extensive renovations, but I'm starting from scratch. I have a vintage baker's rack — it was a flea-market find. I love it, but that's about it. I have an old couch that has definitely seen better days. I could definitely use some help fixing things up."

Alice's demeanor under went a complete shift before my eyes. She'd been ready to send us on our way, but now she stood up straighter, angled her head, and asked me a series of questions about my house: What area of town is it in? When was it built? Are there gables? *Yes?* How many? What's the stone like? Are the windows original?

With each question and answer, she became more animated. "I'd love to see it, Ivy." I guess we'd graduated to first names, now that I was a potential client. "I do hope you'll stop by my booth at the festival."

"Absolutely," I said. I'd make a point of it. Miguel and I hadn't gotten any closer to figuring out where Hank Rivera was, but it was clear to me that Alice and Hank's relationship hadn't ended back in high school. They still had some sort of connection, but Michael didn't seem to know anything about it. Strange, I thought. I wanted to know what it was, though. I aimed to find out more.

CHAPTER 5

After Miguel had dropped me off back at Baptista's, I picked up Agatha, my feisty pug, from my dad's house and drove home. I contemplated changing clothes and heading for the beach to walk, but decided against it. A walk in my historic neighborhood would be just as helpful as I processed through the day. I harnessed up Agatha and headed out, locking the front door behind me. I'd been here for a few months, but I was still learning the different streets. I could walk for thirty days straight and never hit the same route twice.

My mind wandered as I trudged along, Agatha's short little legs moving double time to keep up with me. I thought about my past with Miguel, Hank's disappearance, Jason's concern, Brenda Rivera's convoluted emotions, and whatever Alice Ryder was hiding — because I was sure she was keeping something close to the vest. Finally, I decided a call to Emmaline was in order. Back at home, I sat at the little mosaic table set I'd put on the front porch, put my smartphone on speaker, and placed the call.

"So," I said after a little chitchat, "how long does a person need to be missing for before he's *officially* missing?"

There was a pause before she said, "Um, what?"

I repeated the question, my voice completely serious.

Instead of answering me, she heaved a sigh. "Are you really asking me that, Ivy?"

"Why do you say it like that? Of course I'm really asking you."

"Because you sound like you're part of the Justice League, or something. Or, I don't know, a wannabe X-Man."

"Hey," I said, feigning indignation. "I happen to have a strong sense of right and wrong, that's all. *And* I have a sixth sense."

Emmaline harrumphed over the cellular phone line. "Yeah, yeah, because you're absorbing the bread-shop magic, I know."

"You jest, but it's actually true. Olaya Solis has a gift. The things she bakes —"

"Oh, I know, Ivy. I've been on the receiving end. In fact, I half wonder if Billy ate some magic romance bread that helped him finally take the leap with me."

I shook my head to that, although she couldn't see through the phone line. "He didn't need magical bread. He's been in love with you since high school. Middle school, even."

Silence. And then, "You're so right. He has. No magic bread needed. Okay, so lay it on me. Is it Agatha? Is she missing?"

It was my turn to harrumph. I leaned down to scratch the top of Agatha's flat head. "No, I said *he,* and Agatha's a *she*. And she's right here beside me." I paused, wanting to emphasize my next sentence. "I'm not going to tell you unless you're going to take it seriously."

The conversation had been lighthearted, but now I sensed her sitting up straighter and taking notice. "Ivy, if someone is legitimately missing, of course I'm going to take it seriously. Let's hear it."

"Hank Rivera," I said.

A pause, and then, "As in Mustache Hank?"

"Does everyone in town call him that?"

"Pretty much. That's all I've ever known him as. Have you seen the handlebars?"

Indeed I had. I understood the connection; I just wasn't clear on how such a name had stuck. I pushed on. "No one seems to have seen him for a few days."

79

"Okay," she said, biting, "tell me what you know."

I relayed Miguel's concerns, ending with the odd conversation with Alice and Michael Ryder.

Her response was silence. More than silence. Crickets, in fact. I waited for a few seconds, and then a few seconds more. Finally, I said, "Hello? Em? You still there?"

"I'm here. Just thinking." After a moment, she continued. "So you saw him Monday at Yeast of Eden?"

"Right. About ten o'clock in the morning, or so."

"And then today Jason Rivera called Miguel, who took it upon himself to go see the ex-Mrs. Rivera, and then based on the ex-Mrs. Rivera's comment about Alice Ryder, you both went to see her, too? Do I have that right?"

I wasn't going to get snookered into her telling me I was butting my nose in where it didn't belong. "You have it perfectly right. Look, Em, I don't know the guy. I just know that Jason is worried, Mrs. Rivera seemed pretty sure that Alice Ryder might know something, and Mrs. Ryder was definitely odd when we spoke with her. She couldn't wait for us to leave, and I got the distinct impression that her husband might not know the depth of . . . um . . . the friendship between her and old Mustache Hank."

I heard the tapping of a pencil as Emmaline processed our conversation. "What do you think?" I asked.

"What I think is that I should give Jason Rivera a call. Thanks for the heads-up, Ivy."

"That's it? Can I help?"

She hesitated and I knew she didn't want to just cut me off. She wanted to cut me off with *kindness.* "Don't you have the Winter Wonderland Festival Saturday?"

Of course she was right. I did. But I didn't want to drop my concerns about Hank Rivera at Emmaline's feet and walk away. Unfortunately, at this point I had no choice. "Are you coming to the festival?"

"I hope so. We want to."

I grinned. "We?"

"Oh, stop it. Gloating is not becoming, Ivy."

I took some credit for Emmaline being with my brother. Theirs had been a relationship fraught with bad timing and trepidation. Emmaline had dug her heels in deep, her worry about getting involved with Billy stopping her dead in her tracks. "A friend of mine went to college in Oklahoma," she'd told me. "She fell in love with a guy. They're married now, but it was rough. She's Latina

81

and he's white. She had things thrown at her. People accosted her. It wasn't pretty, Ivy. It wasn't okay. I don't want that to happen to Billy and me."

My answer had been simple. "If you love each other, you need to be together. It's that simple. It doesn't matter that you're black and he's white. Life is too short." We'd learned that lesson good and well when my mother died. I went on: "It never mattered that Miguel is Mexican and I'm white. At least back when we dated. What matters is how you feel about each other."

It had taken years, and a lot of moments when Billy had been free and Em had been with someone else, and vice versa, before they'd both finally found themselves unattached and ready to give their relationship a go. Months later, they were going strong. "When's the wedding?" I asked her, the huge grin on my face infusing itself into my voice.

"You'll be the first to know," she said. We talked for another minute and then she was tapping her pencil again, the *click-click-click* carrying from her desk to my ear. "Gotta go, Ivy. I'll keep you posted."

Bright and early the next morning, all I could think about was if Emmaline had found anything out about Mustache Hank. I drove through town, my mind so distracted that I didn't even register the whitecaps on the ocean water, the pristine sand, smooth and white after high tide and a night undisturbed by human feet, or the rising sun. I parked a few blocks away from the bread shop so I could walk and think. The air was crisp. The salt from the ocean carried on the breeze, making the air fresh. Where in the world was Hank Rivera?

I had no choice but to push the thoughts away as I circled around the back of the bread shop and entered through the back door. It led straight into the kitchen. The stainless-steel countertops sparkled, not yet dusted with flour. The bread racks sat ready for the trays of *batards,* baguettes, scones, croissants, French bread, and every other offering we'd make for the day, and for the Winter Wonderland Festival. Several slots in one of the racks were already filled with trays of long-rise dough, Olaya's specialty.

One of my first lessons from Olaya during my initial baking classes with her was that the factory-produced plastic-wrapped breads in the supermarkets didn't allow the bread to rise for longer than three hours. As a result, the gluten proteins couldn't adequately break down. A long fermentation process, on the other hand — usually twelve to fifteen hours — was needed to allow this natural process to happen. It was the traditional bread-making Olaya had grown up with in Mexico, and was the method she practiced at Yeast of Eden.

The rack also held the day's tray of sugar-skull cookies, already iced and ready for hiding. Olaya, I had learned during the time I'd known her, was a morning person. Early to bed, early to rise. She arrived at the bread shop by 4:30 every morning, starting her day with the sugar-skull cookies, moving on to the long-rise breads, and ending with the quick rise and yeast-free recipes. I didn't know how she kept the pace she did, or how she stayed away. "It is just what I do, *mi'ja,*" she'd told me when I'd asked her one time.

I retrieved a utilitarian white apron from the back room where Olaya kept a collection, as well as all the laundered dish towels, extra supplies, mixing bowls and utensils, and anything else we might possibly need. As I secured the apron ties behind my back, Olaya swept into the kitchen, green caftan flowing around her. Her iron-gray hair was cropped close to her head in a stylish cut that complemented her face. She looked like a free spirit — and she was, on a lot of levels

— but she was also organized and structured, especially when it came to her bread shop. I knew she'd been here for several hours, but she looked as fresh as a daisy. Somehow she managed to bake in her caftan without missing a beat. When I baked, I ended up covered in flour dust, random spots, stains, and bits of dough dotting my apron.

"Hola, *mi'ja*. How are you today?"

I gave a halfhearted smile, still distracted. "Okay."

She perched on a stainless-steel stool near my workspace. "Por que? Why just okay?"

"You know Hank Rivera?"

"Por supuesta. Of course. Chocolate croissant."

I had to chuckle. Some people remembered others by their names, their hair, their voices. But Olaya remembered people based on what they ordered at the bread shop. And she was always right. "Nobody can find him," I told her.

She looked at me, puzzled. "What do you mean? Is he lost?"

"No, I mean that he seems to have vanished. His son called Miguel, looking for him. He missed his delivery to Baptista's. His ex-wife hasn't seen him. He's just . . . gone." I filled her in on my day with Miguel, ending with the Alice and Michael Ryder conversation.

"*Mi'ja*, he cannot be *gone*. He is somewhere; you just do not know where to look."

I reached up and grabbed the container of flour off the shelf, placing it on the counter in front of me. "True, but his family is worried about him. Miguel says that Hank has never missed a delivery."

Her expression clouded. "I do not think he has."

"I called Emmaline Davis last night and filled her in, but I feel helpless. I want to help find him."

"Ivy, but what can you do?"

Olaya's voice was soothing and immediately filled me with calm. She was right. I couldn't do anything more than keep my eyes and ears open. I needed to focus on my tasks and let Emmaline do her job. "What I can do is bake bread," I said. I brought the yeast and salt down from the upper shelf and turned to her. "What's on the agenda today?"

Her eyes were still dark, tinged with concern for Hank, but her response to my question was a chortle. "What are we *not* baking?"

A coil of nerves centered in my gut. I was still a novice, but Olaya was putting a lot of trust in me to help make Yeast of Eden's presence a success at the Winter Wonderland Festival.

She laughed again. "*Calmate,* Ivy. Martina and Consuelo are coming in to help. We will get this done."

I nodded, tapping the pads of my fingers on the cold countertop. "Okay," I said. "What's first?"

The first time I'd officially met Olaya Solis had been the day I'd taken my first baking class. She'd placed a freestanding blackboard in the corner of the kitchen and posted the baked items for the class. Now she pointed to the same chalkboard and I noticed the list of baked goods there.

Chocolate Croissants
Conchas
Almond fig bread
Mini-brioche
Blueberry streusel muffins
Double-chocolate muffins
Lemon poppy-seed scones
Cinnamon-chip scones with maple glaze
Orange cranberry scones
Vermont maple-oat walnut loaves
Roasted garlic Parmesan
Pretzel buns
Cranberry pecan loaf

Pretzels
Stromboli

My stomach dropped. "All . . ." I coughed. "All that?"

"All that," she confirmed. "It will be a spectacular offering of bread."

I got my bearings, wrapping my head around the day of baking ahead. "The line will be out the door."

Olaya shook her head pretty vigorously. "A lot of bread, yes." She lowered her voice as if she were imparting a great secret. "*Pero* Minnie's Bakery will be there."

Minnie's Bakery had a different approach to baked goods than Yeast of Eden. It focused on cookies and cakes, with a spattering of bread. We were the opposite. Bread, bread, and more bread, with just a few sweet treats thrown into the mix. I scoffed. "Minnie's bread isn't any good. You know that. Cookies are fine, but people like the heartiness of bread, Olaya. You do it better than anyone I've ever met."

"True, but people, they like cupcakes. They like cookies. They like *sugar.*"

"They do, but people like bread. They like *your* bread." I nodded toward the chalkboard. "Minnie's has a lot to compete with. Look at your list!"

Olaya stood and smiled. "It *is* a good list," she agreed. "Now, we should get started."

Which is just what we did. We baked and baked and baked. And then baked some more. The breadshop employees handled the front of the store, coming to the back to restock the depleted display cases, but the majority of what we created was for the next day. Finally, when I thought I might drop from exhaustion, Olaya wiped her hands on a red-and-green–striped dish towel, looked around the kitchen, and nodded her head. "We are finished."

I heaved a relieved sigh. The array of delicacies on the four industrial racks lined with baking sheets was staggering. It felt to me as if we had enough items to feed the entire Santa Sofia community. Which, from what we'd heard, might show up at the festival tomorrow.

"Relax tonight, Ivy," Olaya said to me after we'd finished cleaning the mixing bowls, wiping the countertops, and putting up all the ingredients. "It will be a long day tomorrow."

I had the feeling that was an enormous understatement. I needed to start my day at 5:30 in the morning in order to finish the scones and muffins, the final things we needed to bake, and get everything delivered to the boardwalk. Olaya, who I knew would be here much earlier than me, had hired a small local company to set up the bread shop's booth, complete with a black-and-white–striped canopy. She planned to string up the colorful festive cut-paper Mexican garland and paper fans and flowers, a tribute to her culture and the basis for her traditional long-rise artisanal bread baking. I knew there'd be an assortment of sugar-skull cookies thrown into the mix, as well. The booth would be beautiful and full of the best breads Santa Sofia had to offer.

I left Yeast of Eden and headed straight home, driving my mother's pearl-white Fiat, the one my dad had given me. Just being in it made me feel her presence.

I drove along Maple Street, passing a Queen Anne Victorian, several craftsman-style homes, a house that, with a thatched roof, might have been right at home on an English knoll, and myriad other ancient homes, all of which had been lovingly restored. I pulled into the driveway to the right of my gabled house and into the garage. Turning off the car, I closed the garage door behind me and went into the house. Agatha greeted me from her crate with an excited yap. It had been a long day for her to be crated, too, but I knew she just checked out when I was gone, chewing her rawhide bone and sleeping peacefully.

"Let's go! Outside!" I freed her from the crate and she bolted out, spinning herself around in circles. "Outside!" I said again, and she scampered to the French doors leading to the backyard, sliding across the wood floors when her little paws couldn't make purchase. Agatha was a creature of habit — and she was well-trained. Any time I came home, she spun her circles and bee-lined for the door. It was our little ritual.

I swung open the door and Agatha stopped long enough to look up at me with her bulbous eyes. "Outside," I said one more time. That was all the permission Agatha needed. She zipped past me, doing another series of spins once she got to the grass. It took her a few minutes before she spun herself to a stop, nosed around, and took care of business. I'd seen her do her little dance routine more times than I could count, but I still laughed every time. She scuttled around the yard, dodging in and out of the shrubbery, stopping every now and then to bury her flattened nostrils into whatever it was she was sniffing. She could be sweet and cuddly, cozying up to me on the couch or stretching alongside me in bed, but outside and unleashed, she could transform into the Tasmanian Devil.

I left her to her explorations for a few minutes while I went back inside, walked to the front door, and stepped out to get the mail. A mother and young son walked on the sidewalk holding hands, waving when they saw me. A pair of bicyclists zipped by. The January air was crisp and clear and I breathed it in, letting it fill my lungs. When I was at home, it felt as if I had been transported back to a simpler, more people-oriented time period. My neighborhood in Santa Sofia hadn't yet succumbed to the metal-mailbox cluster units so many new developments installed. We still had individualized boxes mounted to the walls of our house at the front porch. I reached into mine and withdrew the small stack of letters and the random catalog that had been delivered earlier in the day.

I thumbed through them as I went back through the house to the yard. The Sur La Table catalog caught my attention. Ever since I'd taken up baking at Yeast of Eden, my own kitchen had undergone a terrific transformation. I'd purchased a top-of-the-line Dutch oven, a set of stainless-steel pots and pans, cookie sheets with silicone baking mats, paring and chef's knives, and — the pièce de résistance — a pale yellow

KitchenAid mixer. Out in the backyard again, I sat down at the outdoor table and perused the catalog while Agatha expended some of her energy.

I went straight to the baking section, mentally adding things to my wish list: A cake stand. A proofing bowl. A baguette tray. I had all the basics; now I wanted the extras. The list, I thought, could go on and on. Meeting Olaya Solis had sparked a new passion in me, and my bank account would pay the price. Working part-time at the bread shop fed my creative soul, but it didn't do much for my pocketbook.

No, what I needed was to get back on track. I had enough money to tide me over for a few months. Which meant I had that long to develop a plan to reinvigorate the personal-photography business I'd left behind when I'd moved back to Santa Sofia from Austin. I'd had a few odd jobs here and there. I'd shot the bread shop to create new brochures. With the tourist population in Santa Sofia, Olaya had needed to update them. The array of breads showcased made everyone's mouth water.

Now I was going to do the same for Baptista's. I'd put some feelers out, thinking that maybe I could branch out and do some photography for other businesses in town.

Before I could think any more about it, my cell phone rang, Mrs. Branford's name displaying on the screen. I swiped my finger across it. "Hello there!" I said, my lips automatically curving into a grin.

"My darling Ivy, what are you doing?"

My smile spilled into my voice. "Right this very minute? I'm sitting in the backyard with Agatha."

"Good," she said. I felt her nod, although I couldn't say whether or not she actually did. "Come over."

It wasn't an invitation: It was a command. I'd come to realize that Mrs. Branford didn't waste time or beat around the bush. She told you what she wanted, and she usually got it. "Now?"

"The Blackbird Ladies are here and I want to do a proper introduction. Plus," she said, her voice dropping conspiratorially, "I heard you saw Miguel Baptista today. I want to hear all the details."

All the details? She sounded like a junior-high-school friend at a slumber party instead of the former teacher and elderly — albeit energetic — woman she was. "There are no details to tell. We went looking for Hank Rivera."

She paused for a split second before responding. "Well, I suppose you'd give me those details instead. I'll see you in a few minutes."

Even if I'd wanted to refuse, I couldn't have. The line went dead, so that was that. I gathered the mail and waited at the French door. "Agatha." I patted my open hand against my thigh. "Come on, girl. Come inside."

She had her nose buried in a bed of flowering white alyssum, but when she heard my voice, she froze. And then, as if someone had pulled a puppet string attached to her head, she looked at me. "Come on, Agatha. Inside."

She looked to the flowers, and then back at me. She hesitated, spun around, and the next second she was bolting across the yard, skidding to a stop in front of me. She tilted her head back and peered up at me with her bulbous eyes. I bent down and scratched the top of her head. "Okay, let's go."

Inside, I tossed the stack of bills on the table, gave Agatha a treat from the container I kept near the door, strapped her into her harness, and headed out the front. Minutes later I had climbed the steps of Mrs. Branford's lopsided porch. I raised my hand to knock, but the door flew open before I made contact. "You made good time, dear," Mrs. Branford said, a sparkle in her eyes. She had on her signature velour sweat suit, this one in burgundy.

"I didn't even stop at GO," I said.

"I'm afraid I don't have your two-hundred dollars, but you can come on in. Hello, sweet Agatha," she said, wiggling her fingers at her, but not bending down. Mrs. Branford was spritely, active, and healthy, especially for her age, but she didn't crouch unnecessarily.

She turned and walked toward the kitchen, her white orthotic shoes noiseless on the original hardwood floors. I followed her, stopping to breathe in the faint scent of lavender. The front room, with its overstuffed floral couch and striped armchair, had the comfort of my grandmother's house. The longer I was back in Santa Sofia, the more connected I felt to my hometown, and Mrs. Branford had been a huge part of that connectedness. But she didn't stop in the parlor, so neither did I. The gaggle of voices coming from the kitchen drew me in.

Agatha and I stopped short at the archway leading to the kitchen. The Blackbird Ladies, minus their unique hats, sat at the round, slat-topped table. It was a pale olive green and naturally distressed from the years it had spent in Mrs. Branford's kitchen. The three older women seated around it looked just as distressed.

"Ladies, let me do a proper introduction," Mrs. Branford said. "This is Ivy Culpepper."

"We aren't senile, Penny," said the one I remembered as Mrs. Peabody. "We met at the bread shop."

Of course I'd met Alice Ryder the day before, and I remembered that the one with the great posture and well-coiffed hair — the one who reminded me of Jane Fonda — as Janice Thompson. "Olaya says you're quite the baker," she said with a subtle smile.

I laughed. "She's being generous."

"Pshaw," Mrs. Branford said. She had gone to the counter and pressed the *on* switch on the electric kettle, opened a tea bag, and waited for the water to boil. "You're a natural."

"I don't know about that. I think I still feel more comfortable with my camera than a spatula, but I do love it." I realized as I said the words that I *did* love it. Being in a kitchen, particularly the bread shop's *cocina*, felt right. I explained all the baking we'd done that day. "So I'm a little tired," I finished.

"I'm tired just thinking about it," Mrs. Peabody said, wiping her brow with the back of her hand.

Alice Ryder, with her short, curled mahogany hair and her tight smile, tilted her head and looked at me. "You're quite the busy beaver, aren't you?"

If the other three Blackbird Ladies noticed the mocking tone in Alice's voice, they didn't let on. Mrs. Branford brought me a cup of tea, her hands trembling very slightly. Aside from the snowy white hair and the map of wrinkles on her face and hands, the unsteady hands were the only physical indication that she actually was in her eighties.

"I *am* busy," I agreed.

"Miss Culpepper and Miguel Baptista paid me a visit today," she announced, and not pleasantly.

Whatever movements had been happening in the kitchen up until that moment suddenly stopped. The silence was piercing. The three other Blackbird Ladies slowly turned their heads to look at Alice, and then as if they'd choreographed it, they spun their heads in unison toward me. Mrs. Branford cocked one eyebrow up. Her forehead dissolved into an array of creases, the eyebrow reaching toward her tightly curled hair. "You and Miguel?"

"Now, now, simmer down," I said, the

Texas expression I'd absorbed during my years in Austin coming out. "That's all there is to it. I'm doing a new menu and promo photographs for him —"

"You're a photographer?" Janice asked. "I'd love to talk to you about my house. I'm almost done renovating and —"

"Janice," Alice scolded.

Janice waggled her head slightly in a little spasm movement. She scratched under her hair behind her ear, clearly ruffled. She looked at me and I got the feeling she was sending me a silent communication, as if she understood that I needed the work and she wouldn't forget to follow up with me on her photography needs.

I dipped my head in a slight acknowledgment that said *Later. We'd talk later.*

"Why were you with Miguel, Ivy?" Mrs. Branford asked, her eyes twinkling.

"And why the visit to Alice?" Janice added.

"Don't jump to any conclusions," I said to Mrs. Branford. "I just happened to be there when Hank Rivera's son called Mrs. Baptista. He's worried about his dad."

Alice scoffed. "There's nothing to be worried about."

Mabel propped her elbows on the table in front of her. "I've heard the rumors, Alice. Nobody's seen him for a few days. We can't be sure there's nothing to worry about."

But Alice wasn't buying it. "Ladies, get some sense. He's a grown man who is perfectly capable of taking care of himself."

"Maybe," Mabel said.

Janice nodded. "Probably."

Alice sat back in her chair, crossed her legs, and folded her hands on her lap. "Definitely. I've known Hank a long time. If I had to venture a guess, I'd say he's gone away on a vacation to clear his divorce-addled mind."

Janice frowned. "I don't know, Alice. I heard business isn't going so well for him."

After Penny Branford handed me my tea, she'd perched on a stool at the counter. Now she leaned forward, a hand on each knee. "You mean financial trouble?"

Janice shrugged. "That's what I heard. My son . . . you know he runs a boarding house in town, and they get their produce from Hank. The scuttlebutt is that some of Hank's contracts haven't paid."

Alice turned to her friend, her cheeks flushed. "Goddammit, Janice. You can't just say something like that. That's how rumors get started."

Janice recoiled, looking hurt. "Ryan told me. Someone at the senior center told him. It's not a rumor, Alice."

Mabel Peabody had been quiet, but now she spoke up. "But if you don't have personal knowledge of it, it *is* a rumor. You can't just spout off gossip as if it's the truth."

Janice's lower lip trembled slightly and her eyes turned glassy at the chastisement of her friends. "Ryan is close with the people he cares for. Why would they lie to him? Maybe I didn't hear it first-hand, but that doesn't make it gossip."

I stood back, observing the dynamics between the four women. So far, Mrs. Branford had been quiet and watchful. Other than posing the question of the finances, she wasn't weighing in on the gossip versus truth. But I knew her, and I knew she'd get in the thick of it before long. If I'd learned anything about Penelope Branford from our first and last stakeout together, it was that she was tenacious and didn't hide that fact.

Alice, Janice, and Mabel, to a lesser degree, continued to argue over what constituted gossip. They went back and forth, back and forth, back and forth. Alice fell in the camp of: If you didn't get information firsthand from a primary source, it wasn't valid. Janice believed that information from a valid source, even if that information had traveled through several people, was still reliable. And Mabel erred on the side of caution. She said that no matter what, you needed to make your own decisions based on your personal knowledge and experiences.

Mrs. Branford cleared her throat before speaking, the voice of reason. "If we want answers, we should go to the source."

"What source?" Mabel asked.

I'd been silent, but now I piped up. "The seniors. Let's talk to Ryan; to your son, Janice," I said, directing my suggestion to her. "Let's go to the source so that, as Alice said, we can be sure."

But Alice wasn't so quick to jump on the suggestion. She leaned her head back, laughing to herself. After a beat, she looked at us. "Why is everyone so concerned about Hank?" she demanded. "Why? A lot of people go away for a few days and no one says or does a thing about it. So why is everyone up in arms about Hank?"

"Because it's out of character for him," Mrs. Branford said. "He was in my class once upon a time —"

"Everyone was in your class once upon a time," Janice said with a throaty laugh.

"— That's what happens when you're eighty-six years old and have been a teacher for more than two-thirds of your life. Anyway," she said, redirecting her conversation back, "I've known Hank a long time. There are kids who are diligent about everything, turning every assignment in on time, taking responsibility for every action. But there are plenty who aren't. Hank was not just one of the kids who was responsible: He went above and beyond. It's hard to forget a person like that. There are only a handful of kids every school year. With Hank it was like he couldn't live with himself if he turned something in late, or didn't give his best. He was one of the most conscientious students I ever had, and he grew up to be the same kind of man."

"He is a good guy," Alice said, and for the first time I realized that she had to be quite a bit younger than the other Blackbird Ladies. How I hadn't noticed it before, I'm not sure. Mrs. Branford had her snowy white hair and wrinkles to match. Janice Thompson had to be in her seventies, but she was put together and had a sophistication to her that the others didn't. Mabel was the free spirit and I guessed her age to be midsixties: Long, dark hair and a vibe that made me think she'd had fun in the 1960s.

And then there was Alice. Late fifties, or maybe early sixties. Hank's son Jason was a grown man. His wife was probably in her fifties. Michael had said that Hank, Alice, Brenda, and he had all gone to school together, so it wasn't outside the realm of possibility that Alice and Hank had been having an affair. It had certainly seemed that way to me when Miguel and I had stood on her porch earlier today, and from her behavior now, it was all the more likely. "How old is Hank Rivera?" I asked.

"Fifty-five," Alice said without even a beat. She drew in a sharp breath, as if she realized that she'd spoken too quickly.

But the others didn't bat an eye. "That's sounds about right," Mrs. Branford said, gazing at the ceiling as if she were counting back the years.

"How many students do you think you've had over the years, Penny?" Mabel asked.

That question sent Mrs. Branford's gaze back up to the ceiling. "Oh, Lord, too many to count. Nine thousand? Maybe ten?"

My eyebrows rose. Either way, the number was staggering.

Janice chuckled. "I'm pretty sure you taught nearly everyone in town." She looked at me with a knowing grin. "She was Ryan's favorite teacher."

Mrs. Branford looked like the Cheshire cat, all knowing and mischievous. "I have had many generations from the same family. Hank and Brenda Rivera and Jason. Alice, I had your kids. Ryan, which, of course, you already said, Janice."

"My kids went to private school," Mabel said, "so they never had the pleasure of being in your class."

"You call that commune one-room schoolhouse *private school*?" Janice said, scoffing.

Mabel didn't say anything for a second and I wondered if Janice had offended her, but then Mabel started nodding, slowly at first, then her head went up and down more rapidly. "Right," she said and she laughed. "In retrospect, that wasn't the best school choice. They learned a lot about, shall we say, herbs?"

My eyes grew wide. Well, well, I was learning all sorts of things about the Blackbird Ladies. Mabel Peabody, the former hippie, sent her kids to school to learn to grow pot, and Mrs. Branford taught everyone else in town. Everyone knew everyone.

And yet no one, it seemed, knew where Hank Rivera was.

CHAPTER 6

The Blackbird Ladies stayed for another hour, the tension from their conversation about Hank Rivera dissolving into the playful banter of longtime friends. Either Penny Branford was a good hostess, or the three other women had nowhere else they needed to be. Probably both. They stayed, and I loved their company. We laughed, I told them about the tragedy of my unfaithful husband and our subsequent divorce, I learned about Mabel's first marriage to a rodeo star and catching her children growing their own marijuana plants in one of their closets. And Mrs. Branford heated up a pot of soup for us. Pretty soon I was wishing for a blackbird-adorned hat of my own.

Agatha slept through the whole thing.

At about 7:30, Alice gathered her things to leave. Janice and Mabel followed suit. We all headed to the front door together, Agatha trotting excitedly by my side. As we approached the door, Mrs. Branford laced her arm through mine. The three departing Blackbird Ladies stepped out onto the porch, turning to say good night, but Mrs. Branford beat them to the punch. "Bye, girls!"

As I started to cross the threshold, she pulled me back in, slamming the door. The force of her movement caused me to stumble over Agatha's leash, my feet tangling beneath me. Mrs. Branford still held me by the arm. "Let go!" I said, hoping she would before she crashed to the floor with me and broke a hip.

But I needn't have worried. "Hold on, Ivy," she said, and she gave my arm a mighty tug, practically lifting me up off the floor. Or maybe she *did* actually lift me up off the floor, because suddenly I felt my feet touch the floor again with a thud.

"Mrs. Branford!"

She chortled at the success of her subterfuge, facing me and rubbing my arms. "Penny, dear. One of these days, you'll call me Penny."

I'd caught my breath and calmed my rattled heart by then. "Never." I just couldn't see it happening. It just didn't feel right.

"Say it."

As I looked at her, I felt my left eye pinch. "Say what?"

"My name. Say *Penny.*"

She spoke slowly, as if I were an addle-minded child. Why did I suddenly feel as if I were being cornered? I steeled my resolve. "Mrs. Branford."

I backed away, but she shuffled toward me, pointing her cane at me. "Penny."

She was trying to coerce me with sheer will, but I just didn't buy her brand of intimidation. "I'm not going to call you Penny —"

"Aha!"

I slapped my hand against my forehead. She'd tricked me. "You sly fox, you."

She patted her tightly-wound silver hair. "That can be my code name when we start investigating." She nodded. "Yes. Sly fox. I do believe it fits."

"Okay," I started to say, but then her words fully registered. "Until we *what*?"

"Sit down, Ivy."

I did. She sat on one overstuffed floral couch and I perched on the edge of the other. "I'm sitting." So was Agatha, right by my feet.

"I think we need to investigate."

All I could do was shake my head. "Investigate what, Mrs. Branford?" I asked, although I knew what she was going to say.

"Hank, of course, because I happen to think Jason is right."

"Right about what?"

"Right to be concerned, because Hank is the most reliable person I've ever known. It is completely out of character for him to just vanish. Something is wrong."

"Slow down there. We are not Cagney and Lacey."

The corner of her mouth lifted in an amused half smile. "I doubt very much that anybody remembers Cagney and Lacey, Ivy. In fact, how on earth do you know that show?"

"Netflix," I replied smugly. *Matlock, Perry Mason, Rockford Files, Murder, She Wrote,* and the aforementioned *Cagney and Lacey.* Vintage TV crime. It was my secret indulgence.

She chuckled. "Ah, yes, the new TV. You never have to watch in real time."

"The point is valid. We are not TV detectives," I said, circling back to her announcement that we investigate.

"No, we're better. Look how we figured out what happened with Janet," she said, referring to the murder that we'd helped solve recently. We'd done some digging, followed some clues, and discovered the truth behind the death of a local caterer and one of Olaya's best friends.

"That was luck," I said. "I've hung up my sleuthing shoes."

She cocked one gray eyebrow at me. "Are there special sleuthing shoes of which I am unaware?" she asked, her teacher genes coming out with her exceptional grammar.

I lowered my head, pinching the bridge of my nose. "Actually, I don't think there are. But again, my point is that we aren't detectives, number one. And number two, we don't actually have anything to investigate. Alice may very well be right." I lifted my chin, adding emphasis to my point. "Hank may just be on a little sojourn that he didn't bother to mention to anyone."

"A sojourn. Pshaw. She's always had a thing for Hank. Their short-lived dalliance in high school has burned like a low flame all these years."

God, I loved Mrs. Branford's vocabulary. It was of another generation, sometimes. "I knew it! When Miguel and I saw her this afternoon, I had this feeling that there was still something between them."

She grimaced, more wrinkles than normal lining her face with the expression. "I have often wondered if they rekindled it at some point, unbeknownst to Brenda and Michael, of course."

Agatha had stretched out on the floor by my feet, so I sat back on the couch, tucking one leg under me. A well-loved quilt with a log-cabin design, soft from years of being laundered, was tossed over the back of the sofa. I pulled it down over me, since it looked as if I'd be staying a while longer than I'd planned. "What makes you think so?"

She patted her chest and gave me a happy smirk. "Detectiving," she said.

I rolled my eyes, but affectionately. I suspected it less about "detectiving" and more about intuition, but either way, Penelope Branford was downright adorable. "Well, Detective Branford, I'm not sure that Hank hasn't just taken a few mental-health days, but I guess it won't hurt to dig around a little bit."

She clapped her hands, letting them fall away from each other dramatically. "Very good! We shall start tomorr—"

My spine stiffened and I fanned my hands in front of her. "No, no. Tomorrow is the festival. I'm there all day. There will be no detectiving tomorrow."

"But of course there will. What better place to start poking the bear than at the Winter Wonderland Festival? Everyone in

111

town will be there."

I considered her point. The place *was* going to be teeming with Santa Sofia's entire population, and then some. "Maybe, but Hank may just show up after his little vacation. That would be nice."

Mrs. Branford shook her head. "It would be, but I don't think so. I think we're dealing with something sinister."

"Something wicked this way comes?"

Mrs. Branford grimaced as she leaned forward and patted my knee. "Ah, sweet Ivy, how right you are. Something wicked, indeed."

I couldn't figure out why she felt there was something threatening or ominous going on with Hank, but she wasn't able to explain it. "Just a feeling," was all she said.

After a few more minutes, I roused myself, awakened Agatha, and gave Mrs. Branford a peck on the cheek. In a dramatic voice — and with a wink — I added, "Until tomorrow, ma cherie."

"Oui, oui."

At the door, I paused and looked at her in earnest. Her face was more drawn than it had been earlier. "Can I do anything for you before I go?"

"No, not at all. It's time for my beauty sleep, that's all."

Agatha whimpered beside me. I placated her with a few soothing words. "Hers, too."

"You know what they say about great minds. Now my dear, I would think that you need your rest, too. Early day for you tomorrow and a long one. If there's one thing I know about Olaya Solis, it's that when she is in for a penny, she's in for a pound. You'll be exhausted by the time the day is done. And we still have a mission to accomplish."

I was getting exhausted just hearing about how exhausted I was going to be by the end of the next day. I said my good-bye and headed across the street, Agatha in tow, and wondered what was really going on with Hank Rivera.

CHAPTER 7

Santa Sofia had its fair share of town events. From the traditional Day of the Dead celebration to the spring Art Car Ball and Parade, we were always up for some merriment. But the Winter Wonderland Festival was nothing short of spectacular. I'd been coming since I was a little girl, minus my years in Austin, and it still struck me as wondrous. Take a little dollop of a vintage fair, an enormous barn that had been remodeled as a town gathering space, and everything wintry, and voilà! It was a unique experience unlike any other I'd ever seen.

I'd woken up at 4:30 the next morning, wondered if I was completely crazy, talked myself out of going back to sleep, and crawled reluctantly out of bed. I'd bundled up, speed-walked a very sleepy Agatha around the block, got myself dressed and ready to go, and arrived at Yeast of Eden at exactly 5:15. Olaya and I spent a few hours doing our "morning of" baking, both for the shop and for the festival, before working steadily with the delivery team to deliver the bread and set up the Yeast of Eden booth. We'd draped cream linens and burlap runners on the tables, adorning the burlap with vases filled with sparkling white branches, white-flecked pinecones, and white twinkle lights. Olaya always brought elements of Mexican culture into everything she did, whether it was the colorful, doily-like garlands hung in the bread shop, her sugar-skull cookies, the occasional special offering of *tres leche* cake, or the sign above the door from the bread shop to the kitchen that read: *BIENVENIDOS A TODOS.* Today was no exception. The skull cookies were there, but today they were plated and for sale, with colorful garlands hanging behind us.

Today's pan dulce sat on a tray under one large, clear plastic rectangular dome. Next to it and spread across the table were all the other offerings we'd prepared, each pro-tected with its own transparent cover. The wintry decorations added a bit of elegance to the display, and on a smaller side table, we'd set up an insulated stainless-steel dispenser filled with Mexican hot chocolate — freshly made with whole milk — *mi abuelita's* chocolate tablets, and cinnamon sticks.

Once we were ready, I reached under the table to retrieve my saddle-brown camera bag. It had been an extravagance, but it had been well worth the price.

I took out my camera, slung the strap over my shoulder, and took a walk around to see the other booths. It seemed as if every business in town was represented, from the mini-mall antique store catty-corner to the bread shop, to the custom glassblowing store on the pier, to the chocolatier a few storefronts down from Yeast of Eden. I spotted Baptista's booth, but turned at the first row instead of heading straight toward it. I'd stop in later, if I had time.

From what I could tell at first glance, there were just as many food booths as there were stalls selling knickknacks. Most of the goods on display were original and unique. As I came across interesting objects, color patterns, and groups of people, I adjusted my camera's settings for the lighting, focused on the subject, and shot.

Everywhere I looked, I saw something attention-grabbing. One booth, in particular, drew my interest. It held curios I wanted to examine more closely. I was always open to something that would fit beautifully into my house and would make it feel even more like home. I admired a collection of antique vases, several ceramic and tin candlesticks, an assortment of ancient books, and a duo of pewter cups. Then I spotted a unique galvanized metal contraption. It had seven small receptacles, each positioned at a movable joint so that it could be formed into a circle. I envisioned it as a miniature conveyor, kind of like a water wheel. It took every ounce of willpower I could muster to resist buying it. Did I really need it? I looked at it more closely, noticing that the rectangular vessels had been stamped with numbers. The whole thing was just so cool. *And* I had the perfect spot for it in my kitchen. It could hang vertically on a narrow section of wall in between the counter where I put the toaster oven and the hallway. I could picture it with a few sprigs of lavender in each small container.

I took a picture of it and then turned away. If I still wanted it at the end of the day, I could always come back for it.

The booth was from a unique little shop a block away from Yeast of Eden: Vintage Bleu. It had been there for a few years, from what I understood, but I'd never been inside. Now I knew what I'd been missing.

"See anything you like?"

The voice was vaguely familiar. I turned and my jaw dropped. I recognized the sleek, long, black hair and fair skin. With the slight blush of her cheeks, she reminded me a bit of Snow White. *"Jolie?"*

From her expression, she was just as surprised to see me. "Ivy!" she exclaimed. I'd met Jolie Flemming at the bread shop during a series of baking classes we'd taken, but I hadn't seen her in a few months. "What are you doing here?"

I held up my camera. "Just taking some pictures."

"Oh my gosh. I follow your Instagram. Amazing pictures!"

"I have a Pinterest board, too. And I'm in charge of the Yeast of Eden website now," I said with a sheepish grin.

A smile leavened her features. "I heard you were sort of an apprentice to Olaya now."

News traveled fast in a small town. "That's what she says, although I'm really just more of a helper." I explained the arrangement to Jolie: "She teaches me what it has taken her a lifetime to learn, and I try to retain a fraction of it," I said with a laugh. "What are *you* doing here? You work at Vintage Bleu?"

She shrugged. "After everything that happened," she said, referring to her mother's death a few months back, "I needed something to get my mind off things. I know the owner and she offered me a job, so here I am."

"Are you doing okay?" I asked. Losing our mothers had created a bond between Jolie and me, although it wasn't a subject we brought up very often. Neither of us wanted to open the wounds we'd been so carefully tending to.

Her smile was genuine but laced with sadness. "Yeah. Doing okay."

We chatted for a few more minutes while I perused the charming vintage goods in the booth. I checked my watch, balking at the time. "Oh, wow. I have to get back to the bread-shop booth." My eyes shifted back to the conveyor thingamajig. It wasn't the end of the day yet, but I didn't have to wait that long to know that I wanted it. It had won me over. "Can you hold that for me?" I asked.

She reached in the pocket of her frilly half apron and withdrew a *SOLD* tag. "Oh yeah, sure. It's cool, isn't it?"

"Very. I can come get it at the end of the day."

"I can bring it by your booth when I go to lunch. It'll give me an excuse to have something from the bread shop. Mmm, do

119

you have any croissants? Ham and cheese, maybe?"

I grinned. "We do. I'll put one aside for you."

She had already turned to my purchase and was tying a *SOLD* tag on it. "It's so good to see you, Ivy."

I thought about Mrs. Branford and her plan to look into Hank Rivera. I doubted Jolie would know anything, but I figured I needed to go ahead and ask. "Do you know Mustache Hank? Hank Rivera," I clarified.

"Doesn't everyone?" She laughed. "Hard to miss that handlebar mustache."

I laughed. "That's for sure."

She straightened an antique kitchen scale with a white base and a red platform. "I know who he is, but I don't actually know him," she said. "Why?"

I embellished my response. "I have a friend who's looking for him. He's sort of gone AWOL."

She raised her eyebrows. "AWOL?"

I shrugged, trying to make light of it. "Yeah, for a few days now. His son is a little worried."

"And you're trying to find him?" I nodded, and she continued. "It's just like you did with my mom." She took one of my hands in hers and gave it a little squeeze.

120

"If anyone can get to the bottom of it, Ivy, it's you. I've seen that firsthand."

I felt heat in my cheeks as a blush crept up. "I hope so. I want to try, anyway. You haven't seen him?"

She thought for a second, but then shook her head. "I haven't seen him around in a while," she said, "but I pretty much go from my apartment to the shop and back again, so I don't think I would."

"Makes sense. Let me know if you hear anything?"

"Absolutely," she said as she straightened a stack of old suitcases that were teetering precariously.

I waved as I left the booth and wove my way through the maze of winter-decorated tables and stalls, taking more photos along the way. The entire place was a wonderland of white and sparkly snowflakes, rustic sticks, and old-fashioned decor. I loved every bit of it.

The festival had officially begun and people were beginning to file in from the cold. They were bundled up in jackets and scarves and I had to laugh; cold in Santa Sofia meant a brisk sixty-five degrees. We were nowhere near artic temperatures, but you'd never know it from the look of the people. Seeing them wrapped up in their coats sent a blast of goose bumps over my flesh.

As I came up to our booth, I rubbed my hands against my folded arms. Olaya was arranging yet another tray of baked goods, this time scones, onto a tiered display, but I was lost in thought. I couldn't get Hank Rivera off my mind. "Cold, *mi'ja*?"

I only half-heard her.

"Ivy?"

"Hmm?"

She peered up at me. "What is going on?"

I focused on her. "What do you mean?"

She raised her eyebrows at me. "I mean, what is going on?"

"Nothing," I said, but even I could hear the overcharged enthusiasm in my voice.

"Nada?" She scoffed. "*Mentirosa*. You lie. You are distracted, and if I had to venture a guess, I would say that you and Penelope are getting yourselves involved in something you should not."

My eyes opened wide. How could she have known anything about what Mrs. Branford and I had cooked up?

I didn't have to ask her because she answered without prompting. "I know Penelope. And I also know that Hank Rivera is not your concern. I thought you were going to leave it to your sheriff friend."

122

I couldn't help but stare. It was like she was psychic. "The man is nowhere to be found. What if he needs to be?"

"*Que?* What if he needs to be, what — found?"

"Yes! If someone vanishes, it's for a reason. There would be a clue, wouldn't there? A trail. Something."

She seemed to consider this as she moved the last scone to the display table. "Are you certain that there is not a clue . . . or a trail of some sort?" she finally asked.

The question surprised me. I had to answer honestly. "Well, no."

She'd finished plating the scones and slid the tray onto the portable rack she'd brought along. "I worry about you, Ivy. You are still searching."

I turned away, swallowing the lump that appeared in my throat. Was I floundering? Losing my mother had been the hardest thing I'd ever had to deal with. My dad and my brother had been my rocks, but finding Olaya and Yeast of Eden, and then Mrs. Branford, had saved me. I still grieved, but I was finally moving forward.

I distracted myself by rearranging the burlap runner and repositioning the sparkling sprigs of holly. My commitment to Mrs. Branford the night before had solidi-

123

fied my concern. "I'm worried about Hank," I said. My hand instinctively went to rest on my stomach. "I have a gut feeling. Something is not right."

"And Penelope, she has this same . . . er . . . gut feeling?"

I nodded. "She does. She wants to do a full-court press and investigate. I reined her in and said I'd dig around with her."

Olaya finished unloading the next tray she'd picked up, and now she looked at me. "And? Have you found out anything?"

I shook my head. "I'm hoping something interesting or helpful may pop up today."

She glanced around the hall. "Here?"

Now that I thought about it, it didn't seem likely, given the fact that I'd be busy serving bread from our booth, but you never knew. Sometimes when you least expected something, you were pleasantly surprised. "It's possible."

Hank Rivera had occupied my thoughts for a long time before I was finally able to sleep the night before. Mrs. Branford had planted a bug in my mind and now I couldn't seem to let it go. But for the next hour, that's exactly what I had to do. The clock had struck 10:00, the doors to the barn had opened, and the people had come in droves, some arm in arm, others holding hands, even more pushing strollers or with small children in tow. Upon entering, there were three possible paths: Straight down the center aisle of the barn and right into the heart of the booths; to the left, which led to a pop-up coffee shop, complete with tables and chairs for people to sit and rest; or to the right, which led to even more booths, displays, and local goods.

Yeast of Eden's booth was right next to Brewer's Coffee. It was the perfect location; everyone needed their coffee, and baked delicacies went right along with that. Once the people came in, a good many headed straight for their caffeine fix, coming right to us next. The line was fifteen deep, with others leaning into every possible space around the tables. Olaya and I fielded the orders while Maggie, a high-school girl Olaya employed part-time, manned the cash register.

The time passed lightning fast and before I knew it, it was 1:00. Just as I realized that Jolie Flemming hadn't come by for her croissant, I heard my name called. Speak of the devil. I looked up to see her waving at me with one hand, the antique conveyor contraption I'd purchased in her other. She turned sideways to edge between a woman and another man with his family, then lifted my purchase over the table to me. I tucked it aside in the back of the booth, next to the bread racks, grabbing the ham-and-cheese croissant I'd set aside for her and handing it over as if we'd done a trade.

"I thought you forgot," I said, looking at my purchase. I didn't have an ounce of buyer's remorse. I loved the antique, whatever it had been used for back in its heyday.

"Never." She put the croissant under her nose and breathed in. "Mmm. So good."

"Been busy?" I asked as I put a small brioche in a bag for the woman next to Jolie.

She nodded, her mouth too full to respond. She touched two fingers to her mouth as she finished chewing, and then swallowed. "Swamped," she said a moment later.

I looked around at the mass of people milling about. I hadn't been to a Winter Wonderland Festival in years, but from what I recalled, the turnout here far exceeded what I remembered. "We haven't had a chance to even breathe," I said as I directed Maggie to another customer.

She nodded, understanding that I didn't have time to talk. "I'll talk to you later," she said, but then she hesitated.

"Do you want another one?" I asked her, then nodded to the man and his family next to her. "I'll be with you in just a sec," I told him.

"No. I mean, yes! I do. Thanks. But that wasn't what I —"

I put another ham-and-cheese croissant in a little white bag for her. Maggie hovered nearby. Jolie handed her a five-dollar bill. While Maggie counted back the change, Jolie leaned forward conspiratorially. "I heard something this morning."

My head snapped up. "About — ?"

She nodded, widening her eyes, a tiny smile on her lips. "Yes," she whispered.

I turned to Maggie, asking her to cover for me for a minute, and then I stepped away from the booth. She followed me and we hovered in the corner by the coffee shop. "Tell me!"

She looked over her shoulder, left and right, and then back at me. "Some people were talking about Mustache Hank a little while ago. I got as close as I could. I didn't hear very much, but I did get the gist."

She paused and I felt my heartbeat climb. "What was the gist?"

"He owes some people some money."

So financial trouble, just like Alice Ryder had suggested. "Who? How much?"

Jolie held her arms out and shrugged. "I heard a snippet of a conversation, not his whole life story, Ivy."

Of course. I was already way too invested in Hank Rivera, but if he really was in financial trouble, that could explain him checking out of town for a few days. Maybe Alice really was right and he just needed time to figure things out. A little time to get away and consider his options. "Do you know who he owes?"

Her eyes looked up toward the ceiling. "Maybe I got it wrong. I was so excited when I heard his name."

"What do you mean, Maybe you got it wrong?"

"I'm trying to remember. Was it that he owes someone money, or does someone owe *him* money?"

"You're not sure what you heard?"

She closed her eyes for a beat, thinking. When they opened again, she dipped her head in a single, assured nod. "He owes someone money. Yes, that was it."

"You're sure?"

She gathered her hair into a ponytail with one hand, looping her fingers around the thickness. "Positive."

"Did you see who was talking?"

She shook her head. "No, sorry. They were around the corner from Vintage Bleu's booth. I just heard Hank's name and did my best to eavesdrop without being obvious. When they stopped speaking, I peeked around the corner, but there were too many people to know who had been speaking."

"Man or woman?" I asked. If Hank had disappeared for a few days to get a handle on his debt, I could understand that, but I wanted to know what we were talking about here. How much did he owe, and to whom?

"It was a man."

"But you don't know who it was?"

She shrugged helplessly. "A woman? Yes. A woman. He said 'Tracy'."

But Tracy could be a man's name, too, so I didn't put 100-percent stock in what Jolie had heard. "Does Hank owe the money to this man?"

She didn't have to think about it. "It didn't sound like that to me. They were just gossiping, I think. Sorry," she said. "That's all I got."

"No need to apologize! Thank you for telling me."

"I need to get back," she said, and with a quick wave, she melted into the crowd.

"Olaya," I said when I slipped back into the booth. "I'm going to make the rounds. Take a few pictures."

She waved me away. "We are fine, Maggie and me. Go on."

I took my camera from my bag and headed into the throng of people. The happy buzz swirled around like snowflake flurries. Everyone at the festival was happy. Outside, horse-drawn carriages took folks on a ride around the converted barn. Winter flowers had been planted in every available space, twinkling white lights sparkled in the trees, and delicate faux snowflakes hung from a nearly invisible fishing line.

I took pictures of the different activities, including the second outbuilding that had been turned into an ice rink. I had no idea how they kept it cold enough, but the rink was solid ice and bundled-up guests, many of them squealing children, made their way around and around and around.

I spent an hour taking different shots, capturing the joyful faces — kids and adults alike. I smiled and laughed right along with the festivalgoers, but the weight of Hank Rivera's disappearance put a damper on my mood.

Back inside the main barn, I wended through the maze of booths. A children's play area had been created in one corner with an arts-and-crafts section, complete with a volunteer to help the kids make handmade snowflakes and hands-on activities put together by a local children's museum. Benches lined the perimeter. They were filled with weary parents already looking for a place to rest before they continued their Winter Wonderland Festival.

I couldn't help but smile at the energy of the kids, snapping a few pictures of them as they engaged in their snowflake making. I continued along the perimeter of the barn, looking at each booth and area, my eyes scanning every corner as I looked for the next photographical scene. I looked through the viewfinder, focusing on a young couple holding hands as they wandered. They were the perfect subjects with their fresh wintry clothes and happy countenance. I knew the shots would end up being some of my favorites.

The girl's blond hair cascaded down her back like spun gold floating over her pale blue jacket. A navy skirt flared from beneath the coat, and she wore dark tights and boots. The young man she held hands with had brown curls, a plaid button-up shirt, and jeans. I depressed the shutter button, refocusing and shooting again as the young woman turned to the man, her head thrown back, her lips parted in a laugh. The booths and the floating snowflakes blurred in the background, bringing the couple, by contrast, into sharp focus. I took a quick look at the digital display and smiled. The picture was everything I had hoped it would be. Better, even.

I looked through the viewfinder, ready to take another picture, when something blurry blocked my lens. I jumped back, lowering my camera. Alice Ryder and Janice Thompson stood in front of me. They were without their blackbird hats, but that didn't matter. They'd forever be Blackbird Ladies to me.

"Hello, Ivy," Alice said, her voice not quite icy, but definitely not warm, either. I got the feeling she was trying to stay mad at me for intruding on her at her home and bringing up whatever it was she had with Mustache Hank, but deep inside she knew she didn't have any reason to hold it against me. I was convinced that she'd get over it.

Janice, on the other hand, was more animated in her greeting. "Ivy, so good to see you!" She looked at the camera in my hand. "I'm so glad I ran into you. I want to schedule a time for you to come take a look at my son's house. It's a beauty. Still a work in progress, you know, but we want to get pictures of it now, and then more when it's all finished."

"I'd love to," I said. I felt in my back jeans pocket for my phone. Empty. "I need to look at my calendar, but I think I left my phone at the booth. Can I get back to you?"

"Of course, dear. You just give me a call when you can. Richie mentioned that he needs a few weeks to finish some tasks in the backyard, so we have some time. I haven't been over there in ages. I can't wait to see what he's done since I saw it last!" She changed subjects, her head jutting forward slightly and her voice dropping as if she were imparting a secret. "Anything new on Hank?"

I shook my head. "No, not since last night. I've been looking around —"

"You think he might show up here?" she asked.

"You never know. Anything's possible." I hadn't really believed it would be that easy. My gut still told me, quite firmly, that something bad had happened, but I didn't elaborate on that with Janice and Alice. They'd heard it all the night before.

Janice tapped two fingers against her lips, peering at the people around her with discerning eyes. "We will let you know if we see Hank," she said, "won't we, Alice?"

Alice nodded, looking less optimistic than Janice did. And less interested, which I found curious, given the fact that she had a different — and more familiar — relationship with Hank than the other Blackbird Ladies did. Of course, I remembered, she still believed he'd just skipped off somewhere to have some alone time and process through his life, such as it was.

I wanted to believe that she was right, but that coil of doubt in my gut told me otherwise.

Janice and Alice waved good-bye and I turned to head back to the Yeast of Eden booth. I snapped a few more pictures along the way, rounded a corner, and there was Baptista's restaurant setup. I thought about passing it up altogether — Miguel and I were on shaky ground, still avoiding our past — but I changed my mind at the last second and veered to the counter.

There was no sign of Miguel, though. I was about to ask after him when the woman working the front turned around. I recognized her immediately — Laura Baptista, Miguel's younger sister.

"Laura!" I said, smiling. So many years had passed since I'd seen her.

Her brown eyes narrowed as recognition dawned. "Ivy."

It was not the enthusiastic greeting I'd expected. I toned down my smile and my voice. "Hey. It's been a long time. How have you been?"

"Yeah, I'm good," she said dismissively.

Her comment didn't invite a response. Either she was distracted with something, or she was not too happy to see me. My gut reacted again. I was pretty certain it was the latter. As I searched for something to say, I noticed a wedding ring on her finger. "You're married? That's great. Kids?"

"A boy and a girl."

I peered over the counter, thinking they might be here. A few people plated up food to the guests in line, but there was no sign of any kids. Laura didn't ask me about coming back to Santa Sofia, my mom, or anything. The conversation was clearly over. "Okay, well . . . I think I'll head back to the bread-shop booth. It's been pretty busy. Tell Miguel I said hello."

At the mention of Miguel, her face changed. Her expression grew darker and her eyes became slits. "Leave him alone, Ivy."

Her voice was venomous. Coupled with the look she gave me, I felt like I'd been slapped. I stared at her. "What?"

She crossed her arms over her aproned chest, glaring. "You heard me. Leave him alone."

I had no idea how to respond. "Um, okay?" I said without thinking.

Her expression turned to disdain. "Um, okay?" she mimicked.

My heart raced, in part with fury at her attitude toward me, in part with hurt. I'd never been anything but nice to her back in high school. Where was this coming from? I batted down the anger creeping up over her menace. "Laura, what's going on?"

She stared at me, openmouthed. "Seriously? You have the nerve to ask me that?"

I stared right back. "Yes, I have the nerve, because I haven't seen you in probably ten years. I have no idea why you're acting like this."

She scoffed. "Is that so?"

I stood up straighter, throwing my shoulders back as if this were a standoff. "Yes, that's so. Why don't you just tell me so I don't have to guess?"

"Why don't you ask Miguel?"

"You just told me to stay away from him, and now you want me to ask him, what — why his sister is being a bitch?"

Her expression darkened some more, if that was even possible. "Priceless," she said. "Look, he's conflicted about you being back, but I don't want to see him hurt again. You drove him away once. I don't want to lose him again."

I pressed my open palm against my chest.

"*I* drove *him* away?"

"Yes, and a zebra can't change his stripes, so stay away from him."

I shook my head in confusion. "What?"

"You heard me."

"Laura, what are you talking about?"

She looked at me as if I were straight from the loony bin. "What am I talking about?"

"Yes," I said, "what are you talking about, Laura?" But apparently she was done. She clamped her mouth shut, threw up one hand, palm out, and then she turned and walked away from the counter, leaving me dumbstruck.

I wanted to leap across the counter, grab Laura by the arm, and demand she tell me what the hell she was talking about, but I thought better of it. Instead, I turned my back on the makeshift restaurant and headed back toward the Yeast of Eden booth. I made it as far as the coffee shop next to our booth when I heard another familiar voice calling my name. "There you are, Ivy. I've been searching all over for you."

Mrs. Branford sauntered up to me, her cane in hand. She was calm and together like always. She'd dressed for the festival, wearing a white velour lounge suit that had a sparkling stripe down the outer pant legs, and a matching stripe on each arm. She had her own brand of hip senior style.

"You look like you've been out for a nice walk."

"I have. All over tarnation and back. This barn is bigger than it looks."

I had to agree. The place was enormous. Hiking around it and fighting the crowds would be harrowing for anyone, let alone an eighty-six-year-old woman. "You have your cane, though. That's good."

She waved her hand, brushing away my words. "It's for show, Ivy. Surely you know that by now."

"I've had my suspicions," I said with a wink. Still, I was glad she had it, just in case.

She winked back, but hers was dramatic, with a cocked head and a crookedly open mouth. "I'm much younger than my years would have you believe, Ivy. Remember that."

"I don't think I could forget if I wanted to, Mrs. Branford."

"Penny."

I pushed my encounter with Laura out of my mind for now and smiled. "Mrs. Branford."

She let the name thing go, moving on to her other obsession. "So dear, tell me what you've found out. Don't leave anything out."

That wouldn't take long. "Do you remember Jolie Flemming?"

"Of course I do," she said. "From baking class at the bread shop."

"Right. She's here. She works at Vintage Bleu now."

"I have always loved that shop," she said.

"Me, too. Pretty great stuff in there."

She adjusted her weight, switching her cane to her other hand, "So, what does Jolie have to do with Hank?"

I got into the spirit of investigating right alongside Penelope Branford. "Well, let me tell you."

"Please, but let's sit down, shall we?" She was quite a bit shorter than my five-foot-eight inches and had to lean around me to look at the options. "Right there," she said, sidestepping me and moving toward the coffee shop's tables and chairs. She looked at one, disregarded it, and moved on to the next one. Which she passed on as well. Finally, she stopped at a table, examined it, and lowered herself onto the chair.

I had no idea what was wrong with the first two, but I didn't ask. I sat across from her and we both leaned in. "Tell me," she said.

"There isn't much," I said and told her what Jolie had overheard about Hank owing

139

people money.

She frowned. "Well, isn't that disappointing? We'd already speculated about that."

It was disappointing. Very. "I had an idea, though." While I'd been serving scones and brioches earlier, I'd gone over the conversation Miguel and I had had with Mrs. Rivera in the home she'd shared with Hank. She'd said that Hank had given up drinking, but what if he'd picked it back up again? "I'm done at five thirty," I said, "and I think I may need a drink after a long day. Something a little stronger than hot tea."

She arched a brow at me, but her eyes twinkled. "I'm not quite following, but who cares? I'm in. Now, what exactly did you have in mind?"

CHAPTER 8

What I had in mind was a visit to the Broken Horse. The former Mrs. Rivera had mentioned the bar in passing, and at the moment that was the only place I could think of to look for Hank. It almost felt personal at this point. No, I didn't know the man beyond having said hello to him that morning at the bread shop, but I was determined to find him.

By 4:45 that evening, the Yeast of Eden booth was down to the last of our baked offerings. There were two French loaves left, a single pumpernickel round, a broken baguette, three olive loaves, a handful of cookies, and the crumbs of everything else. Olaya had calculated almost perfectly. "Impressive," I said as we stacked up the trays and began tearing down the booth. It was a lot of work for a single day and we were exhausted, but Olaya had spread her magic through her bread all day long. People were whistling, they were jaunty, and hardly a child cried all day long. It was as if the breads Olaya had made infused everyone with a warm winter glow that bloomed from the inside out.

"Comes from experience," she said.

As with everything else, experience, more than anything else, impacted how and what one did and the effect it had on others. Olaya claimed to come from a long line of *curanderas,* or medicine women. She baked magic into her breads. Whether you were sick, lovelorn, anxious, or anything else, something in the bread shop would fix what ailed you. Her magic seemed to have worked during the festival.

It took an hour for Olaya, her other workers, and me to close up shop for the evening. We busied ourselves putting the baking trays into the racks and stowing them in the back of the minivan, breaking down the booth — from tables to awning. Mrs. Branford waited at a nearby bench while I finished.

Olaya looked around her, scanning the area for anything she might have left behind. When she was certain we'd gotten everything, she started walking toward the exit. "Penny," Olaya said, coming up to Mrs. Branford.

Mrs. Branford used her cane to stand and

pursed her lips slightly, but there was a trace of a grin. The two women had only recently mended fences after practically a lifetime of bitterness, but their friendship was still a touch tenuous. "Olaya."

"What are you two up to?" Olaya asked as we all continued toward the barn doors.

"Oh, you know, out to do a little detectiving," Mrs. Branford said, a twinkle in her eyes.

Olaya shook her head. "You two. You keep sticking your nose in where it does not belong," she said, but the scolding fell short. She patted me on the shoulder. "You let me know what you find."

"Absolutely," I said. I gave her a peck on the cheek and we went our separate ways at the exit, Olaya heading to the bread-shop van, and Mrs. Branford and me walking to the main parking lot.

"How did you get here?" I asked.

"Uber."

I had to laugh. I knew she usually relied on volunteers at the senior center to take her to appointments and shopping, but Uber was a new choice for her. Mrs. Branford never ceased to amaze me. I helped her into the passenger seat of my car and drove off. I had just turned onto the main street when she said, "Go on back to Maple

Street, Ivy."

Surprise flitted across my face. "You don't want to come with me?"

"Don't be silly. Of course I'm coming. But I know you need to take Agatha out, and I want you to drive my car. It needs a spin."

I should have known she wasn't backing out. And she was right about Agatha. I'd asked Billy to take her out midday, but I hated to leave her alone for another couple of hours without at least a quick trip to the backyard and little scratch on the head.

I dropped Mrs. Branford at her house, and then went home, changed into a fresh blouse and jeans, took care of Agatha, and fifteen minutes later I walked across and up the street to Mrs. Branford's house.

She had an old Volvo coupe 112S. The pale, sage-green color had been resprayed at some point, but Mrs. Branford and her late husband were the original owners and had taken great care of it. The car was immaculate. But since she didn't drive much anymore, it sat in the garage more than it ever saw the light of day. "I'll never sell it," she had said to one of the Blackbird Ladies the evening we'd spent at her house. "And I'm bequeathing it to Ivy."

I'd balked, staring at her openmouthed. I hadn't known her for very long and I certainly didn't deserve to inherit her precious car. I told her as much.

"Ivy, you do not understand. You've given me such joy in the short time I've known you. I already treasure you."

I'd teared up. With my own mother gone, Mrs. Branford and Olaya Solis had become the most present female figures in my life. Emmaline Davis, my longtime friend, would always be there, but ours was a friendship based on history and age, whereas my relationships with the other two older women were different. They were nurturing, without being fussy or trite; wise, without being arrogant; loving, without smothering. I'd come to adore them both, and they'd brought an ease and comfort and peace into my life that had been missing since my mother's death.

"But your sons — ?" I said. "I can't take something that should go to them."

She fluttered one hand in front of her. "Don't worry about them. They'll inherit plenty."

I still hadn't gotten used to the idea that she was leaving her car to me, so I just didn't bring it up. As I climbed the uneven steps of her porch, Mrs. Branford opened the door. "I saw you coming," she said, that ever-present twinkle in her eyes. Before I could say anything or even bend to give her a kiss on her cheeks, she turned and marched toward the kitchen. "Come on," she called over her shoulder. She kept talking as she walked, her voice trailing away as I quickly locked the front door and followed her out to the garage. "— because you've never driven it."

She looked at me expectantly, as if she were waiting for me to respond to something she'd said.

I nodded and said, "Right."

"Okay, then."

We stood there, her wrinkled and age-spotted hand on the hood of the car. Meanwhile, her eyes were on me, still awaiting some response. "Well?" she finally said.

Old cars had quirks. It made sense, then, that she might want to give me the rundown on the Volvo's peculiarities. She and her husband had loved this car. They'd taken care of it. It was a classic, and she was entrusting it to me. "What should I know?" I asked, thinking that this was probably what she wanted to talk about.

"I presume you can drive a stick shift," she said.

My dad had taught both my brother and me to drive using an old Ford truck he'd had. "No frills," he'd said. "Learn the

basics, then add the bells and whistles."
"Yes," I told her.

With that, she launched into her car spiel, something she seemed to have rehearsed. "The clutch sticks sometimes. The brakes are relatively new. I had them replaced a few years ago, but given that the car is rarely driven, they are in excellent shape. At least, I hope so. I guess we'll find out."

I opened my mouth to object, but she kept on before I had the chance. "There is one dent on the back fender. I must have backed into something at some point, but I cannot recall what or when." She tapped one finger against her temple. "The trials of aging. Now, about the inside: The upholstery is tacky if you're wearing shorts. Thank heavens it is January, so no worries there."

I glanced down at my legs. Boots on my feet, jeans on my legs, and no exposed skin to stick to the sage-green seats. "No worries," I agreed.

She dug one hand into her pocket, retrieving a set of keys. She tossed them to me, catching me off guard. But I was quick on my feet. My hand flew up and clasped around the keys.

Mrs. Branford nodded with approval. "I'm thirsty. Shall we go?"

We climbed into the old Volvo, I backed

147

out of the garage, and we were off. The Broken Horse was less than fifteen minutes away on the outskirts of Santa Sofia. The vintage car sat low to the ground. It took some getting used to, but it didn't take long before I got the hang of it. I wove through town and before long we pulled up to the bar. The outside was nondescript. It was a stand-alone building surrounded by wide-open space, a dirt parking lot, and a hand-ful of cars.

I slowed the car, regarding the building. It looked like it belonged in some pioneer town in the old West rather than the beach town of Santa Sofia. The light-brown paint on the facade needed to be refreshed and the four-by-fours holding up the overhang above the porch looked rickety.

Mrs. Branford patted my leg, as if reading my mind. "It's fine, Ivy. It's just a bar."

The car bounced as I pulled onto the dirt expanse. I threw the car into *park* and glanced at her. She was grinning, her eyes wide. The Broken Horse was just a bar, but she looked like a kid in Disneyland. She didn't get out much. It seemed that I was her social director, and looking into the whereabouts of Hank Rivera gave her some-thing to do outside her ordinary life.

The inside of the Broken Horse fit the

outside. A massive display of a Texas long-horn hung behind the bar, a string of lights with big, round bulbs above it. An eclectic collection of bottles cluttered the back bar, as well as a draft-beer dispenser. Through an opening at the back I glimpsed the corner of a pool table and heard the crack of billiard balls against each other, followed by a cheer.

A performance stage was situated in the back corner of the main room. Enormous amplifiers angled out toward the parquet dance floor and although country music played on the speakers, the stage was empty. If there was going to be a band playing tonight, they weren't here yet.

There weren't many people inside, but from the sampling, it was instantly obvious that Mrs. Branford and I were not the typical customers for the Broken Horse. The standard dress looked to be jeans, with a heavy preference toward Wranglers and plain white T-shirts for the guys, some topped with a plaid button-down. The women also favored jeans — of the skintight variety — and tops that showed a little — or a lot, as the case may be — cleavage. Mrs. Branford, in her velour lounge suit and quilted down jacket, and me in my floral blouse, non-Wrangler jeans tucked into my boots, and a wool peacoat, looked as if we belonged at a restaurant or at — I don't know, a painting class rather than at this local dive bar.

If Mrs. Branford felt out of place, she certainly didn't show it. She looked around slowly, as if she were taking in every little detail of the place, then she patted the silver curls on her head, turned, and smiled up at me. And then, feisty elderly woman that she was, she marched right up to the bar. With an open palm, she slapped the counter twice, in rapid succession, and called, "Barkeep! Over here, please."

I stifled a laugh. She was behaving like an actress in a B movie, complete with cheesy lines. *Barkeep?* I shook my head, thinking the bartender would toss us out on our ears if we weren't careful.

But I needn't have worried. Mrs. Branford had that Betty White likability factor going for her. She stretched her mouth into a grin, those eyes glistened, and she even tilted one shoulder down in a slightly flirtatious stance. If the bartender was anywhere near his mid- to late seventies, he might think Mrs. Branford was a hot number.

Alas, he looked to be more my age. But his mid-thirties weren't treating him very well. He was round in the belly, balding on

150

the head, and had bloodshot eyes, either from the dark light in the bar, a love of the alcohol he served to others, some other substance enjoyment, lack of sleep, or some combination thereof. But apparently he responded to being called *barkeep*. He looked at Mrs. Branford, set down the glass he'd been wiping with a white cloth, and ambled over.

"Hello there, young man," she said as he stopped in front of her.

He nodded at her and said, "Ma'am." When he looked at me, his interest quotient seemed to go up. His eyebrows rose and one side of his mouth lifted in a satisfied smile. "Grandmother and granddaughter, out for a night on the town?"

"Something like that," I said, not bothering to go into the fact that we were not, in fact, related.

An eerie tune that sounded as if it had come straight from an old *Twilight Zone* episode sounded from somewhere on Mrs. Branford. She held up a finger, telling the barkeep to wait a minute, pulled her phone from the pocket of her jacket, swiped her finger across the screen, and turned her back to us as she answered.

"A drink?" the bartender asked me.

"No, thanks. We're actually looking for

someone."

His smile faded, but he still wanted to sell me a drink, so he kept talking. "Boyfriend or husband?"

"Oh no, neither."

"That's not who you're meeting, or you don't have a boyfriend or a husband?"

I decided that I really didn't want to answer the personal question he posed, so I chose to ignore it. "We're looking for a friend. Hank Rivera. His ex-wife mentioned that he likes to come here sometimes."

"Old Mustache Hank? Sure, I know him."

Mrs. Branford turned back to me. "That's great, Janice. Thank you." She pressed her finger against the screen on her phone, terminating the call, then turned back to us. She was smiling, though, clearly happy about whatever her friend had spoken whither about.

"Everything okay?" I asked.

"Oh yes, dear. Better than okay." To the bartender she asked, "You said you know Hank?"

"Sure. He's a regular."

So he was off the wagon again. "I thought he'd stopped coming here for a while?"

"He stopped for a while, but more than not, they come back. Hank's divorce brought him back."

I could imagine how difficult it would be to give up alcohol for an alcoholic. "We're trying to find him," I said. "Have you seen him in the last few days?"

He tilted his head back, turning his eyes toward the ceiling. "Can't say that I have, now that you mention it." His eyes narrowed. "Why? Is he in some kind of trouble?"

Mrs. Branford scoffed at that. "If he were, do you think we're the sort of people to track him down?"

The bartender's crooked half smile was back. He looked us both up and down in a very matter-of-fact assessment. "Can't say that you do."

"He's not in trouble," I said. "We just haven't seen him in a few days."

His eyebrows pinched. "And you came here to find him?"

"Like you said, we heard he used to be a regular," I said. "When did you see him last?"

He thought. "Last week sometime, I think. Can't say exactly."

We asked him a few more questions, but got nothing more. "I can give you a call if he turns up," he suggested with a quick wink.

Mrs. Branford jumped in with a response

before I could. "You could give yours and Miguel's number," she said, "or I can give mine."

"Your number would be better," I said, picking up on her cue and hoping the bartender picked up on it, too.

He did. "Miguel?" he asked, frowning.

"They're so sweet together," Mrs. Branford said, smiling up at me, and I knew she wasn't just spinning a tale to get the bartender's attention off me; she really thought Miguel and I were sweet together. Too bad she didn't know about Laura and her demand that I steer completely clear of him. If she had her way, we'd never lay eyes on each other again.

The bartender looked disappointed, but slid a small notepad and pen to Mrs. Branford. She jotted down her number and passed it back to him. "I look forward to hearing from you," Mrs. Branford said, as if she was a character on *Law & Order* and the bartender was a key witness.

We thanked him and left. The second we were out the door, Mrs. Branford grabbed my arm and yanked me to a stop. "That was a dead e— "I started to say, but she interrupted me. "Janice had some information!"

I looked at her expectantly.

Mrs. Branford was positively gleeful. "She

knows where Hank is staying!" she ex-claimed.

"Oh!" I clasped my hands, drawing them up to my face, partly to ward off the chill in the evening air and partly out of excitement. It felt like we were in a Nancy Drew novel and we'd had a break in *The Case of the Missing Produce Man.* "Where?"

"Janice was talking to her son about Hank, and Richie said he just saw him a day or so ago."

I clasped her arm. "He did? So he's okay?"

She nodded, grinning. "He did. He's around here somewhere."

My excitement waned. Just because someone had seen him didn't mean we'd actually found him. "Right. But where? Where did Richie see Hank?"

"Ah, this is where the news gets even better. See, Janice owns an old Victorian house on Rupert Street."

"Oh, right. That must be the one she wants me to photograph."

"Must be. They rent out rooms to seniors. Richie manages the property, takes the tenants to their doctors' appointments, to the store. He's basically their caretaker. When Hank moved out of his house, apparently he moved in there. Of course, he doesn't need the help Richie normally provides.

He's just in a bad place right now."

"Janice just found out?"

She nodded. "Richie told her that Hank wanted to keep it on the down low."

"On the *very* down low if he didn't tell his mother."

Mrs. Branford dismissed that. "Richie runs the place. Hank wasn't missing then, so no reason to raise an alarm or even mention it. When he found out Hank was missing, the alarm was raised."

That made sense. "I think we should go talk to Richie," I said.

Mrs. Branford agreed. "Right away. Once we know he's okay, we can all relax and go back to being normal."

Exactly. But after my encounter with Laura Baptista, I suddenly didn't know what *normal* was.

156

CHAPTER 9

It was late, but Mrs. Branford called Janice back the second we were back in her old Volvo. "He won't mind?" she asked after saying that we wanted to head to Rupert Street right away. There was a pause, and then Mrs. Branford turned to me, grinned, and nodded. "Tell Richie we appreciate it. We'll see you in a little while."

She pressed the red *off* circle on her screen, put the phone in her lap, and rubbed her hands together gleefully. "This is so exciting, Ivy!"

I felt the thrill of the chase, too, but I'd had a few minutes to process, so I was more subdued than my sidekick. According to Janice, her son had seen Hank more than a day before. That still meant that he missed his deliveries and hadn't been seen for a good stretch of time. I wanted to be optimistic, but something still felt off.

We mapped the address on Mrs. Branford's phone. Rupert Street was only about ten minutes away. We made the short drive, arriving just as Janice stepped out of her car. Mrs. Branford was quick to open the passenger door of her car, but Janice had hurried over and helped her out. "You're downright crazy, Penny, out sleuthing like you're Jessica Fletcher from *Murder, She Wrote*. For heaven's sake, you're eighty-six years old."

"Eighty-six years young, Janice. I'm not going to let my age stop me. The minute I do, that's it. I'm a goner. I'll sleep when I'm dead. You're a youngster by comparison, but you'd be wise to follow in my footsteps."

Janice was probably in her late sixties, or maybe very early seventies, but she shook her head, looking as if Mrs. Branford and her crazy antics baffled her. Still, I caught a glimpse of a smile on her lips. "If you say so."

It was dark, but as we walked up the path to the front door, I could make out some of the details of the house. It was big and majestic, with a wraparound front porch, a high-pitched roofline, and a sparsely planted winter flower bed. The front door was stained wood. Up close, I could see that the siding was in need of new paint and the door needed refinishing. Even though it needed some TLC, it was a beautiful house.

As Janice reached out her hand toward the door handle, the bushes to the left of us just off the porch suddenly vibrated. We all jerked back, startled. The leaves quivered again and suddenly a hand shot out through the slats of the railing like a zombie arm stretching up from the grave. "Oh my God!" I yelped, jumping back and nearly knocking Mrs. Branford over.

We stared as the hand strained toward us, the arm it was attached to emerging, followed by a body wrapped in a lime-green bathrobe. A short, stocky, balding head was attached to that body. And the eyes on that balding head were wide open and crazed.

Mrs. Branford twisted her body into an attack stance, octogenarian-style, and flung her cane out like a sword. "Back off!" she practically growled. If she were eight inches taller, sixty years younger, fifty pounds lighter, and dressed in black leather instead of her signature velour sweat suit, she would have been a dead ringer for Lara Croft.

I threw my arm out in front of Mrs. Branford, trying to block her from the lunatic, all the while doing my best not to knock her off her orthopedic feet.

Janice sidestepped, wrapping her hand around Mrs. Branford's arm to make sure she stayed upright, her gold wedding band catching the light from the moon. "Ivy, no! It's okay." She held her palm out to the man. "No, no, Bernie. Bernie! Calm down. It's Janice." She quickly glanced back at us before turning back to the man she was calling Bernie. "It's Richie's mom, Bernie."

He flung his head back and forth, opening his mouth to speak. No sound came out and before he could try, Janice tried again. "Calm down."

The man tightened his bathrobe belt as he gripped the railing, leveraged one foot, then the other onto the outer edge of the porch, and then climbed over. He landed with a thud right in front of us. *"No no no,"* he said, drawing out the three little words until they blended together in a long moan. "My name not Bernie. My name Bernard," he said, and then he spelled it out. "B-e-r-n-a-r-d."

Janice smiled sheepishly. "Bernard. Right. So sorry, I forgot. Bernard." She emphasized his name and then swept her arm out toward us in a welcoming gesture. "These are my friends."

He pressed the back of his hand against his forehead and squeezed his eyes shut, his mouth open, his teeth bared. It wasn't quite a grimace and it wasn't quite a smile, either.

It fell somewhere in between. "Friends," he said, and then he dropped his arm and patted his chest three times. "I Bernard. You friends."

Mrs. Branford stepped toward him and smiled. "You are Bernard," she said, and then she, too, patted her chest. "I am Penny. It is very nice to meet you."

"And I'm Ivy," I said, following suit.

Bernard's flummoxed gaze shifted from Janice to Mrs. Branford to me. "Too many. Too many." He looked up at the darkened sky. "No stars tonight. The garden is dark. Sad. So sad."

We all followed his gaze to the sky. He was right. The sky was dark and a blanket of clouds cast a dark shadow over us. Over everything. "The garden is beautiful, Bernard," Janice said.

Bernard, his mouth still agape, looked back to us. His eyes glistened as they shifted again to Janice. "No, no. Too dark."

Janice nodded sympathetically. "The stars will be back, Bernard. The garden will be just fine."

"They need the light," he said, his mouth forming an exaggerated frown. "They need the light."

"It'll be sunny tomorrow," Mrs. Branford offered.

"Right," Janice said. She turned toward Mrs. Branford and me, tapping her temple with one finger to indicate that Bernard was mentally deficient. She looked back at him. "The sun will shine and the flowers will be just fine."

Although it *was* January, I thought. Even in temperate Santa Sofia, the flowers in winter were never going to be lush and vibrant. But Bernard seemed mollified, so Janice opened the front door, poking her head in and calling out. "Yoo-hoo! Richie, we're here."

The four of us stepped inside to the foyer. It was small, but the floor was done in a neutral tile, the walls were painted a warm cream, and the fronds of a fern splayed in greeting. A man who looked to be in his early forties emerged from behind a corner and met us as we came into the family room. Janice was tall, but he had to bend down to give her a kiss on the cheek. His eyes alighted on Bernard and his face turned stern. "Bernie? What are you doing?"

Bernard's eyes went wide, his mouth gaping again, and he flattened his hand against his chest. "Bernard. My name is Bernard, not Bernie."

"That's what I said," the man I assumed to be Richie Thompson said. He didn't have

162

the patience in his voice that his mother did. "Were you outside? You're not supposed to be out after dark, Bernard. You know that."

"The stars. They are hiding."

Janice nodded, placating him again. "It is cloudy, but the sun will be out tomorrow and —"

"— and the flowers, they will be okay again? Alive again?" Bernard asked.

Richie shook his head, looking frustrated. "The flowers can't come back, Bernard," he said. "They can't be alive again."

Bernard ran the back of his hand over his eyes, back and forth. "Gone is gone," he said, and then he shuffled past us and into the room beyond, stopping at a window that, I presumed, looked out into the back-yard and to the flowers he was so concerned about.

"Shovel?" he said, looking back at Richie. "I shovel tomorrow?" He cleared his throat and this time his voice was forceful and resolute. "I shovel tomorrow. Bring the flowers back."

Richie nodded. "Sure, Bernard. You can shovel tomorrow."

Janice gave a little laugh. "Bernard can be single-minded sometimes. Isn't he darling?" she said to Richie.

"That's an understatement," he said coarsely. From what I'd observed so far, Richie didn't seem to have the patient temperament needed for running a boarding house, particularly one with special-needs tenants like Bernard. But then again, it was the end of the day and we were unexpected guests stopping by to ask about a missing tenant. I probably wouldn't have a lot of patience right now, either, if I were him.

"Darling," Janice said to him as she gestured to me. "This is Ivy Culpepper." He nodded an acknowledgment to me and Janice went on. "And of course you remember Penelope Branford."

"Yep, how are you?" he asked, but he turned back to his mom before Mrs. Branford could answer. "So what's going on? What is this about Hank?"

I answered for Janice. "No one has seen him for a few days. He's missed his deliveries. He's just sort of disappeared."

Richie furrowed his brow. "But, no, he didn't. I just saw him yesterday."

"You said the day before," Janice clarified. "You're sure it was yesterday?"

Richie nodded. "Positive."

Mrs. Branford followed up with, "Did he seem okay? Normal?"

Janice jumped in again before her son could answer. "Did he say anything about his deliveries? He's always been so reliable."

Behind us, Bernard stomped his foot. "No stars. Too dark. Too dark. Too dark. Can't see the flowers. Where are the flowers?"

"Bernie, stop." Richie pursed his lips and narrowed his eyes at Bernard's back. He was worried about Hank, so I couldn't blame him for his short temper, but I found myself feeling sorry for Bernard. Was this the best living situation for him? I didn't know the details of his condition, so it was hard to say.

"Bernard," Bernard said, his voice agitated. "Not Bernie. B-e-r-n-a-r-d."

"Richie," Janice scolded.

I watched the interaction between Janice and her son. Parents would always be parents. My mom had been the same way, rearing me from afar when I'd lived in Texas. Maybe someday I'd be a mother and would do the very same thing to my grown child. Cutting the apron strings was never easy, I imagined.

Mrs. Branford stomped her cane on the floor, bringing everyone's attention to her. "How has Hank been, Richie?" she asked. "His deliveries? His attitude in general? We are quite worried about him."

Richie blinked. "What?" His focus had been on Bernard, who was bent at the waist and tugging the lower edge of his bathrobe toward the floor as if trying to stretch it out.

Mrs. Branford's eighty-six years had earned her the right to feel and say whatever she wanted to, and right now she was clearly exasperated. "Bernard is fine, Richie," she said sternly, and then she repeated her questions. "We are trying to find Hank, and apparently you are the last person who saw him. Richie. Richie! Can you confirm that? How did he seem?"

Finally, after Mrs. Branford repeated his name again, Richie turned to face us. "Sorry. Bernard takes — never mind. To tell you the truth, I didn't really talk to Hank. He hasn't been here very long. Yesterday I just saw him get into his truck, you know? He just drove away."

Janice, Mrs. Branford, and I looked at each other. So Richie *had* seen him, which meant a day ago Hank Rivera was okay. I was the one who spoke up first. "Did he have anything with him?"

"Yes! Good thought." Janice looked excited. "Did he have a suitcase?"

Richie circled his eyes up at the ceiling in thought. "Now that you mention it, he did toss something into his truck. Not a suitcase. Maybe a duffel? I'm not really sure."

I looked around, noting the details of the house's interior. Like the outside, it was in need of a spruce up, but overall, it was pretty nice as boarding houses went. At least from my knowledge of what a boarding house should look like, which was only based on old movies. The whole thing seemed to have been remodeled and didn't resemble the cut-up interior of a traditional Victorian-era house. The heart of the house was the combined kitchen-family room. From what I could tell, bedrooms shot off to either side of the center. A staircase on the right of the foyer led upstairs, where I imagined there were more bedrooms. If I didn't have a home of my own, this would be exactly the type of place I'd want to live. It needed some TLC, but it was still warm and welcoming. "How long has he been living here?" I asked.

"About a month," he said just as an elderly man emerged from a room down the hall and shuffled into the foyer, pushing a walker. His gray sweatpants and T-shirt were both baggy, hanging on his thin, hunched frame like clothes on a hanger, showing no form underneath. His navy corduroy slippers smacked against the tile floor as he walked, the heels of the slippers pressing down so they were more like flip-flops. He had thin and spotty gray-streaked hair swept across his head, but not offering nearly enough coverage of the balding dome. If I had to guess, I'd place him in his eighties, but he wasn't spry and energetic like Mrs. Branford was; he looked every one of his years.

"Why, hello there, Mrs. Thompson," he said, and just like that, the strength of his voice and the suggestive note in his tone made me rethink my first impression of him. Tsk-tsk-tsk. He was an older man wanting to try his luck with a younger woman.

But Janice didn't seem to mind. She gave him a warm smile. "Mason, you're looking well. Ivy. Penny. This is Mason Caldwell. Mason, these are some friends of mine. Ivy Culpepper and Penelope Branford."

He did a little two-step, his hands gripped firmly on the sides of his walker to help him keep his balance, and then gave a little bow. "Ladies."

Janice nodded with approval. "Mason, you're such a gentleman."

"Why, thank you, madam. Care to tell me more? You can join me for a night on the town, although I'm afraid you'll have to drive."

168

Mrs. Branford had been staring at Mason. She took a step forward, cocking her head to one side, considering him carefully. "Mr. Caldwell. Room three-fifteen. Chemistry."

The elderly man spun his head to look at her. "That's right," he began, but then he stopped. "Penelope Branford? Ha! I'll be damned. Room one-oh-one. English lit."

They both laughed as recognition hit. Mrs. Branford made a sweeping gesture with one arm. "Both retired," she said wistfully.

"Thank God!" Mason bellowed. "I can't imagine having to explain to all the angst-ridden teenagers today that I am not, in fact, Walter White, and we won't be learning anything about making meth. That might have done me in. Instead, I get my state retirement, my Social Security check, and I have not a care in the world."

From the window in the other room, Bernard turned to us and laughed. It was a robust and exaggerated bellow, followed by a knee slap. "Mason a funny man. You not Walter White. You Mason. You funny, Mason."

"Thank you, Bernard," Mason said matter-of-factly.

Bernard turned back to the window, staring out into the darkness. "You come back, see Mason be funny," he said.

"Who's he talking to?" Mrs. Branford asked.

"To himself," Richie said. "You get used to it."

"So Janice," Mason said, "how about that date?"

"Mason," Richie scolded. "We talked about this. My mom is off limits."

Janice laughed, more lighthearted than her son, but she echoed his sentiment. "He's right, Mason. That's quite an offer, but you'd be robbing the cradle with me. That wouldn't look good for you."

Mason scoffed. "I don't care one iota what things look like for me. All I care about is getting the most out of every single day. I might not have that many days left."

But Janice wasn't going to let him off easy. "Of course you do! Days and days and days. You're not going anywhere, but if you tried to date me, what would your family say?"

He released one hand from his walker and fluttered his hand in the air. "Family? They don't have anything to do with me anymore. I had the audacity to grow old, and they had the audacity not to care anymore. It's easier for them that way," he said snidely, but underneath it, I could hear the sadness. He'd been abandoned by the people who were supposed to love him the most, at the time when he probably needed them the most.

"Oh, Mason," Janice said. She laid her hand on his shoulder and ushered him from the foyer to the heart of the house where Bernard stood sentry at the window.

"Students," he said. "I have students, which more than makes up for the selfish family I am saddled with. Hank was a student." He looked at Mrs. Branford. "Did you have him, too, Penelope?"

"Oh, yes. Quite a remarkable young man."

"He's been trying to move me into a retirement facility. I bet that's where he is right now, in fact. Mustache Hank, as he's oft called, is quite the persistent fellow."

Richie and Janice both looked surprised. "I don't think Hank's checking out a retirement home for you," Richie said.

Mason looked chagrined. "Oh, but he is. He mentioned it once or twice. He thinks there is more there to keep my mind active. I told him that I'm perfectly happy here, but he wants to take care of me. Former teacher and all that. 'There are movie nights, clubs, dominoes, bingo'," he said, changing his voice slightly to mimic what Hank had told him. "Like I'm going to spend my time playing bingo and dominoes."

"Put me out to pasture before you send me to an old folks' home," Mrs. Branford said. She looked at me. "Ivy, you got that? Out to pasture."

"Got it," I said, although I had no idea what that actually meant or what I had to do with it. First off, I had no claim on her. I wasn't her blood relation, so I wouldn't be making any decisions on her behalf. Second off, retirement communities were costly. Mrs. Branford had told me her sons would inherit plenty, but that didn't mean she had the means to move into a retirement community. And third off, the woman was going to live forever.

"Could he be worried for you over those?" Mrs. Branford asked, pointing her cane at the staircase.

"Certainly not. I had a knee replacement last year. Even if I wanted to, I couldn't venture up those stairs. I would come tumbling down again, much like Humpty Dumpty."

"Mason's room is downstairs," Richie confirmed. "He has no reason to go upstairs."

"Correct," Mason said with a flourish of his hand. If he hadn't chosen the sciences, he could have had a future in theater.

Mrs. Branford laughed. Maybe a little too hardily. I snuck a peak at her, wondering if she was hot or if the slight tinge of pink on her cheeks had something to do with the dapper Mason Caldwell.

"You should rest, Mason. Come, have a seat," Janice said, leading him to the great room. He nodded to Mrs. Branford, and then to me almost as an afterthought. A moment later he was pushing his walker, following Janice to the couch.

"Mason really has nobody?" I asked Richie softly when Mason was out of earshot.

His eyes rolled up. "Of course he does." He tapped his index finger against his temple, just like Janice had done when we'd first encountered Bernard. The implication was that Mason was not all there in the head. He seemed plenty lucid to me, but maybe he was just having a good night. He could very well be the norm for the type of people who'd live in a place like this: People who didn't have others to care for them and who were still able to function in a normal setting, even if their heads were fuzzy part of the time.

"Mason has a daughter in San Francisco," Richie continued. "She needed a place for him while she gets a room ready for him in her house, so he's a short-timer. I admit, I'll miss him when he goes. He's a kick."

"So he doesn't need a retirement home?"

"Not at all," Richie said. "In fact, his daughter is supposed to check him out of here any day now."

If his daughter was coming to get him, why did he think she'd abandoned him? Why did he think *everyone* had abandoned him? Was his mind that far gone? "Doesn't he know that?" I asked.

Richie shrugged. "Sometimes he does and sometimes he doesn't. Good days and bad days. Dementia. Most of the time he's not as lucid as you just saw him, and he tends to make things up, but even now he doesn't remember his daughter. I think the retirement home is all in his head."

My heart broke for Mason Caldwell and for his daughter. He seemed so together. Feisty. Definitely what I would call a fighter, just like Mrs. Branford. To lose one's mind . . . well, that was one of the worst things I could imagine.

"What about Bernard?" Mrs. Branford asked, glancing at Bernard, who was still gazing out into the dark night. She had fallen quiet for a little while, just listening. Thinking. I imagined she was seeing her mortality at the moment, worried that she would succumb to the same faculty losses both Bernard and Mason had unwillingly surrendered to. "Does he have anyone?"

The heels of Janice's shoes clicked against the tile as she came back into the foyer. Before Richie could answer, Janice did. "If he does, we don't know about them," she said. "It is sad to see people all alone." She threaded her arm through Richie's and gave him a peck on the cheek. "I'm grateful for my son."

Richie patted his mother's hand. "Back at you, Mom."

Mrs. Branford cleared her throat. She looked a bit pale. All the talk about dementia and lost families had clearly gotten to her. Given her age, it hit too close to home, so I couldn't blame her. People didn't like to imagine themselves declining in health or in their mental capacity, and Mrs. Branford was no exception to that. She'd had a few instances of forgetfulness since I'd known her, but nothing serious and nothing to indicate that she was on a similar path to Mason or Bernard. "Let's see Hank's room," she said.

"Sure, sure," Richie answered.

Janice sidestepped, turning toward the great room. "I'll stay with Bernie and Mason. You all go on."

As her heels *click-click-clicked* on the tile, Richie led Mrs. Branford and me down the short hallway Mason had emerged from a short while ago. The Victorian had clearly been remodeled, what had probably been a parlor and library cut up to be refashioned into several small bedrooms. I peeked in one of the rooms as we passed. It was sparsely furnished with a bed, a dresser, and a chair in the corner. We walked by quickly, so I couldn't see any more than that, or make out any personal touches that revealed anything about the room's occupant.

Richie stopped in front of the last door on the right and knocked. Mrs. Branford raised her eyebrows at him. He looked sheepish. "Force of habit," he said. "Mr. Rivera?" he called, then turned to us and said in a stage whisper, "Just in case."

In case what? I wondered. From what I'd gathered, Hank's truck wasn't here and Richie hadn't mentioned anyone seeing him return, so it seemed unlikely that somehow Hank was in his room. Still, I held my breath and waited, as Richie had said, just in case.

But there was no answer. Richie turned the handle and pushed open the door, stepping aside so we could walk through. The room looked just like the other one I'd caught a glimpse of. A twin bed came out from the window, the dresser sat against the right wall, and, in this case, a gliding rocking chair was in the corner by the door. I spun around, looking for evidence of Hank. A picture, maybe, or a medicine bottle, or a letter. But there was nothing personal. If I didn't know he was staying here, I'd never have been able to see that he did.

"What the — ?" Richie spun around with an expression of dismay. "He cleared out on me!"

One by one I yanked open the doors to the dresser. Empty. Mrs. Branford opened the closet doors. Also empty. Had Hank had so few belongings that they'd fit into the duffel bag Richie had seen him toss into his truck? Or had he loaded everything else up without anyone being the wiser?

Either way, it was as if Hank Rivera had never been here. The thread of concern that had been loosened for a brief moment suddenly tightened again, winding its way through my insides. Something had driven Hank away. I thought back to the brief conversation Jolie had overheard at the festival earlier. Was it his finances? Was he truly in so much debt that he'd seen no other choice but to run?

Richie fumed, raking one hand through

his hair. "Son of a —" His gaze swung to us and he stopped himself from finishing his rant. "I can't believe it. Mustache Hank. I never would have thought he'd run out like this."

I had to agree. Based on everything I'd heard about him, it seemed very out of character. Mrs. Branford seemed equally puzzled. She swung her cane to and fro, her wrinkled brow furrowing in consternation. We looked at each other, both of us frowning. Suddenly the lighthearted attitude we'd had toward sleuthing took on a new seriousness. "The Hank I know wouldn't do this," she said. "Something must be terribly wrong."

With nothing more to discover in Hank's room, Mrs. Branford and I thanked Richie and Janice, and then left. Before long, I was curled up in bed with a glass of wine, a book — which I couldn't focus on — and my thoughts zipping haphazardly around my head.

The phone call from Emmaline came about an hour later. She launched in the second I answered. No pleasantries. This wasn't Em, friend from high school. Nor Em, girlfriend of my brother. She was calling as Deputy Sheriff Davis, and she was calling with a specific purpose.

"Ivy," she said, not mincing words. "We found Hank Rivera's truck."

"What do you mean, you found his truck?" I asked slowly.

"We got a report about a pickup truck parked at a gas station just outside of town. It's Hank's."

I mulled this over for a few seconds. "What do you think it means?"

"It's a truck in a parking lot without its owner. What do *you* think it means?"

"Well, it could mean that he met someone there and left his truck behind."

Emmaline grunted as if she didn't believe that scenario for a second, but she had to look at all possibilities. "Could be. We're canvassing the area. So far nobody saw anything."

"How long has the truck been there?"

"From what we can surmise, sometime yesterday. The day manager noticed it when he left last night, and it was still there tonight." Which fit what Richie had said about Hank leaving the boarding house the day before. Had he gone straight to the gas station for some sort of rendezvous? I told her about my visit to Richie's boarding house and Hank's empty room. She let out a lengthy and audible breath.

"What are you thinking?" I asked.

Emmaline had a logical head and wasn't afraid to tackle things head-on, but she sighed. Heavily. "I'm thinking Hank Rivera is officially a missing person."

CHAPTER 10

I spent the next morning at the bread shop with Olaya. It was an ordinary day filled with ordinary baking, which I was glad for. The news that Hank Rivera was officially missing put a somber pall over us. We worked without talking for the first few hours, mixing dough, putting it aside for a long rise, rolling out croissants, forming baguettes. I'd realized some time ago that baking had a level of creativity that most people didn't recognize. Sure, a lot of people could follow a recipe, but you had to finesse dough to make it do what you wanted it to do; you had to have patience to let the flour and yeast do its magic. Baking well was like painting a picture that had layers of colors and shadows and negative space, all done to elicit a reaction from whomever was looking at it.

We wanted nothing more than to prompt a response — an emotion — from the people who ate what we created. I'd seen it in action: Almond bread to bring forth wisdom and prosperity. Anise to fight night-mares. For someone searching for love, anything with apples did the trick. Olaya's bread shop was special, her bread magical. That I was a part of it filled me with a level of satisfaction I hadn't experienced from anything else, not even from my photogra-phy. The photos I took affected people. They affected me. But the bread . . . the bread was just as powerful. Maybe more so.

Not even the bread we baked could bring Hank Rivera back to Santa Sofia. It couldn't, but it did make me feel a little bit better.

Finally, I couldn't take the silence any longer. I needed to talk it out. To process through what little we knew and what we might figure out. I was still trying to be optimistic.

"Maybe we're seeing something ominous when we shouldn't. What if Hank is seeing someone?" I asked as Olaya placed another round of dough on a tray for a long rise. She paced her baking throughout the day so there was always fresh bread until clos-ing. And she timed it all just right so there was very rarely anything left over. Any unsold bread was donated to a local women's shelter called Gladiola House.

She turned the next ball of dough onto the floured board she used to knead and dug the heels of her hands into it. "He is a divorced man," she said as she began to work the dough.

I followed her lead, kneading my own round of dough. "Right, so it's possible."

"I like that theory. If he's with a woman, he will come back at some point. But if he did not leave with a woman, then where is he?" Olaya asked.

My question exactly.

During a break from baking, I called Mrs. Branford and asked her to convene the Blackbird Ladies at Yeast of Eden. I knew they were well ensconced in Santa Sofia's gossip and I wanted to ask them what they might know about Mustache Hank's love life.

If I had read things right, then Alice Ryder had had some sort of relationship with Hank. I suspected she might have kept tabs on whatever Hank had been up to. And if she did, I intended to find out what she knew.

Olaya and I kept baking, finishing the last of the baguettes for an Italian restaurant in town just before 4:00. We readied them in a box for the Palermo's driver to pick up on his way to the restaurant. I'd come to know the baking schedule for the local eateries that contracted with Olaya. Daily for Palermo's. Fridays and Saturdays for the Fish Market, a seafood favorite, and Turtle Dove, a local California-cuisine spot. Olaya also baked scones, croissants, morning bread, a few varieties of muffins, and a sweet stromboli for a breakfast- and lunch-only diner.

The Blackbird Ladies had impeccable timing. As the last baguette was bagged, they came through the door of the bread shop one by one. Mabel Peabody came first, followed by Janice Thompson, Alice Ryder, and finally Mrs. Branford. "Here we are," Janice said. "As requested."

Alice pursed her lips. "You summoned us?" It sounded like an accusation rather than a question.

"Oh, come on," Mabel said. "Let's let her tell us why before you jump down her throat, Alice."

Alice primped, patting the flipped curls of her hair. "I do *not* jump down people's throats. I resent that."

Mrs. Branford laughed. "Come now, Alice. You love to jump down people's throats. It's your favorite pastime."

"But we love you anyway," Mabel said.

Alice harrumphed, turning her back on us and sitting at one of the bistro tables. She looked at me with piercing blue eyes. "Why, exactly, did you call us here?"

There were four chairs at the table, including the one Alice had sat in. I pulled up another and swept my arm out so they'd all take a seat. "I called you here because you all seem to have the pulse on all things Santa Sofia," I began.

Mrs. Branford preened, Alice rolled her eyes, Janice nodded, as if there had never been a doubt, and Mabel said, "You know it."

"Hank Rivera is officially missing." I paused, letting that bit of information sink in, and then I continued by filling them in on what Mrs. Branford, Janice, and I had discovered about him leaving the boarding house — potentially with a duffel bag — and Emmaline's discovery of Hank's truck just outside of town.

They all sat dumbstruck for a few seconds, and then Janice broke the silence. "Did anyone see anything?"

"Not as far as I know. Emmaline — er, the deputy sheriff — said they are talking with possible witnesses, but so far no one seems to know anything."

"What does this have to do with us?" Alice asked, her Southern drawl making her words sound extra-snippy.

"You all know him," I said.

They all nodded at that. "Go on," Janice said.

"Could Hank have a girlfriend? Does he have other family? A friend he might have met up with? I'm trying to figure out why he would leave his truck behind. It only makes sense if someone met him there and he left with that person in his or her car."

Mabel angled her head and looked at me. "Why do you want to figure it out, Ivy?"

The answer to that question was complicated. "I feel like I'm invested in finding him at this point, so I want to figure out what happened."

I didn't mention that Miguel had asked for my help, based on how I had recently helped solve the mystery of Jackie Makers's death. I wanted to come through for him. Our history bound us, and there was still a thread of something between us that made me want to stay connected — despite his sister's demand that I stay away from him.

But that was only part of my motive. During the past few months, I had also made a discovery about myself. Looking into my mother's death had unleashed an insatiable curiosity from deep within myself. Emmaline had recently told me that I'd missed my calling; I could have been a detective. She was right. When something was wrong, I wanted to right it. I tried to encapsulate those feelings into something the Blackbird Ladies would understand, but it proved difficult. "I can't really explain it. Miguel asked for my help —"

"Well, enough said!" Janice gave a knowing smile. "What we do for the men in our lives."

"No, but that's —"

"No need to explain any further, dear," Mrs. Branford said. "I told you, you and young Mr. Baptista are fated to be together."

"Por supuesta." Olaya emerged from behind the bread counter. "I believe that is written."

"Written? Fated?" I laughed, but it came out more like a chortle. I didn't believe my fate was already determined, nor did I believe that Miguel and I were destined to be together. If that happened, then it would be because we fell in love again, something that might or might not happen. My fate didn't rest in the stars any more than Hank Rivera's did. "I'm more of the 'we make our own destiny' viewpoint. But thanks for your input."

Alice gave her head the tiniest shake, rolling those eyes again, something that had become her standard action when she was with me. "Let's get back to it, shall we? Hank does not have a girlfriend."

Mabel turned to her. "And how do you know that, Alice?"

"I just do." Alice's annoyance was palpable and I had to wonder again what was driving her irritation.

I took a moment to really consider Alice. She sat stick-straight, her arms folded over her chest as if she were protecting herself. Her lips were drawn tightly together and she looked like she'd rather be anyplace other than here. Given that she had gone to school with Hank and had an actual connection to him, why wasn't she more concerned about him?

Or maybe she was and she didn't want to show it for some reason. Like Emmaline, I was trying to keep an open mind and consider all possibilities.

Mabel dug in her purse, her hand emerging a few seconds later with a tube of lip balm. "Have you talked to his brother?" she said as she coated her lips.

We all swung our heads to stare at her, each of our expressions slightly different. Janice's eyebrows pinched together as if she were puzzled by the question. Alice's eyes went wide with surprise. Olaya, who was still standing nearby, gave an exaggerated frown. Mrs. Branford's open mouth formed an O, as if she were shocked at the suggestion. I went with the straightforward response. "He has a brother?"

CHAPTER 11

I couldn't figure out how nobody had mentioned that Hank Rivera had a brother before now.

"I don't think they're very close," Mabel said.

"They're ten years apart," Alice added.

Mrs. Branford swiped her hands against each other in a moving clap. "Of course. I completely forgot!"

"Mrs. Branford!" I chastised. She was my sidekick in this investigation. How could she forget such an important bit of information?

"Philip, right?" Janice said. "He's got an appliance-repair shop, if I'm remembering correctly."

Alice's face dawned with remembrance. "That's right. Coastal Appliance Repair. I've used him before, but it's been years."

"Could Hank be staying with him?" I asked. Being with family would be far better than staying in a boarding house, at least in my opinion.

Alice shook her head again. "Doubtful. I don't think they see each other much."

Once again, I wondered about Alice's relationship with Hank. Was it as innocuous as she implied, or was my intuition correct that there was something she wasn't telling us?

None of the Blackbird Ladies were able to offer any more information about Philip Rivera, so the subject was dropped — but not forgotten by me. I had committed the information to memory so I could call Philip Rivera the second I got home.

As soon as I was able, I left Olaya and the Blackbird Ladies to their bread, saying I needed to get home to check on Agatha. That part was true. I went straight home to the old Tudor house I cherished, let Agatha into the backyard to take care of business, and played with her for a few minutes. Back inside, I called Coastal Appliance to see if Philip Rivera was in the office. He wasn't. There was only one logical plan of action. I couldn't easily go to Philip, so Philip needed to come to me.

Jackie Makers, the woman who'd recently been killed outside Yeast of Eden and whose murder I helped solve, had owned this

191

house. I'd felt connected to it from the beginning and I'd been saving my money for a decade in hopes of finding a place to call home. When the house became available, I jumped at the chance to buy it. When it came down to it, I felt as if it was meant to be — as if Jackie had offered me her house because I'd brought her killer to justice.

She'd had expensive taste when it came to her kitchen. She'd remodeled and put in a cream-colored AGA range, a farm sink, and a stainless-steel built-in refrigerator. There was a brick arch over the range. A cream-colored exhaust hood hung above the window, but the view to the yard beyond illuminated the space with warm light.

I had to think quickly. "I have a fancy range," I said to the woman on the other end of the line. "The oven-door latch is broken, so the door doesn't close." It was true. It suddenly stopped working, which was a problem, because baking bread had quickly become one of my favorite pastimes. Not having a working oven meant I couldn't do what I'd come to love. Getting it repaired had been on my list of things to do, but since learning that Philip Rivera fixed appliances, it had moved to the top of my list.

She took down the necessary information

and consulted her schedule. "He'll have to order whatever parts are needed. He has a cancellation this afternoon. Can he come by in an hour to see what parts he needs?"

I sat on a stool at the olive-colored island, my forearms resting on the pristine dark-wood countertop. Above it, the wrought-iron light fixture glowed warmly. I'd adorned the open shelves on either end of the island with my sparse collection of cookbooks and a few knickknacks. The only things I collected were antique cameras. Over the years I'd garnered a fair number, all of which were displayed on a built-in bookshelf in the living room. The kitchen, in contrast, held antiques I'd found and loved, a few holy-water founts I'd found in different stores across the country, and the antique galvanized metal conveyor contraption I'd bought at the Winter Wonderland Festival. I'd hung it on a narrow wall next to the refrigerator and had put a sprinkling of dried flowers in each container.

I loved every inch of my house, but with the peaked ceiling and exposed dark beams, the kitchen was my favorite space. The island was covered in beadboard and was painted a warm olive green, but the rest of the cabinetry was a buttery white and had wrought-iron hardware. The old leaded windows were framed in honey-colored wood. The kitchen felt like it was created in the 1920s or 1930s. It was vintage at its very best.

I had one problem: A strange man, the brother of a missing man, alone with me in my house, was probably not a good idea. I was plenty self-reliant and had no qualms about being able to take care of myself under normal circumstances, but this wasn't what I'd consider normal. I couldn't put myself in a potentially dangerous situation by choice and without precautions.

So I called Billy. My brother and I had been best friends growing up — and we still were. He'd come over to be my backup in a heartbeat. He answered and I told him what I needed.

"Sorry, Ivy, no can do," he said. "I'm in the City today. Needed some hardware for a job."

Billy was a contractor. He specialized in taking a house from foundation to finish, complete with custom trims and finishings. Sometimes, like today, that meant he had to go as far as San Francisco to hunt for something obscure or one of a kind.

After we hung up, I went to plan B: my dad. But he didn't answer, which meant he was probably in a meeting.

Emmaline was next. She was deputy sheriff, so she'd be perfect as backup. "I can't, Ivy. We're processing Hank's truck. There's no way I can leave."

The good news there was that, if we were lucky, some clue as to Hank's whereabouts would surface. The bad news was that without Billy, my dad, or Em, I was still without a wingman for Philip's visit.

Which left me with just one option. Even as I made the call, Laura Baptista's words echoed in my head: *Leave him alone, Ivy.* I pushed her admonition aside, half hoping Miguel wouldn't answer the phone so I wouldn't have to deal with whatever Laura had been referring to.

But he did answer.

After a quick greeting, I filled him in on the latest news about Hank, including the discovery of his truck.

"That doesn't sound good," he said, his voice dropping low.

I was still holding out hope that he'd turn up, but the more I thought about it, the more my optimism waned. "He's officially a missing person now," I said. After giving him a minute to process where we were, I told him about Hank's brother, Philip, and how he was coming over within the hour. "I thought it would be a good idea to have someone else here. Billy's in the city, my dad's busy, and Emmaline is doing sheriffing stuff, so I was hoping you could come over," I said.

"Fourth choice, huh?"

I couldn't tell if he was hurt, offended, or simply stating a fact. I thought about defending my choice by telling him about his sister's warning, but thought better of it. Whatever that was about, I didn't want to get into it right now. "Yeah, well . . ."

"It's fine, Ivy. Of course I'll come. I'll be there in a few minutes."

He was true to his word, arriving fifteen minutes later. His six-foot frame filled the arched doorway, the dimples, like long commas on either side of his mouth, framed his smile. Olive skin, dark hair, and green eyes were only part of his appeal. His years of military training had given him broad shoulders, a lean body, and a confident bearing that he hadn't had as a senior in high school. He'd been attractive and fit then, but now he was alluring in the way a teenager could never be. I'd been in love with him as only an adolescent girl can be, but as an adult, he had charisma and countenance that was magnetic. He'd liked me back in high school. Maybe he'd even loved me in his way. But Laura's face as she'd told me to stay away came back to me. Something had driven him away, and whatever it was had been monumental enough that it was still an issue for Miguel's sister, twenty years later.

I was nonchalant with my greeting. "Hey."

His smile faded slightly. "Hey yourself."

I opened the door wider and he stepped in, his gaze immediately falling to the Galileo's thermometer, the housewarming gift he'd gotten me. "Looks good."

It did and I nodded in agreement. Agatha had been sound asleep on her little dog bed in the kitchen, but at the sound of a male voice, she'd jerked awake and bounded into the front room, launching into a barking frenzy as if Miguel was an intruder. She was in full protective mode.

He took an instinctual step back, but chuckled. "I'm not going to hurt her, Agatha," he said, crouching down and holding out one hand. Agatha edged forward and sniffed. She scooted back, then inched forward again, crinkling her shiny black nose as she smelled his hand for the second time.

He stood and Agatha yelped again, in a final halfhearted effort. She spun around, but as I led Miguel to the kitchen, the little fawn pug trotted along beside him. It hadn't taken much for him to win her over. He had that special gift, apparently.

A little thread of nerves wound itself around my insides. It felt strange having Miguel here. Awkward, almost. Although we'd reconnected and he'd called me about Hank, I wouldn't go so far as to say we were friends who hung out together. I didn't know how to make small talk with him. I didn't know if I wanted to. Weren't we past that?

I went back to the stool I'd been perching on earlier, skipped the chitchat, and stayed on topic. "Did you know Hank had a brother?"

He leaned back against one of the counters, hands in the pockets of his jeans. "I had no idea. All we ever talk about is produce."

"Is it odd that Mrs. Rivera or her son didn't mention it?" I wasn't sure if it was or wasn't. On the one hand, Brenda and Hank were divorced, but on the other hand, Hank was the father of her son, so you'd think she'd want to give whatever information was needed to help find him.

Miguel stroked his chin. "I was wondering the same thing. I don't know. We didn't actually ask, and Mrs. Rivera didn't seem to think he was actually missing."

"But what about Jason? He came to you, looking for his dad."

"Looking, yes, but at that point he didn't necessarily think anything was specifically wrong. He was just a little bit worried. If Hank and his brother aren't close, then I can see Jason not mentioning it."

I guess he was right. I was probably reading too much into it. I didn't have any more time to think about it, though, because the doorbell rang. Agatha jumped up and immediately started barking again. She raced to the door, raising her little smashed head up as she yelped with such passion that it sounded hoarse and strained. She only backed away when I opened the door, but she kept up the barking.

I scolded her. "Agatha, enough." She stopped, but kept up a low growl.

The man at the door had a name tag on, but I didn't need it to identify him as Phil Rivera. He was most definitely Hank's brother. Phil didn't have the handlebar mustache, but he did have the same gray eyes, olive skin, broad shoulders, narrow hips, and lanky limbs. He nodded his greeting. "Coastal Appliance. I hear you have a problem with your AGA door?"

"Yes, right. Thanks for coming so quickly." I ushered him in and Agatha took up her barking again. I gave her a stern look and held up a finger. "Hush!"

She did, but her tail was still unfurled, a clear sign that she was on alert. I led Phil into the kitchen where Miguel was waiting. The two men lifted their chins up in a silent, male-oriented greeting. Phil added an additional, "Hey, man."

Miguel returned the greeting with an equally masculine, "Hey."

I showed Phil the oven door. "Beautiful appliance," he said with such reverence he might have been talking about a woman.

I had to agree. "I love it."

He lifted the brim of his cap and scratched his head. "Probably came in on a slow boat from England, eh?"

From what Olaya had told me, Jackie had custom-ordered it and it had taken nearly two months for it to arrive. "I think it needed its own passport," I said with a chuckle.

Phil retrieved a tool from his bag and crouched down in front of the oven. The AGA had five gas burners on top, two ovens, and a broiler in front. The left door opened to the side rather than opening down like a typical oven. "Don't find many of these ranges in the U.S.," he commented as he set to work.

Once again, I agreed. "The woman who owned the house before me was quite a cook."

"Nice piece of machinery."

He played around with the door latch, using his flashlight to peer at the mechanism more closely. "Looks like it's out of alignment. I'll have to order the part directly from the manufacturer, but when it comes in, it'll be an easy fix."

Appliance repair was always a crapshoot. I sighed in relief. "Thanks, Phil."

He looked at me sideways until I pointed to the name patch on his shirt. He smiled. "No problem."

I tapped two fingers against my lips, trying my best to be casual and offhanded. I tilted my head slightly. "Rivera. Rivera. Are you related to Mustache Hank?"

One of his eyebrows arched. "He's my brother. I can't believe people still call him that."

"I don't think he'll ever escape it," Miguel said, speaking for the first time. Guess he'd been waiting for just the right moment.

Miguel and I hadn't strategized about how to approach Phil, so I just went with the first thing that came to mind, which was repeating what he'd just said. "He's your brother?"

"Yeah. I said that." He narrowed his eyes suspiciously. "You know Hank?"

He seemed remarkably unconcerned for someone whose brother was MIA. Unless, I reasoned, he didn't actually know yet. "I've only met him once, but Miguel owns Baptista's Cantina and Grill. Over on the marina?"

Phil turned his gaze upward to Miguel. "Good shrimp tacos, man."

Miguel nodded at the compliment. "Thanks. Hank does the produce for the restaurant. I haven't seen him in a few days."

Phil packed his tools up and stood, scratching his head under his cap again. "Should you have? Seen him, I mean?"

"Yeah, I should have. He missed his last few deliveries."

Phil lowered his cap, adjusting the brim. Now he looked concerned. "Have you talked to Brenda?"

Again, Miguel nodded. "Jason came to see me. He was worried when he couldn't reach his dad." He gestured to me, but continued talking to Phil. "Ivy and I went to Brenda's, but she said she hasn't seen him."

"Not that she would tell you if she had. As divorces go, theirs was not so pleasant."

By definition, I didn't think *any* divorces were pleasant, but I took his point. Brenda or Hank — or maybe both, based on his implication — had presumably been difficult about the divorce proceedings. I thought back to Brenda's response when we'd showed up on her doorstep. She'd been relatively friendly, although she hadn't seemed concerned about Hank's whereabouts at the beginning. It was only after a while that her emotions began to surface. She seemed mostly frustrated — about the money, or lack of it — and what people owed Hank, both before their divorce and after. Overall, I hadn't gotten the feeling that there was horrible blood between the two of them, though. "What happened?" I asked.

Phil shrugged. "You know. Divorce. It's either another woman — or man — or money. For Hank and Brenda, it was a little of both. Don't get me wrong: I love my brother and he's a good guy, but he made a stupid decision and it ruined his marriage."

"He had an affair?" Miguel asked. I could tell from his expression and the surprise in his voice that the very idea seemed out of character for the Hank who Miguel knew. My mind, however, immediately strayed. And yet . . . Alice. There was something there, I was sure of it.

But Phil immediately dispelled the notion

that Hank had been unfaithful to his wife. "No, no. He came close, I'll say that, but no, he's wasn't unfaith — No, it wasn't that."

"Wait, you mean Brenda?" This time Miguel didn't bother to hide the shock. He shook his head, pressing his fingers to his forehead as if he was trying to make sense of this new information. A second later he shot me a look with an expression I couldn't quite read. It was a mixture of disgust and disbelief.

Phil frowned, hesitating. "Um, yeah." He turned back to the range, but stopped, facing us again. "Why are you so interested in Hank?"

I answered with my own question. "If he didn't cheat, what kind of bad decision did Hank make that ruined his marriage?"

Phil hesitated before answering. "Money. What else? He's in the hole so deep I doubt he'll ever be able to get out."

Brenda had said money was an issue, but with that one sentence, his brother painted a much more dire picture of the problem. I imagined that the truth was somewhere in between.

Phil folded his arms over his chest. "Now, once again, why are you so interested in Hank?"

I couldn't tell if there was any love lost between Phil and his brother, but I decided there was no point in mincing words. "He's missing."

Whatever he had been expecting, it wasn't this. If I'd had any thought that Philip Rivera had something to do with his brother's disappearance, I'd have reconsidered based on his reaction. His response seemed utterly genuine. His jaw dropped and his eyes bugged as his head jutted for ward. "Wait, what?"

"His truck was found, but he hasn't been seen since yesterday —"

"Yesterday?" He scoffed and turned back to the range again. "That's not new. He disappears every now and then. Thinks he can somehow solve his problems, or escape them, or something. Of course, that never happens and he comes back in worse shape than when he left."

Miguel spread his fingers and ran them through his hair. "So you're saying he's done this before?"

"What I'm saying is that he's done this plenty of times before. It's not like he doesn't try, or that he doesn't have good intentions. He does. He's always been a hard worker. He started his business with nothing. Loves the earth, you know? He's had a garden since he was knee-high to a grasshopper. But it's a tough business to be successful in, especially with those corporate growers taking over everything. Hank gives people the benefit of the doubt, letting them run up credit because he thinks they're good for it. I see that in my business, too. Sometimes they pay, sometimes they don't. With his debt, I think he sometimes just needs to . . . you know, take a hiatus from life."

"But he's never — I mean *never* — missed a delivery before," Miguel said.

Phil scratched his temple, thinking about that. "He just drops it off outside the kitchen door, right?"

"Usually. We meet once a week to talk about the order for the following week."

"When he checks out, he gets someone to do his deliveries. Brenda and me have both done it. His right-hand guy, Daniel. I think Jason's even done it once or twice."

"He didn't get anyone to do it this time," Miguel said.

Which, to me, meant that something different was going on with Hank this time around. What if he'd finally hit rock bottom? If he was in financial straits, maybe he couldn't see a way out anymore.

Suddenly I wasn't worried that he was off

somewhere on a bender. Now I feared that he was off somewhere contemplating ways to resolve his desperate situation. "Does he have life insurance?" I asked.

Phil nodded, and I drew in a heavy breath. It wasn't unheard of for someone in Hank's situation to think he was worth more dead than alive. For Jason's sake, I hoped against hope that this was not the case with Hank Rivera.

CHAPTER 12

Emmaline called me within fifteen minutes of Phil Rivera leaving my house. "Ivy Culpepper, you need to cease and desist."

"What do you mean?" I played innocent, although I knew just what she was talking about.

"Look, Hank's officially a missing person. We hadn't talked to his brother yet, so imagine my surprise when Phil Rivera called *me* instead of the other way around."

"Phil just happened to be the technician who came over to repair my broken oven door. I couldn't pass up the opportunity to ask him some questions."

She scoffed. "He 'just happened' to be the tech that came?" She emphasized *just happened* with utter sarcasm. "And I have some swampland in SoCal to sell you for a dollar."

"Have you found out anything?" I asked, already knowing the answer. If she had, she would have led with that.

"Nothing. I don't want you to interfere."

"What you see as interference, I see as helpful assistance."

"But here's the thing, Ivy. You're not actually an employee of the Santa Sofia sheriff's department. Nor are you a licensed private investigator."

"Maybe not, but I did help solve that other case —"

"Beginner's luck."

"Tenacity," I argued.

"Coincidence," she countered.

"Smarts."

She sighed. "Okay, okay. Look, I know you're good at this. You have a natural curiosity and decent deductive skills —"

My jaw dropped. "Decent?"

She sighed. "Better than decent," she admitted. "Look, I can't stop you from poking around, but would you *please* keep me in the loop? I do *not* want to be blindsided again."

"Agreed."

"So what's next, Veronica?"

"Veronica?"

"As in Mars."

"Subtract twenty years from my age, and maybe that reference will work," I said. "She was only in high school during her prime investigative years."

"But just as obstinate as you are."

I couldn't disagree with her there. Veronica Mars was a TV detective after my own heart. If you overlooked her age, her blond hair, as compared to my curly ginger mass, and her slight physique as opposed to my five-feet-eight inches, then we were practically twins. "What's next?" I mused, getting to her question. "Phil told us —"

"Us?"

"Miguel," I said, glancing over at him. My farm table was made with reclaimed oak from a barn, sanded and refinished, and was one of my favorite pieces of furniture. He looked comfortable sitting at it, leaning back in his chair, one leg crossed at the ankle.

There was a pause while Emmaline weighed her response. We'd been friends so long that I could almost read her mind. I was fairly certain that I knew her thoughts and the order in which she was having them.

1. For years, I had given her a hard time about the unrequited love between her and my brother.
2. Oh, the irony. The tables had turned: She and Billy were finally together while Miguel and I were . . . *not.*
3. Should she drive home that point with

a sarcastic barb?

4. No, she should be the bigger person and get back to the task at hand, namely Hank Rivera.

5. Oh, what the hell. Jab, jab, jab.

"Miguel, huh? Showing him some of that Southern hospitality you learned in Texas?"

"Actually," I said, ignoring her, "I have an idea."

"I bet you do. High time you got back on the horse. I'm sure he'd take you for a ride wherever you want to go." She said it suggestively, double entendre fully intended.

I rolled my eyes. "You've been hanging around men too long."

Miguel couldn't help but overhear my part of the conversation. He arched one brow. Which made me wonder if he could also overhear what Emmaline was saying. She did have a voice that carried. I smiled, rolling my finger in the air as if to say Em wouldn't stop talking. I played it off as if we were not talking about him.

"Only your brother," she said. "What did you tell me about that? Oh, yes: 'I should get over my fears.' 'We only have one life to live, so why waste it without our soul mate?' 'Stop standing on the edge; take a leap of faith!' You're excellent with the cliché."

"It takes one to know one," I said, cringing after the words left my mouth. Behaviorally, people often reverted to childhood family roles. The same was true with dear old friends. *It takes one to know one?* I thought the words again at the very same time that Miguel mouthed them, a big, laughing question mark on his face.

All I could do was shrug. There was no way to explain our juvenileness.

"Back to it, Ivy," Em said. "What's your big idea?"

"Right. Phil mentioned that Hank has a right-hand man. Daniel. And he also said Brenda, Hank's ex-wife, cheated and that's at least one reason for the divorce."

I'd half expected a gasp, but instead I got a snort. "Now *that's* cliché."

But I begged to differ. "No, what would have been cliché is if Hank had had the affair. Brenda hadn't struck me as the type, or at least my brain hadn't automatically gone there."

"I guess you were wrong, then."

"If Phil is right, then I definitely was."

"Still waiting for the idea, Ivy," she said, as if her hair was going gray as the seconds passed.

"We should go see Brenda again under the pretext of getting information about this guy Daniel."

I felt Miguel's eyes on me. I turned and faced him. His expression was tense. Was he against me going back to talk to Brenda Rivera?

"I don't have the manpower to send someone —"

I leaned against the kitchen counter and waved my free hand in the air as if I were warding her away. "I'm not asking you to. *I* want to go."

"I know you do, but —"

"No. No buts. You didn't ask me to —"

"I should be telling you not to —"

"Even if you did, it wouldn't work."

"Don't I know it," she muttered.

"So? Do I have your blessing?" Not that I needed it. I'd be going with or without it.

She sighed, reading my mind. "Does it matter?"

I shook my head. "You know me too well, Em."

"Let me know what you find out, okay?"

Emmaline hung up. I lowered the phone to my side and turned to Miguel. "She gave her blessing," I said, trying to ignore the sense I got that something in Miguel was brewing under the surface.

"Yeah. She might give a little more this time." His voice was gruff, and if I didn't know better, I'd say it was almost tinged with anger.

But if either of us had a reason to be mad, it would be me. He was the one who had driven away, leaving me in the dust. "Something wrong?" I asked, folding my arms as a barrier.

He dropped his foot to the floor, put his open palm on the table, and stood. "Nope."

Except clearly there was. I pressed. "Miguel, I know you. Something's wrong."

The look he gave me could have withered a flower. "We don't know each other anymore."

My head spun. Where was this coming from? "I don't —"

"I've been trying, Ivy. I welcomed you back to town, into my restaurant. Hell, into my life." He paced the length of the kitchen while I stared at him, trying to comprehend what he was saying. He swung his arm out toward the front of the house. "That damn Galileo's thermometer was a peace offering, you know? But . . . I don't want to do this again."

"I didn't know we were trying to," I said, although my insides felt like they were being crushed. "You were the one who called me to take pictures for the menu, remember?"

He raked his hand through his hair again, his eyes darkening. "I shouldn't have. I don't —" He stopped, dug his keys from his front pocket, and headed toward the door. "I'll see you tomorrow, Ivy."

I gaped at him. "Tomorrow?"

"Tomorrow," he repeated. "I got you involved in looking for Hank. I need to see it through with you."

He said it as if it was going to be torture. "I'm perfectly capable of handling Brenda Rivera without you."

"I want to find Hank," he said, making it sound final.

"I do, too," I said.

He headed for the door. "Great, then I'll see you tomorrow." And he was gone.

My emotions were going haywire, waffling between disappointment and anger. He acted as though I was pursuing him, as if I was trying to get back together, when all I'd done was be friendly. I shook my head, my anger growing. He'd been friendly, too. Asking me to come to the restaurant, going to see Brenda together the first time —

I stopped, remembering. I'd invited myself to go along to see Brenda. Maybe he'd never wanted me to. Maybe he'd thought about rekindling what we had, but realized it wouldn't work for him.

Well, okay then, Miguel, I thought. What's done is done. I thought again about Laura telling me to stay away from him. Well, she was going to get her wish. I'd stay away from him, and he'd stay away from me.

After we went to see Brenda Rivera one more time.

CHAPTER 13

The phone rang bright and early the next morning. I reached for my cell, swiping my finger across the screen without looking at the name, and muttering a slightly disgruntled, "Hello?"

Penelope Branford's voice shot into my ear, bright and awake, neither of which I was. "Well?"

I tried to erase the sleepiness from my voice. "Well what?"

"I was right."

"Mrs. Branford — ?"

"Penny," she corrected.

"Mrs. Branford," I insisted. It was as if I had to maintain the respect that came with the formality, even though we had become partners in crime. Or partners in crime fighting, I should say, "It's too early."

She harrumphed, a sound I had grown quite accustomed to. "Actually, Ivy, it's not."

I pressed my fingers to my eyes, clearing

217

away the fog so I could focus on the clock. Nine o'clock! I rolled over, scanning the bed in search of Agatha, hoping she hadn't hopped down to take care of business inside without me realizing she'd left the bed.

She hadn't. Her little body was stretched out beside me. She lay on her back, her stomach exposed, front legs curled in the air. I laid my hand on her belly, closing my eyes again.

"Well?" Mrs. Branford said again, and suddenly I knew what she was talking about. She knew everything that happened on Maple Street. I'd grown up watching old reruns of *Bewitched;* Mrs. Branford was like Gladys Kravitz, the nosy neighbor who was always watching — minus the annoyance.

"Miguel was here," I said.

"Ha! I knew it. He was there a long time, wasn't he." She phrased it as a statement, not a question.

"No, not really. Just long enough." Just talking about Miguel made every word he'd said the night before come rushing back. My stomach roiled all over again, my confusion front and center.

"And . . . ?"

"And nothing."

"Aha!" she said, and then she stopped. "Wait, nothing? No kissing? No declaration of love?"

"No nothing," I repeated. And maybe that was a good thing. My high-school relationship with Miguel had crushed me and I'd rebounded straight into marriage. Luke Holden was a swashbuckling cowboy from Texas. We'd met at UT in Austin and he'd swept me off my feet. I'd been vulnerable, still aching for Miguel, and had succumbed to Luke's charm. He'd wined and dined me, taking me home to meet his family in Louisiana, spending long weekends together in Hill Country outside of Austin, filling my empty spaces with attention. We'd spent the first year together in romantic bliss. No responsibility. Living the college life. And truly, he had helped me get over Miguel.

After a year and a half, we'd gone on a weekend getaway to Nashville and ended up married in a quickie wedding at the Rhinestone Chapel. We'd gotten a marriage license in one easy step, and with no waiting necessary in Tennessee, we chose the first chapel we'd found. An Elvis officiate had been our only choice. That should have been a red flag. Like most girls, I'd dreamed of a white wedding, a princess gown, a dashing groom, a tiered cake, my dad walking me down the aisle, my mom, teary but happy.

I'd had none of those things.

But that had been my own choice, however misguided, and it was a misstep that I'd lived with for nearly eight years.

Ultimately, Luke Holden had been my biggest mistake.

I'd finally left him for good when I couldn't ignore the obvious. On a random Sunday afternoon when my car had been low on gas, I'd taken his to an anniversary party I'd been contracted to photograph. When I'd taken one of my camera bags from the front passenger floor, I'd discovered a wayward oil-blotting makeup wipe under the seat, a product that I didn't use. That had been the catalyst for what had become my first sleuthing experience. I didn't ask Luke about it; I didn't want to hear a lie and have him try to turn things around on me. I could just hear him saying how hurt he was that I didn't trust him, how indignant he was that I'd question his morality, and how disappointing that I could even think he'd be so low as to cheat on me. I wasn't going to face him blindly with only a flimsy piece of blotting paper as my proof of his infidelity, so I dug around. I looked at his cell phone, his computer history, and finally I hit pay dirt. I found a contact for someone named Mike. I'd never heard of Mike. When I clicked on the text history, it was crystal clear that Mike was, in fact, Heather, and that Luke had been carrying on with her for months.

At that point, I didn't bother to confront him and give him the opportunity to deny it. I just showed him the screen shot I'd taken of the incriminating texts and told him I was divorcing him. End of story.

It had been a lot of years since my marriage to Luke dissolved, but there hadn't been anyone significant since. I often wondered if I'd ever find a partner. A soul mate. I'd just started taking to heart what Mrs. Branford and Olaya believed, thinking that maybe Miguel and I would end up together again. But now it was clear we wouldn't. I had been foolish to believe that we could rekindle those old feelings. We might be older, more mature, more cautious, but that didn't mean we belonged together. Mrs. Branford had that all wrong.

I changed the subject to something I knew would get her off the current topic: Namely, the hunt for Hank Rivera. "I'm going to see Brenda today."

"Rivera? As in Hank's former wife? Again?"

"Yes, yes, and yes. I have some new information," I said, and proceeded to tell her about Phil Rivera and his big reveal about Brenda's unfaithfulness.

"I'll be ready in a jiffy," she said.

I smashed the pillow over my head, wishing I could fall back into an oblivious sleep where Hank wasn't missing and Miguel hadn't just crushed my heart. Instead, I got up and took Agatha out to run in the yard while I got ready. In the bathroom, I looked in the mirror, wondering how bad my curly hair looked and how much I'd have to contain it before I left. It was more unruly than usual. Disheveled was my hair's normal state, exacerbated by the ginger tint and long, loose Shirley Temple–like curls. People tended to notice me because of the curls, my bright green eyes, and the arresting color of my hair. Things I got a lot: *You're a curly-headed version of Emma Stone. Is that your real hair color? Perm or natural?* My answers: I know, and thanks. One-hundred-percent real. One-hundred-percent natural.

Now, looking in the mirror, I tamed it as much as possible, pulling it back into a haphazard ponytail. I put on my minimal makeup, dressed in jeans, a long-sleeve T-shirt, and a lightweight vest, crated Agatha, and steeled myself to face the day.

CHAPTER 14

Miguel seemed to have a sixth sense. He drove to Brenda Rivera's house separately from Mrs. Branford and me and arrived about thirty seconds after we did, although we hadn't prearranged a time.

We greeted each other with a strained hello, but otherwise didn't talk. Mrs. Branford looked at me, a question mark on her face, but I kept my expression blank. I didn't want to think about Miguel anymore. Much as I tried to ignore it, though, what had happened the evening before with Miguel and me was like a elephant in the room between us.

Mrs. Branford, however, he greeted warmly. He bent and kissed her cheek. "Good to see you," he said.

"The pleasure is all mine," she said with a wink, "but you know I'm a little too old for you."

He cocked one eyebrow conspiratorially

before leaning down again and whispering something in her ear. She blushed, the pink tinge spreading from her neck to her cheeks. "Mr. Baptista, you are a scoundrel," she said with a happy grin. If she'd had an old-fashioned handheld fan, I imagined her playfully swatting his arm with it before flicking her wrist, popping it open, and holding it in front of her face.

With me leading the way, we headed up the walkway. Miguel and Mrs. Branford walked side by side. At the door, I turned to look over my shoulder. "Ready?" I asked.

They both nodded, so I raised my hand, and rapped my knuckles against the door. We waited. No answer.

I sighed, disappointed. Mrs. Branford put into words exactly what I was thinking. "I know we couldn't have called ahead to make sure she was here, but damn."

But then the door was suddenly thrown open and Brenda stood there. She was already tall, but she gained a good four or five inches on the step into the house and she towered over Mrs. Branford and me. She met Miguel's gaze at equal height. I looked up at her. "Mrs. Rivera, sorry to barge in on you —"

She rolled her eyes, her mouth twisting in annoyance. "Yet here you are, just as expected."

As expected? So Philip had called Emmaline and Brenda the day before. "Is now a bad time?" I asked, hoping to smooth out her irritation.

"It's as good a time as any," she answered, but she didn't invite us in this time. No offer of a couch to sit on, or iced tea to drink.

Miguel put his hands in his jeans pockets, his brown nubuck shoes rooted to the ground. "Brenda, we're still trying to find Hank."

"I already told you everything I can. We aren't married anymore. He's not in my life."

"He's not, but does he still want to be?" I asked. "We're wondering if maybe he was depressed. If anything might have happened between you to make him —"

I didn't know how to ask if he was suicidal over the affair she'd had.

In a split second, the anger on her face dissipated and the veneer she'd been wearing cracked. She pressed her lips tightly together, breathing heavily through her nose, as if she were trying to regain the control she'd momentarily lost. She was indignant, but with herself, not with us. "I cheated on him, okay? Is that what you want to hear?" she blurted. "He was destroyed. I betrayed him in the worst possible way. I wasn't just unfaithful, it was with his —"

She stopped herself from finishing the sentence, but my jaw dropped as I filled in the blank. With his brother? With Phil? Was he seriously the one she'd slept with? A cheating spouse was horrible. I knew that from experience. Brenda cheating with Hank's brother? That really *was* a betrayal in the worst possible way.

"Phil told us everything," I said, implying — or rather stating explicitly — that he'd revealed the truth about their affair. I was fishing for more information, but I had no idea if she'd bite.

Mrs. Branford looked at me, a puzzled expression on her face. Miguel said nothing. But Brenda Rivera stared at me wide-eyed, her anger crumbling right in front of me. "He told you about us?"

Mrs. Branford's mouth formed an O as she realized what Brenda and Phil had done to poor Hank. It seemed reasonable to assume that this was what had caused him to run away, if that's what he'd done.

She dipped her head, one hand cupped at her forehead. Her body trembled. "I pushed him away," she sobbed. Her voice broke as she continued. "If anything happens to Hank, it's my fault."

Miguel reached out and gently touched her arm. "Do you want to sit down?"

She stood motionless, as if she were unable to move.

"Brenda," Miguel prompted. "Come on. Let's go inside."

Nodding, she let him guide her into the house, turning and practically stumbling into the kitchen. Whatever grief she'd been holding inside the last time we were here had unfurled in a torrent of emotion. She was torn up inside, that much was clear.

Brenda had already collapsed at the kitchen table by the time Mrs. Branford and I came into the room. She looked up at us, her eyes red-rimmed. "Did I do this to him? Where is he?" She moaned. "Oh my God, where is he?"

There were four chairs at the table. Mrs. Branford, Miguel, and I took the remaining three. "Can you think of anything new, Brenda? Any place he might have gone?" I asked.

Miguel cupped his hand over hers. "You thought of the bar he sometimes goes to. Are there other places? Somewhere else he might have gone off to?"

Brenda rubbed her eyes. "Maybe to Daniel's?" she suggested.

His right-hand man, from what Phil had

said. "You think Hank might be staying with him?" I asked, wondering why she didn't mention Daniel before and if Jason had thought to look there.

From the imploring look she gave Miguel, I suspected the answer to my second question was *no*. "Will you check?" she asked him. "I — I hurt him. I know I did. I don't have a right to ask anything, but — but I *am* worried. And Jason . . ."

Before anything else, she was a mother. Whatever pain she'd caused Hank, whatever her actions had done to her marriage, she also recognized that she'd destroyed the only family her son had known. Jason was a grown man, but I knew from personal experience that it didn't matter how old you were. A family torn apart, whether by accident or design, took its toll on everyone.

"We'll check," Miguel said, gently squeezing her hand.

With her other hand, she wiped the tears pooling in her eyes. "You'll let me know?"

"Absolutely," I said.

"Of course, my dear," Mrs. Branford said at the same time.

And Miguel nodded.

"One more thing," I said. She waited and I continued. "Do you know if Hank is seeing someone?"

She wiped away a final tear. "What, like dating?"

I nodded. Exactly like dating. "Do you think he might have gone off with someone?" A thought just occurred to me. "Maybe he did the online-dating thing, or something?"

"Hank?" She laughed at the absurdity of the idea. "He's in the dark ages. No computer. Order forms in triplicate. I had to force him to have a cell phone, which he eventually gave back to me. He prefers to do things like when he was younger. Before all the technology. Can't teach an old dog new tricks." Her eyes teared up again. "That's . . . that's what he always used to say to me."

After a few more minutes, and with Daniel Sanchez's address in hand, it seemed we'd gotten all the information we were going to. We left her to her grief and got back in our cars, Mrs. Branford with me, and Miguel on his own in his truck. We were an unlikely trio, but we were all determined to find Hank for our own reasons. And one way or another, I felt sure we'd succeed.

Turns out we didn't have to go very far to look for Daniel Sanchez. He lived in a modest house about a mile away from Brenda Rivera. But finding his house didn't mean we found him. His fifteen-year-old daughter opened the door for us. The door opened right into the main living area where another kid, younger than the girl standing in front of us now, slouched on the sofa, staring at a flickering TV.

The girl looked at us blankly, waiting for us to give her some clue as to what we wanted. Miguel made the first move. "Hey. We're looking for your dad, Daniel. He around?"

She looked at us like we were crazy. "He's at work."

I stepped forward, shouldering past Miguel to stand in front of him. "When does he get back?"

She shrugged. "I don't know. Like, around six, I guess."

I glanced at my watch. It was barely eleven in the morning. That was too long to wait to talk to who, so far, was amounting to Hank's only friend. "Do you think he'd mind if we stopped by his work to see him?" I asked.

She dipped her chin toward her chest and peered at me through her eyelashes. "Who'd you say you are?"

Miguel spoke again. "We're actually looking for Hank Rivera. We were under the impression that Hank and your dad work together."

Her expression changed, becoming less hostile at the mention of Hank. "Well, they *did* work together, but then Mr. Rivera had to let my dad go. Business was bad, I guess. Which is okay, in my opinion. Not that business is bad for Mr. Rivera, but that my dad didn't work for him anymore. He found a really good job at Crenshaw. Rubber products, or something. He runs one of the lines, I think? He likes it. It pays way better." She stuck her leg toward us, pointing to her foot. "See? I got new shoes." She practically glowed with pride and my heart swelled. Like most kids, the world revolved around her, but still, she was happy for her dad.

"He works at Crenshaw Company?" Miguel asked.

The girl smiled big and pointed her finger at him. "That's it, yeah. He works the day shift, so he, like, gets home around dinnertime."

Mrs. Branford had been standing by, silently taking in the conversation. Now she edged her way forward. "Have you seen Mr. Rivera lately?" she asked.

I looked at her, impressed. It was an obvious, yet good, question. I wished I'd asked it.

"Like, last week sometime? He was here

all the time for a while. Now he comes around maybe once a week?"

I heard a loud screeching sound in my head. "Wait, what?"

"He was here all the time?" Miguel asked, piggy-backing on my question.

Mrs. Branford finished off our thoughts. "As in he lived here?"

Being interrogated, which is what it felt like we were doing, wouldn't be fun at any age, but Daniel Sanchez's daughter was only a teenager. She could spook and we'd be done.

But she didn't spook. Instead, she rolled her eyes as if we were dense. "Jeez, no. He didn't, like *live here* live here. God, my mom would have freaked. He just stayed for a while. Like when he was in between places or something."

Mrs. Branford seemed unfazed by this revelation and by the girl's derision of us. "When was this, dear?" she asked calmly.

The girl's lips moved in and out as she thought. "A few weeks ago, I guess. I don't know. I don't really remember."

"How long was he here?" I asked, hoping we could get something from her.

She shrugged. "Like, a week? Maybe a little more. I don't know. I wasn't really paying attention."

Mrs. Branford reached out and patted the girl's hand. "You've been a big help, dear."

She looked at each of us in turn, but didn't seem to know what to say. So she kind of shook her head, shrugged her shoulders, and retreated back into her house, shutting the door. Mrs. Branford, Miguel, and I looked at each other. "That was interesting," I said.

"Where to next?" Mrs. Branford asked, pointing her cane in front of her as if it was a sword and she was leading the charge.

"I have to get to the bread shop," I said. I'd been able to get the morning off, but Olaya needed me. The Winter Wonderland Festival was over, but there were still restaurants to bake for, preparation for the new class Olaya was going to offer on yeast doughs, and a few private-catering contracts we needed to supply bread for. I was a novice, but she still needed my help in the kitchen.

"I have to get back to the restaurant," Miguel said. He led the way back down the walkway. "See you later," he said, but it was more of an innocuously broad *see you later,* not a specific-to-me parting.

"Sure," I said, but I had no intention of calling him to join our next investigative adventure.

He gave me a backward glance, as if he were trying to decipher some hidden meaning in my single-word response. Then, coming up empty, he gave Mrs. Branford a wave, got into his truck, and sped away.

"Well, well, well," Mrs. Branford said. I braced myself for the onslaught of her commentary, but she surprised me. "That young girl was quite helpful, don't you think?"

"Quite," I agreed, blinking away my relief. I didn't want to talk about anything but Hank Rivera.

"You sure you have to go to Yeast of Eden?" She was clearly disappointed. I didn't blame her. If I could, I'd head straight over to Crenshaw Company and hunt down Daniel Sanchez. But Olaya had come to count on me as much as I counted on her.

Our meeting with Hank's former right-hand man would have to wait.

CHAPTER 15

There were a million things I loved about Santa Sofia. My father and brother were here, my mother was buried here. I had memory after memory after memory, from elementary-school plays to high-school homecoming and prom, to days laying out at the beach with Emmaline and my brief attempts at surfing. And, of course, Olaya and Mrs. Branford.

But the view of the coastline as I drove along Beach Road came in a close second to most of my favorite things in town. Beach Road wasn't an original name for a coastal highway — if you could even call it that — but it was accurate. It ran alongside the sandy expanses of public beaches at the ocean side, but at times it worked its way inland and ran alongside parts of our own special forest. La Mujer wasn't as renowned as Los Padres National Forest, but all Santa Sofians loved it. Our beach town was located northwest of San Luis Obispo, which sat inland. We didn't have Los Padres, but we had a large variety of vegetation and our trees were spectacular. Coastal redwoods, a variety of pine trees, oaks, and a fair number of willows, cottonwoods, alders, and syca-mores made up the green space.

I stayed on Beach Road as I headed back to town from Daniel Sanchez's more inland residence, my thoughts on Hank Rivera and the end of his marriage. I felt for the man. My marriage had ended after only a frac-tion of time compared to the length of Hank and Brenda's marriage. The betrayal of a cheating spouse after more than half your life together had to feel like an earthquake at a fragile fault line.

"You're taking the scenic route," Mrs. Branford commented.

I blinked, my thoughts retreating. "Oh, yeah. Distracted, I guess."

"Thinking about Hank?"

The more time we spent together, the more Mrs. Branford seemed to know just what was on my mind. I told her my thoughts on divorce and what Hank might be feeling, but followed it up with my reservations. "I just . . . I wonder if that was enough to make him vanish from his life."

"Divorce is like a loss," she said, "and

people deal with loss in a lot of different ways."

I knew she spoke from her own experiences. She'd almost lost Jimmy, the love of her life, to another woman, namely Olaya — hence their strained friendship — and then she *had* lost him when he'd died a little more than ten years ago. Mrs. Branford knew what it was like to have a broken heart, of that I had no doubt. She hadn't run away from her life like Hank did, however. She'd stayed the course and eventually, both times, her heart had healed.

I cracked my window for a moment, letting in the brisk ocean air. I breathed deeply, letting the air filter through me. "I don't know if it's intuition or skepticism or something else," I said, "but I feel as if there is more to this story. Something else that made him run away. Do you think that's possible, or am I trying to make things more complicated than they probably are?"

She adjusted the sleeves on her turquoise velour lounge suit as she considered my question. "In my experience, Ivy, human nature is unpredictable at best. I think anything is possible."

I did, too. But no matter what the situation was with Hank, the problem was trying to actually figuring it out. We had so little to go on.

Mrs. Branford reached over and patted my arm. "Don't ignore your intuition. You have it for a reason."

I tossed that over in my mind. She was right. Intuition didn't need reason or logic to back it up. It was a sixth sense that was indefinable. At the moment that felt like all I had to go on. I had a hunch that there was more to Hank's disappearance than betrayal and a broken marriage. I tossed around the other possibilities in my mind, throwing them out for her to chew on "What could motivate someone to pick up and simply leave their life? Money troubles? We know Hank had that. Betrayal? He had that, too. Love? Blackmail?"

"Any of the above," Mrs. Branford said.

I went with the financial angle first. "If he isn't getting paid by people who owe him, then he can't pay the people *he* owes. That could have put him in a never-ending downward spiral that he couldn't control. But," I said, playing devil's advocate, "wouldn't Brenda have known that things were *that* bad?"

Mrs. Branford sighed. "Ivy, people tell you what they want you to know, or they spin it so they control the message. Rhetorical fallacy one-oh-one."

She always came back to her years of teaching English. "Okay. So maybe Brenda knows how bad things are for Hank and she's trying to mislead us. But why? Why would she do that?"

"I just explained human nature, my dear. I don't actually have the answer."

I pondered the possibility of Brenda knowing just how bad Hank's financial situation was. The problem might have been real, but did it explain Hank's response? People trying to escape their life — if that's what was happening with Hank — did it for some very serious reasons. Were his finances that bad? And if Brenda knew, then why keep it a secret? I came back to one of the questions I'd asked Phil and his response. Hank had life insurance. Was Brenda hoping Hank didn't come back so she could collect on that insurance? Was she the beneficiary? I made a mental note to share this theory with Em. She could find out the details of Hank's policy easier than I could.

"So one scenario is that Hank ran away to — what — think things through? Come up with a solution to his problems? Or does he not plan on ever coming back?"

"There's no way we can know that," Mrs. Branford said. The soft curls of her white hair bobbed slightly with the movement of the car. "If he didn't leave a clue that we're somehow missing, and if this Daniel Sanchez fellow doesn't know anything, I don't see how we'll ever be able to find him."

I didn't, either, but I wasn't about to give up. I wanted to know the truth if only to satiate my own curiosity.

I went back to my list of reasons Hank might have disappeared. "Nothing in the blackmail or the love columns," I said.

Mrs. Branford tapped my hand on the steering wheel. "That we know about."

"Good point." I continued my thought process. "What if he actually fell in love with someone else? I mean, he and Brenda were already split, she had an affair with his brother —" I had trouble saying those words without getting a bad taste in my mouth — "so why wouldn't he move on?"

"It isn't always easy to find love, Ivy."

That was an understatement. My eyes strayed from the road to her. "Did you try to date after Mr. Branford passed away?" He'd been gone a decade, which meant she would have been a spritely seventy-six-year-old when he'd passed. I knew love was hard to find at any age, but I imagined even more so during your third act.

Her hand fluttered. "No, no. Me? No.

240

Jimmy was my one and only. But Hank is young —"

"He's in his sixties, right?"

She looked at me, hitting me with a clear-eyed gaze. "Which, relative to my age, makes him a spring chicken."

I smiled. "Point taken."

"He has plenty of time to find someone new. With Internet dating as rampant as it is, the possibilities seem nearly limitless."

Internet dating. But Brenda had said Hank didn't do computers. Still . . . "Oh my God," I said, a new idea surfacing. I shot a furtive glance at her, my hands tight on the steering wheel. "What if he got over the technology phobia? What if he's been cat-fished?"

She looked at me, the expression on her face showing that she wasn't familiar with that particular urban idiom. "It means to be lured in," I explained. "Like you hook a cat-fish by the mouth, pulling it in? You trick someone online into thinking you're some-one you're actually not. They believe you, and so they've been catfished."

"Ah, hoodwinked," she said, but then her eyes narrowed and one corner of her lip rose in distaste. "People just don't court each other anymore?"

I shook my head. "Not so much." Setting

dates, full conversations, breaking up with people — it all happened over text these days.

"Catfished," she repeated, shaking her head. "It's a crazy world."

A crazy world, indeed. I continued with my hypothesis: "What if he met someone on one of those Internet dating sites?"

"By that you mean someone who wasn't actually who they said they were," she clarified.

I slowed to a stop at a stop sign, used my finger to push the turn signal down, and went left into Santa Sofia's quaint downtown. "That's exactly what I mean," I said.

Mrs. Branford breathed out heavily. "I am not a shrinking violet, my dear, but sometimes I just do not understand."

I sighed, feeling as dismayed as she did. There were a lot of great things about social media, but it also brought out the dregs of society, and within those dregs, it brought out the worst of the worst. "I'm not saying that's what happened. I'm just suggesting it as a possibility, that's all."

She pursed her lips, a map of fine wrinkles framing her mouth. "Like I said earlier, I believe anything is possible." She didn't say it in a hopeful way, though. Her voice, just like my thoughts, was edged with dismay.

Parking at this time of day right in front of Yeast of Eden was always a challenge. Even the back lot was usually full. But as I pulled up to the bread shop, there was a spot open right in front, and, as if it was a sign, I knew Mrs. Branford was right. Anything was possible.

As usual, as I stepped inside the bread shop, a warmth as comforting as a heated blanket on a freezing evening settled over me. Olaya worked behind the counter, placing six chocolate and six almond croissants into a white pastry box for a customer. Jamie, a high-school girl with raven hair, fair skin, and dark fingernail polish worked alongside Olaya helping another customer.

I caught Olaya's eye and waved.

"Hola, *mi'ja*," she said with a smile. She tallied the bill for the customer on her order pad, talking to me at the same time. She looked over my shoulder at Mrs. Branford. "The bird girls are here," she said, pointing to a corner table.

The bird gir— ? I turned around and spotted Mabel Peabody, her vibrant red hair pulled back into a loose bun at the nape of her neck, sitting with her back to the bread shop. Her gauzy black culottes floated around her legs and the chair, her raglan-sleeved taupe jacket baggy on her thin

243

frame. Janice Thompson, brown hair perfectly coiffed, as usual, sat on one side of Mabel while Alice, with her red-lipped tight smile, sat on the other side of her. They each had on their hats, looking as if they were ready for a tea party.

The Blackbird Ladies.

Mrs. Branford saw her friends and made a beeline for them. She came to a stop next to the open chair, her back to the window. "Who among you," she blurted, "has ever heard the term *catfishing*?"

"Mrs. Branford!" I hurried up to the table, putting my hand on her shoulder. She was an entire head shorter than me, so with my scolding tone and towering height, I felt more like a reproachful parent than a surrogate granddaughter. "You can't . . . you shouldn't . . ." I trailed off, not sure what I was trying to say. Should she not say anything about my hypothesis? If not, why? What harm would it do to share the idea that Hank had been duped into a friendship — or a relationship — with someone who was not, in fact, on the up and up?

Mrs. Branford reached across her body to pat my hand atop her shoulder. "It's a legitimate question, Ivy," she said. She turned back to her friends. "I, for one, have never heard that term. Ivy and I are fearful —"

"*Fearful* might be a little strong," I interjected, wanting to keep this as just a theory, not a foregone conclusion.

"Ivy and I are fearful," Mrs. Branford reiterated, ignoring me, "that this may be what has happened to Hank."

The three women stared at Mrs. Branford, each of them wearing their own version of a flummoxed expression. Alice Ryder cocked her head to one side, those lips of hers pursed tightly. "Hank has never, to my knowledge, gone catfishing."

"I don't have much knowledge of Hank and his fishing habits," Janice said, "so I'll defer to you on that one."

Only Mabel's expression cleared as understanding replaced confusion. "I've heard of it," she said. "There was a middle-school girl last year. Right here in Santa Sofia." She looked at her friends. "She was on Instagram, I think. Or that Snapchat, maybe? One of the social-media things kids use. She thought she was talking to an eighth- , or maybe ninth-grader from Santa Barbara, but it wasn't."

Janice's eyes opened wide. "I remember that! She was missing for a week, at least, wasn't she?"

I swallowed, a lump in my throat. I hadn't heard this story. "Was she okay?"

Mabel nodded. "She was. It was a miracle, really. She took a bus to Santa Barbara and met the guy near the university. If I'm remembering right, he was a student, but he was from the area. I think his family had a house, or he had a place of his own? I can't quite remember. I don't recall the details, but she managed to escape."

"She got herself to a garden center, didn't she?" Janice asked.

"That's right," Mabel said. "Wherever the man took her, it was away from the main drag, but she stumbled upon a nursery."

Alice waved her hands in front of her. "I'm confused. What does this have to do with fishing?"

I explained the term to all of them. Alice's upper lip curled. "That's a real term? Cat-fishing?"

"Yes. That girl? She was catfished."

Alice closed her eyes for a second before continuing. "And you think this may have happened to Hank? That he was catfished?" She said the last word with utter disdain, snarling into it. "He's a grown man. How could that even be possible?"

Mrs. Branford sat down in the last chair at the table, propping her cane against the window behind her. "I've been thinking about that ever since Ivy brought it up."

Alice glowered at me as if Hank being catfished was my fault. I ignored her, keeping my attention focused on Mrs. Branford. She hadn't shared her theory with me yet, so I was all ears.

With everyone's attention on her, Mrs. Branford went into teacher mode. She cleared her throat and sat up as tall as she could, placing both hands flat on the table. "He was desperate."

We all waited. I leaned forward, ready for the next part of her explanation, but nothing came.

Janice rolled her eyes. "He was desperate? That's your great revelation?"

Mrs. Branford gave a single, succinct nod. "That is my revelation. How does this catfishing work? I asked myself that and what I came up with is this: It can only work if people are vulnerable. What makes people vulnerable and therefore open to new friendships? New relationships?"

"A broken heart," I said, once again nodding with approval. Mrs. Branford was good.

She tapped the tip of her nose with her index finger. "That's right. Whether it be broken, bruised, or torn apart altogether,

247

that's what a catfisher would need in order to hook in a victim."

I didn't know if *catfisher* was actually a term, but her logic made perfect sense. A person who was in a good emotional place wouldn't succumb to a catfisher. At least I didn't think so. If you were mentally healthy, emotionally stable, and/or emotionally mature, I couldn't imagine you'd be susceptible to that sort of duplicity.

"His divorce wasn't yesterday. Was Hank that brokenhearted?" I asked, my gaze naturally straying to Alice. If anyone would know Hank's recent state of mind regarding his love life, I suspected it would be Alice.

"I don't think he was catfished," she blurted. Instead of the typical snobbery in her voice, this time she sounded resigned. She drew in a breath, and then she let loose. "Goddammit," she muttered, looking at each of her bird girls in turn, but completely avoiding my gaze. She shook her head, biting her lower lip. "Goddammit," she said again. "I have something to tell you."

CHAPTER 16

The sounds of the bread shop faded away. We all stared at Alice, mouths agape, eyes wide. Mabel leaned forward, concerned. She patted Alice's hand. "Sweetheart, what's wrong?"

Mrs. Branford looked up and caught my eye, silent communication transpiring between us. She raised one steel-colored eyebrow and I knew that she was thinking the same thing I was: Alice had been having an affair with Hank. I'd suspected it since the first time I'd met Alice at her house with her husband, but getting ready to have her confess it to us, validating my suspicions, didn't make me feel any better.

"Goddammit," Alice said again, louder this time.

"Oh, for Pete's sake." Janice rolled her hand in the air in an effort to keep Alice talking. "What is it?"

Mabel's eyes suddenly went wide and she

inhaled sharply. "Oh, Alice, no."

Mrs. Branford and I looked at each other again. It seemed that Mabel had come to the same conclusion we had.

Alice had pinched her eyes closed, her lips pressed together in a hard line, but they flew open with Mabel's inhalation. "Oh my God! How long have you known me, Mabel?"

"Practically our whole lives," Mabel said, leaning forward. "So spill it, sister. What is going on?"

"I did not sleep with Hank, if that's what you're thinking." Her voice was emphatic; I wanted to believe her.

"Then by all means, tell us the big secret," Janice said impatiently.

Alice's normally silky hair suddenly looked a little lackluster. She brushed it back behind her ears. "Hank has always had a soft heart," she said. "He trusts people. He *believes* them." She gave a harsh laugh. "He believes *in* them. In high school, he'd give his last dime to some poor classmate who didn't have enough money for lunch, even if it meant he'd go hungry that day."

She looked down at her hands, spreading her fingers on her lap. "He got himself into a big hole," she continued. "He trusts people, giving them the benefit of the doubt, and they repay him by . . . by forcing him into debt."

Janice rolled her hand again, prompting her to continue. "We know all this, Alice. Get to the point."

"We were not having an affair," she said again. "People don't pay him, so he can't pay his creditors. He was struggling, so I . . . so I . . . I loaned him some money."

We all stared at her, but it was Mabel who spoke first. "Come again?"

"I loaned him money. *A lot* of money," she said, her voice quivering slightly.

Janice went next. "Alice, he's not a good businessman, for God's sake. You know that. Why would you loan him money?"

Alice threw up her hands. "I know, I know, I know. Oh my God, what if he never comes back? What if he doesn't repay it?"

"Honey," Mrs. Branford said. She leaned forward and patted Alice's hand. "Why wouldn't he? People might owe Hank, but he pays his debts, doesn't he? Surely he intends to settle up with you?"

"He's missing, Penny!" And then she broke down. Her tears came fast and furious, welling in her eyes and spilling over her cheeks. This was a side of Alice I wouldn't have thought even existed. The tears stopped at her jawline, hovering there like spheres of dew hanging onto a vibrant green leaf. "I'm worried about him."

Mrs. Branford's chest rose with the deep breath she drew. Her nostrils flared, just slightly, but enough that I knew she was struggling to keep her emotions in check. "I'm worried, too, Alice," she said.

I looked at Janice and Mabel and saw the same reaction. Alice had opened the levy and now the Blackbird Ladies had let their worries for Hank flood out. The four friends needed a moment, so I stepped away from the table and moved to the bread-shop counter. The last customer had been served, a school-aged girl held one of Olaya's sugar-skull cookies, and Olaya stood at the cash register, taking in the four women at the table. "Finally it has hit them," she said.

I nodded. She was right. The Blackbird Ladies had been burying their emotions about Hank's disappearance, but the reality that he was, in fact, missing and that he might never come back was sinking in.

Olaya wiped her hands on the blue-and-white French dish towel she had on the back counter. She had a million of that very same towel. "I love it, and it's perfect," she'd told me once when I asked her why she had so many of the same towel. "I never run out of these, even if I get behind on the bread shop's laundry.

She tossed the towel under the counter below the register, and then looked back at me. "It has finally hit them that perhaps Hank is not coming back. Or worse yet, that perhaps Hank is already dead."

I stood stock-still. This was the very word I'd avoided saying. "Dead? As in . . . dead? Nothing is pointing at that."

"Yet. I have a feeling, Ivy. I cannot explain it anymore than I can explain the results of one eating my breads. The *bruja* legend in my family is strong, and I believe it is true. I have a feeling," she repeated.

When I'd first met Olaya Solis, she'd known I would show up for her baking class. She'd understood so much of what was in my heart. She'd credited it then to the long line of *brujas* in her family; I'd just chalked it up to a lucky guess. But now she'd said what I'd been afraid to even contemplate. Whatever had made Hank run off and leave his ex-wife, his son, his business, and his life behind was one issue, but I had to concede that it was possible something sinister had happened to him since.

Would Hank Rivera ever come home to Santa Sofia?

Was Olaya right? Was Hank already dead?

CHAPTER 17

"Everyone just calm down!" Penelope Branford stomped her cane against the floor, interrupting the tear-fest that had been going on for the last ten minutes. She'd wiped away her own tears and sat up straight, as if to get back in control of her emotions.

I'd let the Blackbird Ladies process the possibility of Hank being gone for good, staying with Olaya in the kitchen instead. But that just made me wonder more about Olaya's feeling. Could Hank have come to some tragic end? Could he have orchestrated it himself in an effort to wipe his debt clean? He might have thought killing himself would free him from whatever he owed others. As Mrs. Branford had said, anything was possible.

Janice, Mabel, and Alice each gathered up their emotions, letting composure slide over them again. Janice exuded poise. Even under duress, like now, she managed to pull herself together and didn't look any worse for wear. Alice's hair had already been lifeless, but now, after she'd run her splayed fingers through it in her distress, she looked wholly disheveled. No amount of lipstick could distract from the dark circles under her eyes or her slouched shoulders. Only Mabel, with her sparse makeup and naturally vibrantly dyed hair, looked the same as she had.

Janice cocked her head and looked at Alice, frowning sympathetically. "I don't imagine you'll see that money again."

Alice's eyes grew glassy. She nodded. "I know. I don't think he's coming back."

Mabel looked from Janice to Alice. "Ladies, surely you aren't giving up on Hank so easily. He's resourceful."

"But what if he doesn't want to be found?" Alice said. "Maybe he saw an opportunity and decided to take it." She buried her face in her hands. "Oh God. Michael is going to kill me."

"Oh no," Janice said. She laughed, but it wasn't from humor. It was an ironic staccato sound that somehow demonstrated understanding and sympathy for what Alice was feeling. "Michael doesn't know you lent Hank money," she said matter-of-factly.

Alice nodded, misery etched on her face.

"I can't believe he did this."

Mrs. Branford patted Alice's hand encouragingly. "We don't know that he did anything," she said. "Remember the catfishing theory."

But Alice shook her head. "Do you really think someone duped him? Why would they? To what purpose?"

To these questions, Mrs. Branford shrugged. I jumped in. "I'm not an expert, but it seems to me that there isn't one reason why catfishers . . . um, catfish. It could be a dating scheme. Or maybe someone knew about the money you lent him."

Janice didn't look convinced. "Did the man even have a computer?"

"Does," Mabel said, "not *did.*"

Janice's hands trembled, her emotions getting to her. I got the feeling she was already preparing herself for the worst. "Does. He does not use a computer, does he? And he is no Sean Connery," she said. "I doubt very much that women are — were — are knocking down his door."

I stifled a wry smile. Janice and the Blackbird Ladies were of a different generation. Sean Connery was my favorite James Bond, but he wasn't the Hollywood hunk I'd have referenced. George Clooney? Yes. Ryan Gosling? Most definitely. But Paul Newman? Robert Redford? Sean Connery? These men had been incredible in their heyday, but they weren't the epitome of gorgeous men for my generation. Cultural references could certainly date a person.

"No, maybe not," I said, getting back to Hank. "But that doesn't mean he couldn't have been the target of a catfishing scheme."

Alice looked skeptical. "Don't you think it's more likely that Hank ran off with my money?"

This surprised me. Hank was her friend and she'd given him a loan, but she was ready to believe that he'd absconded with the money rather than consider other alternatives.

"Alice, think about what you're saying," Mrs. Branford said. "You've known Hank since we were all kids. He couldn't possibly have fled with your money."

"How much money are we talking about?" Janice asked, her eyes narrowing with concern.

Alice took a napkin from the table and dabbed at her tear-filled eyes. "Fifty thousand dollars," she said, the words catching in her throat.

Next to me, Olaya drew in a stunned breath. Mabel put into words what I imagined all of us were thinking. "Fi—fity —

thousand dollars? Alice, are you out of *your ever-loving mind*?"

Alice hung her head. "I know, I know."

I leaned down and whispered in Olaya's ear. "How could she hide that much money from her husband?"

As if reading our minds, Alice continued: "I cashed out some of my retirement."

The three other Blackbird Ladies stared at Alice with varying degrees of disbelief on their faces. This time Janice put to words what we were all wondering. "Alice, why in the world would you do that?"

Alice's hard edges had completely softened — despair had a way of doing that. The haggardness had taken over. The weight of losing tens of thousands of dollars had taken its toll, as had the burden of keeping the loan from her husband in the first place. "He was so desperate," she said, shaking her head. "I tried to talk myself out of it." Her eyes widened, but were glazed with distress. "He had such a hard time asking in the first place, and then I said no. I didn't even have that kind of money. But then, a month later, he came back again. He was fraught with anxiety. Worried about how he was going to keep going. I think he hated to do it, but he suggested my retirement.

Could I take a loan against it? Or cash it out?"

"It was his idea?" Mabel asked.

Alice nodded. She flicked away a tear that had slipped down her cheek. "He never had any intention of paying me back," she said suddenly, her voice shaky. "I see that, now."

But Mrs. Branford shook her head. "Hank is not a swindler," she said. "He is as honest as the day is long. You know that." Alice, Mabel, and Janice each looked uncertain, but Mrs. Branford turned and considered each one of them. It was as if she were doing some sort of Jedi mind trick so they'd believe what she was saying. "Hank is a cultural icon in this town. Tell me what you think of when I say his name. Hank Rivera." It was a rhetorical question, so she went on without waiting for an answer. "His handlebar mustache, right?"

We all nodded. "It is one of a kind," Olaya said.

Mabel agreed. "Only Hercule Poirot does it better, and he's fictional."

Mrs. Branford continued: "What else do you think of?"

She waited, like any good teacher, giving us the chance to think before we tried to answer her question. "He gives good veggies," Mabel said. "The best around."

Again, they all nodded, murmuring in agreement. "A vegetable hero," Alice added.

"He's got a good heart," Janice said. The comment seemed a little on the sentimental side for her, but the dual crisis of Hank's disappearance and Alice's missing money seemed to have impacted her. She wanted to believe the best about him. "There has to be a good explanation about the money."

Mrs. Branford spoke up. "Hank is a straight shooter. A man like him doesn't simply change his stripes overnight. Janice is right. He couldn't have borrowed the money with the intention of running off with it. He's a produce man, not a swindler," she repeated. She'd summoned up metaphors and imagery as only an English teacher could. But despite — or maybe because of — her vivid description of Hank, I believed her. There had to be more to the story.

"What was your arrangement with the money?" Olaya asked Alice.

Alice looked at her, puzzled. "Arrangement?"

"*Si.* Why did he need it? How did he say he planned to pay it back? Did you make an arrangement about that?"

Clarity crossed Alice's face. "He needed to pay his creditors."

"Por supuesta," Olaya said. "Of course, *pero* how does he intend to pay you back? If he is in debt now, what is his plan? He certainly cannot earn that amount of money from his produce business to keep going *and* to pay you back."

"I guess I just trust — trust — trusted him."

Janice threw up both her hands in frustration. "Michael has every right to be furious with you. How could you be so naive. Alice?"

Her nostrils flared. "Because it's Hank!"

The mutterings of the women grew, both chastising Janice for her bluntness and Alice for her naïveté. Mrs. Branford let it go for a minute before knocking her cane against the floor again. "Enough!" she said. "All we can do is speculate, and that isn't going to get us anywhere. We need to get back to the issue at hand. We need to —"

Mrs. Branford and Olaya caught each other's eyes. "Find Hank," they said in unison.

A series of customers came into Yeast of Eden just then and Olaya summoned me back behind the counter to help her. The baking for the day was just about done, but there were still loaves of bread to pull from the oven, trays to be cleaned, counters in need of wiping, and baked goods to bring to the front. The Blackbird Ladies spent the next hour going round and round about Hank and how to find him — and recover Alice's $50,000 — while Olaya and I took care of the bread shop.

Three hours later, the Blackbird Ladies had gone their separate ways, and Olaya and I had exhausted every angle we could think of in regards to Hank's disappearance. All we had were theories, not a shred of proof supporting any of them, and still not a clue where Hank actually was. We were back where we'd started. Which was basically nowhere.

A short while later, I stood at the enormous stainless-steel sink, pulling down on the retractable faucet and spraying the aluminum baking trays until they sparkled. One by one, I slid them back into the baking rack. As I worked, I got lost in my thoughts, circling through what I knew once again. Brenda cheated on Hank with Phil, Hank's brother. Hank and Brenda divorced. Hank borrowed $50,000 from Alice Ryder, stayed with Daniel Sanchez, his right-hand man in the produce business, for a little while, and then moved into the boarding house run by Richie Thompson. At some point, he made an arrangement to meet someone, left his truck at the gas station on the edge of town, and vanished. Had he been catfished? Or had he decided to disappear on his own for some reason?

"Hank," I muttered, "where are you?"

CHAPTER 18

It was still early by the time I finished up for the day at Yeast of Eden. I still had things to do. I'd uploaded the photos from the Winter Wonderland Festival and put one on Instagram, but I hadn't taken the time to look critically at them. Once I did, I'd be able to update the Yeast of Eden website.

But I couldn't focus on photographs at the moment, not with Hank circling around in my head. I'd heard so much about him from so many people that I felt as if I knew him.

Which meant I couldn't let well enough alone. I'd given it a lot of thought and I'd finally decided on two courses of action in my search for Hank Rivera. First, I wanted to understand how Hank ran his business and finances to get some insight into the why and the how of the $50,000 loan from Alice Ryder. In order to do that, I wanted to talk to one of his clients, as well as Daniel Sanchez, his right-hand man. I had to track down Daniel and find a time when he could talk. As for the client, it made the most sense to go with the easiest access I had. As longtime clients of Hank's, that meant the Baptista family.

I could try to come up with another option, but that would take more time — and Hank needed to be found now. So, should I heed Laura Baptista's wishes and stay away? It seemed as if it was Miguel's wish, too. But I wanted to be expeditious, so maybe I wasn't in the conundrum I thought I'd been in.

I also wanted to pay a second visit to Richie Thompson's boarding house. I wanted to see if there was a communal computer the tenants were able to use. I hadn't seen one the first time I'd been there, but maybe I'd missed it. If there was a house computer — and if Hank had used it — maybe it would hold a clue as to where he had gone.

With cell phone in hand, I started to call up Mrs. Branford, my partner in sleuthing. But before I could press *call,* the phone vibrated in my hand. I jumped, startled. I didn't know the number, but as soon as I answered, I recognized Janice Thompson's cultured voice. "Ivy, darling, I'm so glad I caught you."

I didn't say that the majority of people didn't have landlines anymore and that everyone was reachable 24-7. I said hello, and Janice carried on. "You mentioned a few days ago that you are a photographer."

She left the sentence there for me to respond to. "I am."

"Tell me more," she prompted.

What did she want to know? "Well, I had a studio in Austin, but —"

She drew in a sharp breath, stopping me in my tracks. "Are you going to open a studio here? You can't leave Olaya."

"I'm not leaving Olaya!" I held the phone away from my ear, stunned at the force of my reaction.

"I believe you," Janice said as if she were trying to calm me down.

"I mean, I love the bread shop. And Olaya. I'm doing okay with my freelance work, and I don't think I want to open a place of my own again." I'd started selling the occasional photo to an online stock-image site, as well, but I didn't elaborate on that endeavor. "I'm happy doing what I'm doing," I said, and after I'd said the words, I knew it was true. I was happy.

"Olaya mentioned that you do a lot for her. Website, brochures, and things of that nature."

"She's my most steady client at the moment," I said, "but really, once you have a photo of a baguette, you're good."

"I guess that's true. A baguette is a baguette is a baguette."

I laughed at her adaptation of Gertrude Stein's "rose is a rose is a rose". One piece of bread, once photographed, was the same as any other. Of course, that wasn't actually true if you were talking baguettes compared to croissants compared to pan dulce compared to a rustic loaf. But the idea was clear. "There is only so much bread I can photograph," I said. "Once I have a good shot, there really isn't a need to do it again."

"Which leads me to the reason for my call," she said. "I mentioned that my son has been renovating his house. He took a few before pictures, but I told him that we should do some more to really capture what it's currently like. Then, when it's done, we can take some more to show the difference."

"Do you mean the boarding house?" I asked. When she'd first mentioned it, I thought she'd said she was renovating her own house. If it was Richie's place that was undergoing the renovations, that certainly worked out in my favor. I wouldn't have to talk my way into visiting; I had an open invitation, and if I was photographing the house, I'd be able to look around for a computer. Of course, I could just ask Richie again, but I liked the idea of snooping around in the place Hank had been living before he vanished.

"Yes. It's such a beautiful place," she said. "Historic. He bought it for a song because it needed a lot of updating. Well, you saw it. He's done some, but he still has a ways to go. The kitchen needs redoing. The library. Several of the bedrooms."

"I just bought an older house, myself," I said. "A lot has been remodeled, but I have some things I want to do. Someday."

"It takes a lot to bring an old house back to its former glory. So," she continued, "the reason for my call. I want to document our progress and the changes. I thought I'd make one of those photo books as a gift for Richie. Before and after. What do you think? Is this a project you'd be interested in taking on?"

Several thoughts went through my mind. The first one was all about the photography. Did I have the right lens and lighting to do a quality job photographing an historical Victorian house? I quickly cataloged my lenses and equipment. If enough ambient light shone through the windows, I probably wouldn't need a flash. My wide-angle had a 14-24mm lens. The 2.8 aperture qualified it as a fast glass, so it would work well in low light. As long as it wasn't *too* dim. I could probably shoot the exterior with the same lens. I had a light stand, if I needed it, although I'd need a helper. Janice could do that. Or Richie. The forecast showed clear skies for the next forty-eight hours, so the morning light should be good. "Is tomorrow okay?"

"Perfect! I'll let Richie know. He had his house-cleaners there today, so everything should be in good shape."

We agreed to meet at 7:00 the next morning, which left me plenty of time to try to track down Daniel Sanchez. I made the call to Mrs. Branford and filled her in on the plan to hunt down Hank's former right-hand man. "Want to come along?" I asked.

"My dear, sweet Ivy, does a bird have feathers?"

I laughed. "I'll take that as a *yes*. I'll pick you up in fifteen minutes."

After we hung up, I slipped on my coat, called Agatha, and went through the French doors off the kitchen and into the backyard. As usual, the little pug immediately spun around in circles, her little tail wound up like a curlicue. I waved my hand toward the corner of the yard. "Go potty!"

She went off, sniffing and circling, sniffing and circling, sniffing and circling until she finally found the spot she was looking for to take care of her business. And then she was off like the Tasmanian devil. I sat in one of my two Adirondack chairs and watched her as she ran this way and that, her short little legs and squatty body looking almost lean as she loped across the yard, then back again.

"Knock-knock!" I jumped, startled by the click of the gate and sound of Mrs. Branford's voice. Her lounge suit tonight was navy blue. White stripes ran the length of the pants legs on either side. Her snowy white hair was coiled into perfect elongated curls and tonight — for the sleuthing occasion, I guessed — she wore sparkly diamond studs. She had been a teacher her entire adult life and her Jimmy hadn't struck it rich, so my guess was that they were faux. Much more practical and the choice I always made, too. No one ever knew the difference. She was an elderly Sporty Spice. "I was going to pick you up!" I said, standing.

"I couldn't wait," she said. The expression on her face was priceless. If she were a little kid, she'd be rubbing her hands together with glee. "Let's go."

"Yes, ma'am." I patted my outer thigh and called to Agatha as I walked to the French doors. I held the right door open for Mrs. Branford. Agatha trotted inside next to her, and I followed, locking the door behind me.

A few minutes later, Agatha was snug in her bed. I didn't think our outing would take very long, so crating her wasn't necessary. I reserved that for the times when I was gone for six or more hours. Agatha was a precious dog, but she wasn't always trustworthy after a certain period of time.

We passed through the kitchen and into the garage. I opened the garage door and slid behind the wheel. Mrs. Branford circled around the car and got into the front-passenger side, propped her cane beside her, and promptly buckled up. She was a stickler for the rules. "What do you think Daniel Sanchez will tell us?" she asked as I backed out onto the driveway, hit the garage-door button again, and headed down Maple Street.

I had no idea and told her as much. I wanted to find out what state of mind Hank had been in when he'd crashed at his friend's house. Had he been a man in despair? Had he been preparing to leave his son, his business, his life behind? "I am just hoping he can give us a little insight," I said. "I don't know Hank, but from what everyone says, he is a good guy."

"He is not the kind of man to steal a fortune from a friend and leave town," Mrs. Branford said. "There is no way that is what happened. There is more to this story."

I nodded. "But what?"

"That, my dear, is the fifty-thousand-dollar question."

By the time we arrived at Daniel Sanchez's house, we still hadn't been able to come up with any new scenarios. It was temperate for a January evening, even in Santa Sofia. Still, I'd donned a lightweight coat before we'd left and now, stepping out of the car at Daniel Sanchez's house, I realized it had been a good decision. It had been twilight when we'd left my house, but as the light waned, a breeze had blown in off the coast. The temperature dropped and I pulled my coat around me. Better to be prepared. My mom had lived by that motto and had taught me well.

It was a clear night, but dusk had given way to nightfall and the darkness dropped onto the street like a blanket. Daniel's daughter, with her new shoes, had said that her dad worked the day shift at Crenshaw Company and got home every day around dinner. It was 6:30 now. Light gleamed from each of the windows in the house, vertical blinds slatted just enough to block passersby from seeing inside. Faint shadows moved around for a moment behind one window, and then vanished.

A single porch light illuminated the front stoop and for the second time, Mrs. Branford and I walked up the short path to the Sanchez house. "Second time's a charm," she said.

"If we're lucky," I said, hoping we hadn't jinxed our success. Had Daniel Sanchez's daughter mentioned our visit or would showing up on the doorstep after dark, two strangers looking for his former boss, be a complete surprise? How would Daniel react?

"Hank is a good judge of character," Mrs. Branford said. "Look at Mason Caldwell. That man might be curmudgeonly bugger, but he's got a big heart. Hank sees that."

I'd had my hand up, ready to rap my knuckles on the door, but I stopped short. She'd said *curmudgeonly* as if it were a good thing. I turned to her. "You *do* like him," I said, suddenly feeling like a middle-school student teasing her best friend.

She didn't refute it, only smiled mischievously. "Knock on the door, Ivy," she said.

Oh yes. There was most definitely a twinkle in her eyes.

Mrs. Branford and I both jumped as the door behind us wrenched open suddenly. I turned and looked up at the man looming there. "Mr. Sanchez?" I asked, offering a sincere smile.

He was a tall man. Slick-backed dark hair, a blue-collared shirt, blue jeans, and a thick mustache over his lip. He didn't return my smile. "That's right," he said.

No small talk. No pleasantries. My hope that the conversation would flow easily waned, but I forged ahead, introducing Mrs. Branford and myself.

"You were here yesterday," he said. "My daughter told me."

He made no move to open the door and invite us in. Mrs. Branford leaned on her cane, her hand trembling. "Yes, looking for Hank," Mrs. Branford said, affecting a shaky voice. I smiled. She was good at putting on an act for the sake of acquiring information.

Daniel Sanchez looked her up and down, frowning. "Do you need to sit down?" he asked.

She lifted her hand, the handle of her cane clutched in her thick-knuckled hand. "What a sweet boy," she said, her voice still quivering. "Thank you."

He looked over our shoulders, as if a bench or chair would appear behind us. When it didn't, he looked over his own shoulder, grabbed the doorknob, and stepped back. Daniel Sanchez seemed less than thrilled that we were on his doorstep, but as Mrs. Branford took a gingerly step forward, he put one hand at her elbow and the other behind her back, carefully ushering her over the elevated door frame and into the entry of the house. Chivalrous. It was the only word that came to mind.

I followed them in, closing the door behind me. I was not Emmaline Davis, deputy sheriff, but I did my best once-over scan of the house, quickly taking in as much as I could. It was clean and neat. A few photographs hung on the wall to the right. A staircase leading upstairs was straight ahead. A bench sat against the wall just beyond the front door, several pairs of shoes lined up underneath it.

I glimpsed a bit of the kitchen all the way down the main hallway in the rear of the shotgun-style house and, to the left, sat the main family room. The TV was on a *Sponge-Bob SquarePants* episode. The girl who'd answered the door reclined on the back of the sofa, her eyes glued on the cell phone in her hand. A younger boy, maybe nine or ten, sprawled on the floor, eyes on the television. Neither one cared a bit about the two women now talking to their dad.

If there was a Mrs. Sanchez, she wasn't in plain sight, but a moment later, clanking came from the kitchen. I guessed she was the one jostling around in the back of the house. Daniel Sanchez situated Mrs. Branford on the bench and turned back to face me. He scooped his hand through his hair, making it stand on end. "Since you're here again, I guess you're still looking for Hank?" he asked.

Good deduction. "We've been trying to figure that out for a few days, Mr. Sanchez," I said.

"Danny," he said.

Mrs. Branford spoke up, her voice no longer trembling. "We have a few theories, Danny, but other than that, we are still very much in the dark. We know he stayed here with you for a while. We are hoping you might shed some light on his state of mind."

Mr. Sanchez — Danny — closed his eyes for a long second. As he opened them, he drew in a deep breath. "He was pretty broken up after Brenda and Phil. He didn't want to stay in his house. *Couldn't* stay there."

"We had to help him," a woman said from behind me.

I spun around in surprise and came face-to-face with an attractive, dark-haired woman. She was several inches shorter than me, wore loose jeans, and a plain-colored T-shirt.

Danny looked miserable, but he swept his arm toward the woman. "My wife, Nancy."

Nancy wiped her hands on the floral terry dish towel clutched in her hands, nodding at us. "You're trying to find Hank?" she asked us.

"*Trying* being the operative word," Mrs. Branford replied. "Did you have any idea he was thinking of running away?"

Her choice of words sounded funny, as if Hank were a child instead of a grown man.

Nancy glanced for a moment at the pictures hanging on the wall. "I guess we all have something to run away from."

Her words were weighted down, as if they were being pulled straight from her heart, falling to the floor with a thud. I followed her gaze to the photos. They were school pictures. The girl and boy in the family room, and the older boy. The boy who I hadn't seen here in the house. Had he run away? Or died? Wherever he was, or whatever had happened to him, I felt Nancy

Sanchez's pain into the depths of my soul. I'd lost a mother; but it was clear that somehow she'd lost a child, and that was the worst pain imaginable.

Danny took his wife's hand and gave it a tender squeeze. He began speaking, his words coming slowly. "We gave Hank a place to stay while he got back on his feet. He's been good to me, you know?"

Nancy nodded her head, her lips pressed tightly together. I got the impression it was her way of trying to keep her emotions in check. "He was a good boss for Danny," she said.

Danny rooted both of his feet to the floor, rocking back on his heels slightly. He'd let go of Nancy's hand and now folded his arms over his chest. "He taught me his business," he said. "It's just too difficult to compete with the big growers. He tried to keep it together with the private-restaurant contracts and local organic markets, but that hasn't ever been enough."

Nancy looked at us, her eyes wide. Imploring. "You need to find him," she said. "Jason? He's grown up, but everyone needs their father." Her lips tightened into a thin line again, as if to bolster her strength. "And every father needs his son."

The sentiment hung between us for a moment. Their loss was rooted deep and I wondered what had happened to their other child.

Mrs. Branford had been a teacher for half a century and had sons of her own. I could see the empathy on her face as she looked at Nancy Sanchez, as if she could completely relate. She held her cane upright, clutched the handle with one hand, reaching out with her other and letting her fingers flutter against the back of Nancy's hand. "I lost my only daughter," she said, her voice quavering, and this time I knew it was for real. "You never get over it, do you?"

Nancy shook her head, her eyes pooling.

My breath caught in my throat. I looked at Mrs. Branford. She had a melancholy expression on her face and I instantly felt my eyes get glassy with tears. I wanted to sink down next to Mrs. Branford and hug her. She hadn't told me that she'd had a daughter. That she'd lost a daughter. In all my turmoil over the last months and my struggles in dealing with my own grief, I was shocked that she hadn't shared this thing that clearly connected us. And yet, I realized, it wasn't about what might have helped me in that moment. It was her story. Her life. Her loss. And I respected that it had, until this moment, been her secret.

She didn't actually speak to me, but I could almost hear her in my head softly saying, "It's a story for another time."

Nancy ran the backs of her fingers under her eyes to clear away the tears pooling there. "Never," she whispered.

Danny squeezed his wife's hand again. He cleared his throat before speaking again. "Hank visits his father every day."

Nancy's eyes widened. *"Dios mio,"* she said, making the sign of the cross. "How could I have forgotten that? Poor man. He's probably worried sick."

"He has a father around here?" I asked. No one had mentioned that fact. Not Brenda, not Phil, not Alice. What else did we not know about Hank?

"At an old folks' home," Danny said matter-of-factly.

Mrs. Branford looked as shocked as I felt by the news. "His father doesn't know his son is missing?" she asked.

Danny shrugged helplessly and I could see the blanket of burden fall over him, the one that made him feel that he needed to go see Hank's father. To let him know Hank was missing, and to possibly prepare him for the worst.

"We'll do it," Mrs. Branford said. She pressed her hand firmly on the cane handle and propelled herself up to standing. "You should not have to do that."

Nancy's shoulders sagged in relief. "You will?"

But Danny's brow furrowed. "I'm Hank's friend. I should go."

Mrs. Branford jumped on his obvious reticence, but I spoke first. "No, no. You stay with your family, Mr. Sanchez. Danny," I corrected. "We'll go."

"We need the address," Mrs. Branford said, already turned halfway toward the door.

Nancy straightened up. "I have it. Remember?" she said to her husband. "He came by, what, two weeks or so ago?"

Danny thought about it. "That sounds about right."

Nancy turned to Mrs. Branford and me. "He left a business card here in a pile of his receipts and things. He was trying to help a teacher or something," she said. She slipped her fingers along her temple and into her hair. "Now, where did I put it?"

"What teacher?" I asked, immediately wondering if it was Mason Caldwell. He had been a teacher, and Hank seemed to think Mason needed help.

"I don't know his name. Someone he recently ran into again, though. An old teacher from high school, I think. Here's the thing about Hank," Danny said. "He wants to do everything he can for everybody else. Sometimes that interferes with what's best for him."

Danny nodded. "Right. So anyway, Hank hadn't seen the guy in years, but he still recognized him. They got to talking, and Hank told him about Brenda. The teacher — what was his name?" He shook his head, drawing a blank. "Anyway, this teacher told Hank where he'd been living and said there was a room. Before we knew it, Hank was leaving here and moving in there."

Nancy picked up the thread of the story. "I started making Hank a few dozen flour tortillas every week. It's hard to go from your own house and home cooking in your own kitchen, to nothing. I wanted him to feel loved."

"Right," Danny said. "Flour tortillas for Hank, and then you started making corn for his dad."

"They're healthier," she said, as if she needed to explain the reason Hank's dad got the corn tortillas.

"And better," Mrs. Branford said.

Nancy flicked her gaze to Mrs. Branford. "I agree," she said, and then she continued with her story: "Hank came by one day to get the things he'd left behind. He picked up some tortillas. Said he'd decided the boarding house was fine for him, but he thought his old teacher would like the place his dad is at."

The story was interesting, but I couldn't quite see how it was going to help us. "You both have been such good friends to Hank," I said. "You've done so much. Let us go talk to Hank's father. He may be able to help us."

Nancy threw one hand up suddenly. "Oh! I know where it is!" She turned and hurried down the hall and back into the kitchen, reappearing a few seconds later. She had a business card and brochure in one hand, her dish towel and a gallon-sized plastic bag filled with perfectly round, thick corn tortillas in the other. She handed me all three items. "Would you give these to Hank's dad?"

I took the tortillas and nodded.

"We definitely will," Mrs. Branford said, and then she winked. "If there are any left by the time we get there."

Her off-the-cuff remark had the desired effect. We all laughed, lightening the tension and the sadness in the modest little hallway. "Let me get you some," Nancy said, and before either Mrs. Branford or I could object, she was off again, returning with a second baggie filled with tortillas. "It's not quite a dozen," she said sheepishly, as if she'd let us down.

"Mrs. Sanchez," I said, "you don't have to —"

"I want to." She offered a faint smile that didn't quite reach to her eyes. I knew she tried hard for the two kids in the TV room, but the pain of her loss would never quite go away. She spoke to both of us, but settled her gaze on Mrs. Branford. "You are very sweet. Thank you."

I knew she wasn't talking about us trying to find Hank, or bringing tortillas to Hank's dad. No, she was talking about something so much more than that. She was speaking to a kindred spirit, to her heartache, to another woman who'd lost a child — and who'd ultimately survived.

CHAPTER 19

We left the Sanchez family to their evening, both Mrs. Branford and I aching from the hollowness we'd seen and felt in both Nancy and Danny. Nancy Sanchez might not understand it now, but somewhere in the depths of her heart she'd recognize that Penelope Branford, who'd also lost a child, had managed to make a new normal and ultimately to move forward. I didn't know Mrs. Branford's story yet and I knew she still had to ache inside, whatever had happened, but she had not let her loss define her, and I hoped that Nancy Sanchez would also be able to recapture her life at some point.

We walked back to the car in silence. I helped Mrs. Branford navigate the curb, get situated back into the passenger seat, and after I'd put the tortillas on the backseat, we drove away. It took a good minute for either of us to speak, and even then it felt as if we were skirting around the heavy stuff.

"Poor family," I said.

"They'll be okay," she said.

I'd been trying to find some words to express what I was feeling, but I couldn't pull any from my brain. Nothing worked. "You never told me," I managed after a while, but I couldn't finish the sentence that was circling around in my head. The fact was that she hadn't told me and there had to be a good reason for that. It wasn't my place to push her into revealing something she'd buried within herself.

I caught Mrs. Branford's shrug from the corner of my eye. It wasn't a dismissive movement, but more of a deep breath saddled with the idea that it just *was*. "Losing a child isn't something you bring up in casual conversation with new people in your life," she said.

I felt a pricking behind my eyes. I blinked the feeling away and kept driving, listening as she started talking. "Her name was Katherine." I caught her grin from the corner of my eye. "I named her after Katherine in *Taming of the Shrew*, you know. It was not the way of things when she was growing up — to be a strong girl. To have opinions. To speak your mind. But my daughter was not going to be a shrinking violet, to coin a phrase. I raised her to be bold and daring. She was one of the smartest people I ever knew. Quick-witted, book smart, but also intuitive and wise. I used to tell her that she was an old soul stuck in a young girl's body. Of course, she didn't understand that when she was just ten years old, but when she hit her twenties, suddenly it made sense."

There was a park up ahead, the parking lot lit just enough to feel safe. I pulled in so I could listen to Mrs. Branford talk without the distraction of driving. She was lost in her narrative, so she hardly noticed that we'd stopped driving and that I'd turned my body to face her. She continued without a break. "She was close with her brothers. Jeremy — he's the one who lives in San Francisco. He has struggled with addiction on and off. He's in a good place now," she said, "but I don't think he'll ever get over Kat's death. She would have been fifty this year," she said, almost to herself. "She was a good girl."

"What happened?" I asked, wondering if the question would push her too much toward memories she didn't want to have resurface.

But she answered matter-of-factly. "Cancer, of course. She fought as long and hard as she could, but it eventually took her."

She looked at me then, the daze in her eyes clearing. "It took part of me, too. I understand what that woman is going through," she said. "For a long time I didn't think I'd get over it. That was when Jimmy . . ." She trailed off and I filled in the blanks. It was when her husband had almost sought comfort with Olaya Solis. In the end, he hadn't, and Penelope and James had lived out his days together. Statistically, they were not the norm. I hoped Danny and Nancy Sanchez could beat the odds, too.

"You remind me of her. Of Kat," Mrs. Branford said in an uncharacteristically soft voice, and my eyes filled. I didn't think there could be any greater compliment.

Before trying to find Hank's father, I called Richie. Hank had stayed at the boarding house, so there was a chance Richie knew some specifics about where Hank's father lived. It was worth asking, but Richie didn't answer. I called Janice next, for the same reason, but again, no answer.

"We're on our own," I told Mrs. Branford.

"I'm up for the challenge," she said.

I was, too. I'd do whatever it took to find Hank.

The retirement community where the senior Rivera lived was called Rusty Gates, and the tongue-in-cheek approach to senior living didn't stop there. We pulled up to the main building, which advertised the Out with a Bang recreation center. Mrs. Branford squinted her eyes at the sign, opened them, squinted them again, and then let loose a deep belly laugh. "Well," she said, "I guess this is where the road ends."

I laughed along with her. "I guess it is." We doubled over, and after we finally pulled it together, I realized that the hilarity of the retirement community and the emotions tied to it were spillage from the sorrow of the last hour. Feelings have a way of reversing themselves.

I hopped out to look at the map while Mrs. Branford collected herself. "There are four resident buildings, two on either side of the rec center," I said as I slid back into the driver's seat.

"A needle in a haystack," Mrs. Branford said.

"Maybe," I said, "but let's check it out anyway." I drove to the left, winding around the rec center. The first resident building lay straight ahead. The sign marked it clearly: AGED OAKS. Mrs. Branford and I looked at each other, each of us doing our own version of a titter under our breath. "Aged Oaks, really?"

"If you can't laugh in the face of death, then it just looms there, scary and ominous. I'm eighty-six years old, Ivy. I've had ups and downs. I've experienced loss, but it hasn't all been bad. I had Kat for as long as I was able. It's been a good life. And I'm not ready to leave it just yet. I'm tired. My knees hurt. My joints hurt. My heart hurts sometimes. But the minute I stop wanting to get up in the morning and get out into the world for the day, I'm done. But let me tell you, Ivy, if and when I am ready to go to a retirement community, this place is where I want to be."

Oh no, now that I'd found her, I wasn't going to lose her. Mrs. Branford was quickly becoming my rock. "If you ever get to that point," I said, "we'll get you a place here, but that's a long way off."

"Deal," she said.

I pulled up in front of Aged Oaks, put the car in *park* and left the car running, and ran out to try the front door. It was locked and used a keyless entry system. I cupped my hands around my eyes and peered through the glass. I didn't see anything or anyone. There was no way to tell who lived in this particular building. I got back in the car. "If it were an apartment complex, there would be people coming and going, but —"

"But the old folks are probably already in bed. They're just staying."

"Right." We sat, thinking about how to get in, but neither of us had any big brainstorms.

"There's always Phil," Mrs. Branford said.

"Right," I said again. "There's always Phil."

Although I couldn't say why, I didn't want to call Phil to ask him what building his father lived in.

I started to back out of the parking space, when a car approached and slipped in two spaces down from us. "Maybe we won't need Phil after all," I said, pulling forward again and putting the car back into *park*.

The driver's-side door of a pale green sedan opened and a woman stepped out. I leaned over my steering wheel to get a better look. There was something familiar about the woman. Her hair? Her posture? Maybe both. I sat back suddenly, recognition surfacing. "That's Consuelo."

"Consuelo Solis? Olaya's sister?" Mrs. Branford squinted her eyes to try to get a better look, but she sat back, frustrated. "My eyes don't work like they used to."

"It's definitely her," I said. I opened my door, got out, and hurried around to the other side, lifting my hand to wave.

291

Consuelo looked my way, shading her eyes from the glare of an overhead streetlight with her hand. "Ivy, is that you?"

I held my arms wide. "Surprise!"

The back driver's-side door opened and another set of legs swung out, these draped in a blue-and-gray caftan. I smiled. If there was such a thing of perfect timing, this was it. The head followed the legs and Olaya emerged from the car.

I rushed forward and wrapped her up in a hug, relief washing over me. If Mrs. Branford was like my grandmother, then Olaya had become my favorite aunt.

She tightened her arms around me for a moment, and then she patted my arms and pushed back. "Ivy, why are you here?"

With perfect timing, Mrs. Branford stepped out of the car. "Hank Rivera, of course," she said. "His father lives here —"

"Here somewhere," I interrupted. "Problem is that we have no idea where."

The passenger door of Consuelo's car opened and yet another woman swung her legs out. Under the bright parking lights, I could see that these were clothed in light-colored loose pant legs. "Connie," the woman called, her voice frail.

Consuelo rushed to help the elderly woman from the car. She guided the woman to the back of the car where we stood. Her voice was louder than normal as she said, "Dorothy, this is a friend of mine. Ivy."

The elderly woman, Dorothy, cocked her head. "Ivy? What a funny name." She looked to be in the same age vicinity as Penelope Branford, but with her feeble voice, sagging skin, and spindly frame, Dorothy seemed so much older.

"It *is* a funny name," I said. I'd often asked my parents where the name had come from. The answer was always the same. My mom's two favorite options were Ivy and Mathilda. But my mother didn't like nicknames, which pushed Mathilda out of the running. She wouldn't have been able to resist calling me Mattie or Tilly or some other shortened version. There was also no poetic story or famous literary character that bore my name. It wasn't inspired by some person or ideal like Mrs. Branford's Katherine had been. I was just Ivy and I had figured out how to make my own way in the world with a name that was all my own.

I must have had a curious expression on my face, because Consuelo answered the question I hadn't yet asked. "We volunteer with a local organization," she said. "We take seniors for outings."

"It's called Helping Seniors," Dorothy said. "These ladies come to see me a few times a week. I don't know what I'd do without them."

I bit my upper lip. Everywhere I turned, there was something pulling at my heart-strings. I'd read the statistics. It was like Mr. Caldwell had said: Elderly people living in a senior living situation were often the forgotten ones, yet here were two of the Solis sisters doing their part to lesson that isolation.

Dorothy was petite and her thin frame was hunched. I walked on one side of her and Consuelo walked on the other so we could guide her. Olaya and Mrs. Branford walked behind us. "Olaya said Hank Rivera is missing," Consuelo said as we walked Dorothy up the pathway toward the door.

"For several days now," I said.

Dorothy stopped her forward shuffle and looked up at me. "My ears aren't working. Who are you looking for, dear?"

"Her hearing aid is on the fritz," Consuelo said.

I put my hand to my mouth to hide my smile. Dorothy was adorable. "We're looking for a friend. Do you know Hank Rivera? Mustache Hank?" I asked, speaking loudly enough for her to hear me.

"Mustache Hank?" she asked, her face crinkling in her puzzlement. "That's a peculiar name. This is a seventy-five and older facility. Does he meet the age requirement to live here?"

"No," I said. Hank was a spring chicken compared to the average Rusty Gates tenant. "We *are* trying to find him," I said, but further clarified, "but at the moment, we're trying to find his father. He lives here. Somewhere."

We'd made it to the front entrance. Consuelo swiped the key card, the lock clicked, and the door opened. "What is his name, dear?" Dorothy asked me.

I felt ridiculous admitting that I didn't actually know the name of who we were looking for, but I admitted it anyway. "All we know is that the last name would be Rivera," I said.

She lifted one arm, pointing a heavily knuckled finger toward the back of the lobby area. "There is an information and mail center, and the emergency and nurse's station. Straight ahead. They take good care of us here at Rusty Gates. We want for nothing, except our youth," she said with a feeble chuckle.

I'd wondered about their emergency services with such an elderly population, but the nurse's station eased my mind. "Thank you, Dorothy," I said. Olaya took my place at the woman's side. She and Consuelo took Dorothy to the elevator while Mrs. Branford and I headed straight through the lobby. After a full evening, Mrs. Branford was moving slowly. I kept pace with her, commenting on the cleanliness of the lobby and the pleasant aroma of vanilla bean. A moment later, Olaya suddenly came up alongside me. "Dorothy thinks they might not talk to you since they don't know you."

"But they know you," I said.

Olaya tapped a finger to her nose. *"Exactamente."*

"Good thinking." Mrs. Branford nodded with approval.

"Should we wait for Consuelo?" I asked, but Olaya shook her head.

"No, no, we can leave her here. I will drive back with you two."

"That's fine with me," Mrs. Branford said, "but I call shotgun."

I laughed out loud at that one. Surely, she'd picked up that turn of phrase from past students, but it was hilarious coming out of her mouth now as if she were fifteen years old.

Olaya's reaction was just as juvenile. She

heaved a disgruntled sigh, pursing her lips and breathing out through her nose. She topped it off with an *aw, shucks* snap of her fingers.

"How long have you volunteered here?" I asked once they were ready to move on.

"Years and years. Our mother was here for a short time. My sisters and I — one of us came to see her everyday, but we saw so many people . . ." She paused, swallowed. "So many people are alone in the world."

I hadn't known how deep Olaya's compassionate spirit went. Penelope Brandord and Olaya Solis, the two women I'd come to love as family, both had undiscovered depths to them. "So you volunteered to brighten up their lives?"

"No, not right away. We would come to see our mother, to take her to the hairdresser, to the library, to the bookstore, the grocery store, the senior center in town. I would take her to the bread shop, or I would bring a loaf of bread here to her. So many of the others here, they always looked so sad. I thought to myself, a little bread. It makes my mother so happy, maybe it can make others happy, too."

"So you started bringing bread to them?"

She nodded, sparkling silver strands in her short, cropped hair glistening in the diffused light of Aged Oaks's lobby. "Just the left-overs at the end of the day at first. I'd come every afternoon and we would . . . how does the Bible say?"

"Break bread," Mrs. Branford supplied.

"Yes. *Exactamente.* We would break bread. The staff, they told me how it helped people. They had something to look forward to, they said."

I could see why. The idea that someone was coming to see them, that in itself would be uplifting enough. Add in bread, which seemed to fulfill a basic need, and it couldn't help but raise spirits.

"The staff, they said the people were sleeping better. Eating better. Smiling more."

"I'm not surprised. Your bread does that for people," Mrs. Branford said, and it was true. Olaya had a reputation that had traveled far and wide. People came from all over to experience magic of Yeast of Eden.

"Our mother, Dios la tenga en la Gloria," she said, making the sign of the cross, "she passed, but *mis hermanas* —"

She stopped when she saw Mrs. Branford's baffled expression.

"God rest her soul," Olaya said, switching to English for our sake. "My sisters and I, we continued to come. We take the people out as we did for our mother. I bake extra each day to bring here. Maybe we are making a difference. We hope we are."

I wasn't often at the bread shop at the end of the day, so I'd never realized that Olaya had a surplus, or that she made a trip here to Rusty Gates with it. I took her hand, squeezing lightly. Hidden depths, I thought again.

We'd stopped a few feet from the information and mail desk, but no one was around. An antique brass call bell sat on the counter. I reached out and depressed the button three times. It sounded with a tinny *ting, ting, ting.*

A young man, probably in his late twenties, appeared from a back room. He wore blue scrubs, which I thought might be overkill. Then again, there was no doubt he was the one to flag down if there was a medical problem. The rectangular plastic name tag clipped to his shirt confirmed his position: Steven Lang, RN. He looked surprised to see the three of us standing before him expectantly. "Can I help you?"

"I hope so," I said, resting my open palms on the counter. "We're looking for one of your tenants. A Mr. Rivera?"

"Are you family?"

The answer, of course, was no, and from

his expression, he seemed to know that. If we were family, wouldn't we know where he was, at least generally speaking? "We're friends with his son," I said, hoping that would be enough.

Nurse Lang considered our multigenerational trio, must have considered us harmless, and moved the mouse next to his computer, waking it up. He searched for a minute, finally saying, "There's an Enrique Rivera. Is that him?"

Olaya leaned close to me and whispered. "Enrique is Spanish for Henry."

And Hank was short for Henry. I couldn't say with complete certainty that this was our man, but I went with my gut. "Yes, that's him. Can you tell us which building he is in?"

The man narrowed his eyes, revisiting his earlier suspicions. "So you're friends with his son? And why do you need to see him?"

As I thought about how to answer, Olaya cleared her throat, an indication that she was going to field this particular question. "We know his son. Mustache Hank — you may have heard of him?"

"Is that a real name? Mustache Hank?"

"It's a moniker he picked up years ago," Mrs. Branford said. "He has a handlebar mustache, hence the name."

The nurse shrugged. "Never heard of him, sorry."

Olaya continued: "I am a volunteer with Helping Seniors."

"Oh, right," the young man said. "That's a good organization."

Olaya nodded, her eyes dropping to his name tag. "It certainly is, Mr. Lang."

"The bread's from Yeast of Eden, just off the PCH, isn't it?"

PCH was the acronym for the Pacific Coast Highway, also known as California State Route 1. It was the highway that ran along most of the state's Pacific coastline. "One and the same," Olaya said.

"I've heard it's good," he said.

Olaya smiled. "Stop by sometime. I'll give you a croissant, on the house."

His eyes opened wide. "You're the owner?"

"Owner, baker, magic maker," she said, tilting her head in a slight bow.

"From what I hear, there *is* magic in the bread. I'll be by tomorrow!"

She nodded with approval. "I will keep an eye out for you. I have bread to deliver to Senõr Rivera," she said.

If Nurse Lang noticed Olaya's empty hands and wondered where this bread was, he didn't let on. I forged ahead while I could. It was 8:00, and while that wasn't late for a person my age, it was quite possibly past the witching hour for the seventy-five and older crowd. "Which building is Enrique in?"

He punched a few keys on the computer keyboard and his eyes scanned the screen. "He's in the Eternal Peace building," he said after a second. "I'll call over there and let them know you're coming. When you get there, press the button on the speaker, let them know I sent you. They'll buzz you in."

We thanked him, and then followed his directions, driving to the Eternal Peace building. Olaya did have a bag of bread in the car, from which she pulled a loaf of sourdough, and I brought Mrs. Sanchez's tortillas with me. We looked for the doorbell. It took a minute, but I finally noticed the little round button on the keyless entry mechanism. I hadn't noticed the identical swipe pad on the Aged Oaks building. Clearly, I hadn't looked closely enough.

The attendant buzzed us in, directing us to apartment 315. We took the elevator up to the third floor. It was a nice facility. Clean. Muted colors that were comfortable to live in. We passed amenities like an exercise room, an entertainment area with a grand piano and chess and checkers set up on a few tables, and even a mini–coffee lounge complete with a barista during daytime hours. If I ever had to leave my home and live in an old folks' home, this would definitely be the type of place I'd want to be.

We arrived at Enrique Rivera's apartment. I knocked and we all stood back, surrounding the doorway in a woman-made semicircle, and waiting with bated breath.

Enrique was elderly and we had no idea how mobile he was, so we waited as patiently as we could. After a solid minute and a half, I knocked again. From inside, we heard a muffled, "*Esperate.* I am coming."

Finally, the doorknob rattled. And rattled. And rattled some more. At long last, the door wrenched open and before us stood a man who was the spitting image of Hank Rivera. Or rather Hank was the spitting image of this man — right down to the handlebar mustache. The man standing in front of us was a generation older than Hank. He had a spattering of dark hair still visible, but most of it was white. All except for the mustache, which was as black as muddy coffee. If I hadn't seen Hank's, I'd have wondered if it was genuine.

He ran his forefinger and his thumb along

one side of the handlebar, twisting it at the end to emphasize the curl at the tip. "It is mine," he said, as if he'd quite literally read my mind. "Many people ask it."

"It's lovely," said Mrs. Branford.

"Gracias, mi amor. *Entonces,* am I able to help you?"

CHAPTER 20

It seemed as if most of the people I'd met lately were on the far side of sixty. Enrique Rivera, however, was the most dapper. "We're friends of Hank's," Mrs. Branford said, answering his question.

He smiled at the mention of his son. "Oh! Que bueno. *Las amigas de Hank* — his friends, they are also friends of mine." He bowed slightly and slowly stepped back to open the door wide enough for us to enter. "Come in, come in!"

I'd wondered if Phil had told his father that Hank had vanished, thinking that he must have, but Enrique seemed too joyful. He couldn't possibly know that his son was nowhere to be found. Should I sugarcoat things or be direct? I hadn't decided, but once he welcomed us in, it didn't feel right to hold back. Beating around the bush seemed unfair and cruel.

Enrique slowly made his way to an upright

chair, the plaid upholstery faded and worn. Olaya, Mrs. Branford, and I sat side by side on the small couch across from him. I cleared my throat, hating to be the one to make Enrique's affable smile dissolve, but I had no choice. "Sir, we've been looking for Hank now for a few days. He seems to be . . . um, missing."

The man frowned, leaning forward, his hands on his knees, elbows out to the side. "No intiendo. I do not understand. Hank is missing?"

"That's right," I said. "He's missed his deliveries. He left the place he's been staying and no one has seen him since. We're all worried and —"

I'd been hoping that Hank's father might know Hank's whereabouts, but it was clear that he didn't. "That cannot be," he said, shaking his head as if he hadn't heard us correctly and he could fling the words back out and unhear them. Worry instantly clouded his eyes.

I didn't know what to say next. My gaze met Olaya's; a thread of understanding passing between us. She steeled herself, looked at Enrique, and spoke to him in Spanish. He replied and they slipped into a conversation in their native language. Mrs. Branford waited patiently and I listened intently, trying to understand the gist of what they were saying. Unfortunately, my high-school Spanish wasn't up to par.

By the time Olaya was done, the debonair mustached man had dissolved, his smile gone, his shoulders slouched. He looked up at her. "Su camion?"

She nodded. "The truck was found, but there is no sign of Hank."

As the color drained from his face, Olaya moved from the sofa, crouching in front of Enrique. She put her hand on his. "Lo siento," she said.

I recognized those words. *I'm sorry,* she told him.

"We are still looking," I said to him. He needed hope to hold onto. We all did.

He nodded. His nostrils flared as he looked at Olaya, and then at Mrs. Branford and me. "What can I do?"

I felt for him. Inaction made you feel powerless. "Could you answer a few questions?"

Enrique drew in a tremulous breath, steadying himself. "Por supuesto," he said. He followed it up in English: "Of course. If it will help find my son . . ."

He trailed off. I pushed on before he could slip away into his worry. "Did he seem okay the last time you saw him?" I asked, wishing we hadn't been the bearers of bad news for this man.

"Okay? Yes. He was Hank. He was normal. We talked about Brenda. And Jason. He brought me tortillas. He always brings me tortillas."

"From Nancy," I said, and I held out the bag we'd brought with us. "We saw her earlier. She sent these for you."

He ignored the tortillas. "Daniel, he did not know where is Hank?"

"No," I said. "I'm sorry. Mr. Rivera, did Hank say that he was going away? On a little vacation, maybe?"

He shook his head. "I am trying to remember, but no. I do not think so, no."

"Can you think of anything different? Something he might have said that was unusual?"

He thought for a moment, and then his eyes sparked. "He has a friend. An old teacher, I think? He has been talking about the man to move in here," he said, his English a little off. "He ask me if this man, if he could call me, if I would talk to him."

"Mason Caldwell?" Mrs. Branford asked. "Was that the name of the teacher? Of the man Hank wanted to move in here?"

Enrique's expression was uncertain. "It is possible. I do not remember. Caldwell,

308

Caldwell," he murmured to himself. *"Posiblemente."*

"Mr. Rivera," I said, deciding to simply ask the other thing I needed to. It had taken many years and a failed marriage to be confident enough to simply be direct. There was no point in backsliding now. "Do you know what kind of financial situation Hank is in?"

The horizontal lines of Enrique's forehead deepened as he considered how to respond. "Hank, he works hard always. He builds his business from the ground. From nothing. *Pero* some things for Hank, they are difficult," he finally offered. "He can grow anything. He has many contracts, but he must do more than grow, yes. Crops for the week to the restaurants in town. It is not make enough money to keep going."

I caught Mrs. Branford's and Olaya's eyes, a knowing look passing between us. This information brought us back to the money Hank borrowed from Alice Ryder. I reviewed the possibilities relating to this money in my head:

1. Hank had had good intentions in borrowing the money. He'd planned to pay his debts and get back on his feet, but the temptation of having

the money was too much and he
ran away from his problems to start
over.
2. Maybe Hank's intentions were
never good. What if he borrowed
the money from Alice with the
intention to disappear from the
beginning?
3. Or maybe he confided in an online
friend, who then arranged a meeting.

A new idea barreled into my head. From
everything I'd heard about Hank, he was
honorable and responsible. He took care of
others more than himself, allowing his
clients to postpone payments, not burden-
ing others any more than necessary with his
problems. He'd stayed with Daniel Sanchez
only briefly, moving into a new place pretty
quickly after leaving his home. That's when
he borrowed the money, not before. Why
move into the boardinghouse and then bor-
row money to disappear? My guess was that
he wouldn't have bothered. So what else
could he have wanted the money for?

My idea grew until I felt sure I should add
it to my list of possibilities.

4. What if the money he borrowed

wasn't to pay off his debts at all? What if it was to help Mason Caldwell, who he seemed so determined to help, get settled here at Rusty Gates?

In the end, I decided that a more focused conversation with Mason Caldwell was in order. Which made me anxious for morning to come and for the photo shoot at the Thompson boarding house.

By the time we took our leave, Mr. Rivera looked distressed and beaten down. He walked us to the door, but the confident swagger he'd had when we'd first arrived was gone. It felt as if he were the victim of a hit-and-run: We'd delivered bad news, and then abandoned him to deal with it alone.

"Can we call someone for you, Mr. Rivera?" Olaya asked.

He shook his head. "I can do it, but thank you. You'll let me know if you find him? Or find out anything?"

I promised we would.

My cell phone rang before we were out of the parking lot. Mrs. Branford was still riding shotgun. She jumped in her seat at the sound. "I will never get used to some of these newfangled technologies," she said.

No, I didn't think she would. At least not

without some prodding. She had a flip phone, which was as advanced as she got.

Her cane rested next to her leg. She held on to the top and twirled it. "Go on, Ivy, answer it!"

From the rearview mirror, I could see Olaya leaning forward, equally anxious. Then it hit me: They thought it was Miguel on the phone.

I knew better. "Simmer down, you two," I said as I hit the button on my dash to answer.

All I could hear was distant chattering and the sound of cars in the background, but nothing I could identify. I tilted my head to the side, keeping my eyes on the road, but trying to get a better angle to pick out something distinguishable.

"Hello?" I said, then more loudly, "Hello!"

It sounded as if whoever was on the other end of the line was fumbling with the phone. Finally the noise stopped. "Ivy," someone said.

"Em!" *It's Emmaline,* I mouthed to Mrs. Branford and Olaya.

"Hold on," Emmaline said. She seemed to cover the phone as she spoke with someone. "Hey," she said, coming back.

"What's going on?" I asked. It was late for her to be working, but that's what it sounded like.

"Ivy," she said, her voice shifting from the commanding tone I'd vaguely heard to something softer. If I didn't know better, I'd say it was almost regretful.

My heartbeat started to quicken. "What? What's happened? Is Billy okay?"

She was quick to answer. "He's fine. No, Ivy, it's not that."

I heaved a relieved sigh. "Then what is it? What's wrong?"

"Ivy," she said again. "We found Hank's body." Beside me, Mrs. Branford gasped. She clutched the side of the door. From the backseat, Olaya let out a sob. My blood ran cold as Emmaline said, "He's . . . dead."

After Emmaline's bombshell, my hands wrenched to the left, nearly driving my car up onto the curb. "Dead?"

"That can't be right," Mrs. Branford said.

Emmaline's voice came back over the line, sharper in tone again. "Where are you, Ivy?"

I pulled the car over to the side of the road and clutched the steering wheel. I hadn't known Hank, but I felt knocked out by the news just the same. "We just saw Hank's father," I said.

There was a long pause and for a moment I wondered if she'd covered the phone again and was dealing with one of her officers. But then I heard her letting out a steadying breath. "Where and how?" she asked succinctly. She was no longer Emmaline, friend. She was all deputy sheriff.

"We paid a visit to . . . to Daniel Sanchez, Hank's right-hand man. He mentioned that Hank visited his father every week. We —"

"Who is *we*, Ivy?"

"Penelope Branford and Olaya Solis," I answered.

Another sigh. "Okay, go on."

"We figured that no one had told Enrique — that's Hank's father — that his son was missing."

"So you were the messengers," she stated.

I didn't need to answer, so I asked a question instead. "Can you tell us what happened?"

She paused for a beat before answering. "I guess so. The media is already here. It'll be on the eleven-o'clock news and in tomorrow's paper."

"Where's *here*?" I asked, and then she dropped another bombshell.

"His son found him in the large plastic garbage can on his mother's driveway."

In the rearview mirror, I saw Olaya clasp her hand over her mouth, her shoulders trembling. Tears spilled onto her cheeks, her silent crying more heartbreaking than if she'd let out wailing sobs.

Mrs. Branford stayed facing forward, stone-still. Her chin quivered and her eyes glistened, but she was stoic.

Grief emanated from them both, seeping through my skin until my hands shook and my eyes pricked. I fought the tears, staying focused on Emmaline and what she'd just said.

Hank Rivera was more than dead. He'd been murdered.

CHAPTER 21

I'd spent the night tossing and turning, wondering if we could have somehow saved Hank. If we'd found him sooner, would he still be alive?

I braced myself for the day ahead. The search for Hank Rivera had turned into a search for his killer.

We weren't the Blackbird Ladies, but after the night before, Olaya Solis, Penelope Branford, and I were united in our goal. "You don't have to come with me this morning," I said to each of them over the phone, but they'd both insisted.

"I am not sitting here at home to wallow in my grief, Ivy," Mrs. Branford said. "I'll be waiting for you."

Olaya just harrumphed. "I'll be at the bread shop."

I picked them both up and we headed to Richie Thompson's old Victorian boarding house. I was determined to have a conversation with Mason Caldwell. Did he know about the money Hank had borrowed from Alice? Was it possible that he intended to help him move into Rusty Gates? I'd had a new idea during the night. If Mason had known about the money, could he have somehow killed Hank and kept the money for himself? That was the question I needed an answer to.

We arrived promptly at 7:30, gathered my equipment from the back of my car, and trudged to the front door, loaded down with camera bags, a light stand (just in case), and a mind full of sadness. Janice opened the door before we even had a chance to ring the bell. The moment I saw her, I knew she'd heard about Hank's fate. I had to admire the woman. Her eyes were red-rimmed, but she was perfectly coiffed, nary a wrinkle in sight. Botox and fillers, I thought, lightly touching the pads of my fingers to the corner of my eyes. I'd started to get the telltale signs of aging, but I wasn't sure how I felt about trying to eliminate them. I was living my life and whatever wrinkles I ended up with would be hard-won. Did I want to hang on to my youth, or did I want to age gracefully, wearing the evidence of a life well lived?

I guess time would tell.

Janice stepped out onto the porch and she and Mrs. Branford wrapped their arms around each other. Olaya and I looped arms as the two Blackbird Ladies embraced. Their words were unspoken, but their emotions were the same. I suspected that everyone who'd known Hank Rivera would feel the same grief.

After another minute, the two women separated. Janice held the door wide and took the lightweight bag Mrs. Branford had carried up the walkway. "Come in. Richie is brewing a pot of coffee."

Olaya held out a white pastry box. "Croissants and pan dulce," she said.

Janice tried to smile. "Ham and cheese?" she asked.

"Por supuesto," Olaya said. "Just for you."

We deposited my gear in the entryway and followed Janice into the kitchen. The house was cut up, as was traditional for homes in the early twentieth century. Open floor plans were not a thing. But French doors led from the dining room to the kitchen, and two other sets led from the kitchen and the entryway to the main living area. An old-fashioned PARLOR sign hung above the French doors, announcing what the room was. With the doors open, the house felt bigger and airier than it might have otherwise. We passed into the parlor. Straight ahead were three side-by-side windows — the ones Bernard had stood at the other night. In the morning light, I could see that each was framed in what looked like the original refinished oak molding and faced the backyard. A door opened to the backyard, where muddied Crocs, a pair of rubber boots caked with mud, blades of grass, and a spattering of white flower petals, a pile of gloves, and some gardening tools were scattered. Had they been Hank's?

As Janice set out the flakey croissants and rich pan dulce and poured cups of coffee, I looked around, hoping to catch a glimpse of Mason Caldwell. He wasn't around, but Bernard, wrapped up in his green bathrobe, sat on the couch staring at the windows. It seemed to be his favorite view in the house. I turned back to the kitchen and took one of the mismatched mugs on the square island, added a splash of cream, and took a sip. "Does he know?" I asked quietly, gesturing toward Bernard.

Janice shook her head. "We think it might be too much for him to handle right now. Best not to mention it."

From my limited experience, Bernard's mental state was fragile. Janice's reticence about how Bernard might take the news of

Hank's death seemed warranted.

Mrs. Branford cleared her throat. "Is Mason around?"

I was still pretty certain that her interest in Mason Caldwell ran deeper than our plan to question him, but her heart wasn't into flirtation at the moment.

"He's here somewhere. Do you want me to get him for you?" Richie said. His face was drawn and sallow, his eyes sunken. It looked as if he hadn't slept at all the night before.

"I would appreciate that," Mrs. Branford said. I felt the strength of her determination. We'd been so intent upon finding Hank when he was missing; now we both wanted only to find his killer.

Richie walked to a little antique desk in the corner of the kitchen. He depressed a button on a little black device, there was a beep, and he spoke. "Mason, you awake?"

He let go of the button and waited. A few seconds later, a voice came back at us. There was a fair amount of static. It was difficult, but I could make out the response. "Of course I am. I'll sleep when I'm dead."

From that lone comment, I could see why Hank would want Mason Caldwell to move to Rusty Gates; he'd fit right in with his morbid humor.

Richie depressed the button on what I now knew was a portable intercom system and waited for the beep. "Someone's here to see you."

The voice replied, "Of the male or female persuasion?"

Mrs. Branford marched to the desk. "This button?" she asked Richie. He nodded, stepping back so she could take over the communication. She pressed it, waiting for the beep as he had, and then spoke. "Mr. Caldwell, last time I checked, I determined that I am indeed female. I'd like to speak with you, if you are so inclined. Over."

There was a pause and for a moment I thought Mason Caldwell might not reply, but then the voice came back. "I am indeed so inclined, Mrs. Branford. I'll be there in a hop, skip and a jump. Cliché, I know, but it aptly conveys my eagerness to visit with you." There was another pause before Mason's static-filled voice added, "Over and out."

I tried to bring a little levity to the room. "Mrs. Branford," I said in mock scolding. "Are you leading the poor man on?"

She patted the loose curls in her white hair. "Of course not. I may be old, but I'm not pushing up any daisies just yet."

"The daisies'll come in the spring," Bernard said from the couch. "Right now we have white winter jasmine and sweet alyssum. Hank planted them. Do you know Hank? He planted flowers. They die in the winter, I told him, but he planted flowers and said they would bloom. And they did."

Bernard mentioning Hank opened up the subject for all of us, although we stayed in the kitchen, speaking in hushed tones so we wouldn't upset him. "We saw the news last night. Is it definitely Hank?"

"It is," I said.

Richie leaned back against the counter, running his hand over his face. "Do you know what happened?"

Now that this had turned from a missing person to a murder, Olaya, Mrs. Branford, and I had decided to hold our cards — what few cards we had, anyway, close to the vest. What if Bernard was involved, for instance? Or even Mason Caldwell. Of course, my gut was telling me that neither were a likely option, but I'd learned that you just never knew. "Not really," I said, answering Richie's question. "I don't know any more than you do," I said. It was the truth. Emmaline had given me the bare minimum.

The room fell silent, as if in respect for Hank. The fact remained that the man had vanished into thin air. While I had a few theories, none of them felt quite right, but suddenly time was of the essence. There was a murderer on the loose.

Richie had seen Hank with a suitcase, but where were the rest of his belongings? Surely, he had acquired more than one case worth of stuff in his lifetime. If he had been lured away by someone, who was that person, and how did they become connected with each other? I dived right in, turning to Richie. "Did Hank have a computer here? A laptop?"

Richie was mindlessly scooping rounded spoonfuls of sugar into his coffee. He stopped scooping and started stirring, looking at me. "Not that I know of. He spends — *spent* most of his time in the yard," he said.

"Spent," Bernard said from where he sat on the couch. "Hank. In the yard. Always in the yard."

"Yes, Bernard," Janice said, controlling the tremor in her voice. "You're right. Always in the yard."

Bernard stayed on the couch, but went back to staring out the window. I circled back around to my earlier question. "Is there a desktop?" I asked, looking around. "A computer everyone uses?"

"No!" Bernard stared out the window, but

he was clearly agitated. "No computers. No computers! Danger, danger."

Richie strode over to Bernard, laying a hand on his shoulder. "It's okay, Bernie. Calm down."

"Bernard. My name is Bernard. B-E-R-N-A-R-D. Bernard."

Richie jerked his head as if he were giving himself a mental slap. "Sorry, man. Old habit. Bernard. Relax, okay?"

Janice lowered her voice. "He used to go by Bernie. He switched one day because of Hank. They were out there planting flowers and Hank started calling him Bernard. He liked it, and it stuck."

"He connects with Hank, that's why it stuck," a voice said. We heard Mason Caldwell before we saw him stride into the parlor, a little jauntiness in his step. At least as much as he could muster, anyway, given the aluminum three-footed cane he was using instead of the walker he'd had the first time we'd met him. He had traded in his baggie sweatpants for khaki chinos and his corduroy slippers for a pair of brown leather shoes. He looked well worn, but stylish — in an old-guy kind of way. He was aiming to impress. He headed straight for Mrs. Branford — slowly — and swept her hand up in his, bowing slightly to give it a little kiss. It was crystal clear whose attention he was hoping to garner. "Good morning, Penelope. I hope it's all right if I call you that. Such a delightful name."

Bless her sweet heart. Despite the emotions coursing through her over Hank's death, Mrs. Branford blushed a bright shade of pink. "I usually go by Penny," she said, "but coming from you, Penelope sounds so lovely."

"And you call me Mason."

We introduced Olaya to him, and to Bernard, who had finally grown quiet again. And then we broke the news.

Mason stared at us, shock clear on his face. "Dead?"

Richie had rejoined us in the kitchen and leaned back against the counter. He spoke to all of us, but ended by looking at me. "Can I run something by you?"

"Yes, of course."

He lowered his voice and beckoned us closer. "I don't want to get Bernard riled up." We circled around him so his voice wouldn't travel into the other room, and Richie continued. "We're pretty sure Hank was on medication. A mood stabilizer, I think."

"A mood stabilizer — as in depression?"

"Mmm, no. Bipolar," Richie said.

325

My heart instantly sank. I knew two people with bipolor disorder and if they stopped their medication, their swings between mania and depression were scary. Highs and lows were no laughing matter. This could definitely explain why Hank disappeared in the first place. "How do you know?"

Richie notched his chin toward Bernard. "Bernie is on medication for it. Clozapine, I think? About a week ago, he went around saying Hank had taken his pills. I finally had to ask Hank straight up. He showed me his own prescription bottle. It wasn't the same medication, but it had the *pine* at the end. To stabilize the chemicals in his brain, he said."

Olaya frowned. "That could explain some things."

Right. "If he was depressed, whatever hopelessness he felt would have been intensified. It might have been enough to push him over the edge."

"Or if he was manic," Janice said, "he might have thought he could do anything. He could have gone off on some crazy adventure, thinking he could save his business."

"And then someone killed him?" Olaya shook her head. "I do not think so. He was in a garbage can at the house of his ex-wife. That is not random. Whoever killed him knew where she lived."

A chill ran up my spine. That little fact eliminated the possibility that Hank's death was a crime of opportunity committed by a stranger. He had been killed by someone he knew.

The money he borrowed from Alice came to my mind again. From what I knew, mania could lead to financial disaster. According to both Brenda, the ex-wife, and Enrique, Hank hadn't handled the financial end of his business very well. Could it be because of his illness? It would certainly explain a lot. What if Alice lent him the money and then realized that it had been a mistake? If Hank hadn't been willing to give it back, could she have killed him for it?

Or . . . what if she'd told her husband, Michael, and he'd gone after Hank? Surely Michael knew where Hank lived with Brenda, and he'd have been able to heave a dead body into a city garbage can.

I filed that theory away and came back to my questions. "If Hank had his own prescription, why would he need Bernard's?"

Richie pondered this while he took a sip of his coffee. He made a face, his tongue snaking out from between his lips. The sugar. He poured the coffee out in the sink as he said, "No idea."

"Any chance you have his prescription bottle?" I asked, already knowing the answer.

"Nah. He cleared out everything," Richie said, and then he repeated, "Everything."

"Does Bernard stay on his meds?" I asked, wondering if he was reliable enough for us to believe his theory that Hank took some of his pills. To my mind, he didn't seem stable enough to be responsible about it.

"He does, but only because I give them to him," Richie said.

Olaya was working hard to keep her composure. She had swallowed her grief and was fully focused on the moment. "Would he not be better off in a facility of some sort?" she asked, glancing over at Bernard. He still sat on the couch, but now he rocked back and forth, back and forth.

Richie frowned. "I take care of Bernard," he said, "and I will for as long as it works for him."

My first impression of Richie had had me thinking he wasn't the most compassionate caretaker, but I'd recalibrated my thoughts. He seemed to have a soft spot for Bernard. The soft morning light was fading quickly. "Did you still want me to take the photos?"

I asked. I'd come prepared, but I wouldn't be surprised if they wanted to postpone.

"I do. It'll be a good distraction," Janice said. Richie nodded his agreement.

Having something else to think about would dissipate the stress we were all feeling, and might allow my mind to absorb new ideas. "Okay."

"Where should we start?" Janice asked as she led us back to the entryway and my equipment.

"I'll get the exterior shots first," I said. "Front, then back."

She frowned. "I hadn't thought about the outside. The flower beds aren't up to snuff."

I got my wide-angle lens locked onto my camera and headed for the door. "I can come back in the spring," I said, "but I'd like to at least get some test shots."

She looked unsure, but led me to the front door. The entire group, excluding Bernard, started to follow me outside like an entourage. I held up my palm, halting them in their tracks. "You all should stay inside," I said. "Unless you want to be in the pictures."

"It's too cold out there anyway," Mrs. Branford said.

Mason moved next to her. He'd do his best to keep her warm.

The door closed behind me and I got to work. I wanted to capture the entire house straight-on, and then try a few from different angles. I crossed the street and got to work, adjusting my camera settings as I worked to capture the best lighting. I hurried, wanting to get to the backyard before the softness of the light gave way to the harsher midmorning glare.

I ended in the front yard with a shot of the house numbers and the birdbath in the front shrubbery. As Janice had said, the dirt had been freshly turned and the flowers were not in bloom, but the greenery was still pretty.

The temperature had dropped slightly the night before and was holding at a steady 55 degrees. Not freezing by any stretch, but cold enough that I was shivering by the time I went back inside.

My two comrades in crime fighting were sitting with Bernard, Janice, and Mason in the parlor. I scooted past them and opened the single French door leading to the backyard.

Once outside, I looked around, trying to decide how best to capture the yard. Bernard had been right: the flowers weren't abundant, but there were a few varieties blooming. Mounds of white alyssum and the delicate miniature flowers of winter jasmine dotted the landscape, giving wisps of color here and there. The house itself, with the windows, a trellis patio cover, and relatively fresh paint was lovely. I shot from a few different angles, stepping through patches of dirt and over small embankments in the yard to capture the best angles of the house. I stood in the furthermost corner of the yard and took a few final shots of the yard itself. I'd come back in the spring, like I'd told Janice, but now I'd have a pretty good idea about which angles worked and which did not.

I turned my back to the house to shoot the flowers, zooming in on a few of the flower petals, the greenery, the crocuses poking up through mounds of dirt. I started to review the digital images I'd taken so far, when something touched my shoulder, lightly at first, then clamping down. I jumped and yelped, nearly dropping my camera.

I spun around to find Bernard looming over me, dislodging his hand in the process. "You should not be here," he said. "The flowers. The flowers. Leave them alone."

I raised the camera, depressing the button to show the digital display of the flowers I'd just photographed. I held the screen up for

Bernard to see. "I'm not going to hurt them, Bernard. I love the flowers, too," I said. "When I take pictures, they are with me forever."

He barely glanced at the pictures, instead bending to pluck a scrap of a dead branch from a cascade of alyssum. "No, no, no," he muttered, clasping the piece of wood in his fist.

"It's okay," I said, gently pinching the dead branch between my thumb and forefinger and pulling it free from his grip.

"The flowers," he said. "We have to take care of the flowers."

"Of course. You do a good job, Bernard."

He smiled, big and grateful. "I take good care of the flowers. No branches. No branches. Hank. He watch for me. Take care of me. I take care of his flowers now."

"Of course. You do a good job, Bernard. No branches." I guided him back toward the house. "You just tend to the flowers."

"Flowers, yes. No dead branches. Flowers. Only flowers."

I watched him picking up branches and leaves and moving them from one dirt mound to another. He was an interesting man with an interesting face. The whites of his eyes and teeth fairly sparkled against his dark skin. I snapped a few pictures, capturing the contentment on his face as he cleared away branch after branch, and then gently touched the flower petals. He looked up at me, not smiling, but not agitated anymore, either.

Before we went inside, I stopped him. There was something about him. Something I couldn't put my finger on. His mind might not be 100-percent there, but that didn't mean he couldn't help me. "Bernard," I said slowly. He looked at me. "Do you know what happened to Hank?"

His eyes twitched and he looked away. "Collin's dead, did you know that?"

"Who's that?" I asked.

"Martha left," he said by way of answer. "They all go away, but me? No, no. I not leave. I never leave. I rake. I can rake for you? Take away the leaves." He bent and scooped up a handful of brittle, brown, curled leaves that had fallen from the trees. "I take away the dead leaves?"

"Sure, Bernard," I said, not wanting to upset him.

But he was upset. He half nodded, half shook his head, the force of it making me wonder if his brain was rattling inside his skull. "I take care of his flowers now," he said. He slapped his open palm against his chest. "I take care of the flowers, now."

I tried to follow his train of thought. "Hank's flowers?"

"No dead branches. Not one. I tend Hank's flowers. No one else. Just me. Just me."

It was clear that things inside Bernard's head were muffled, but I asked one more time for good measure. "Bernard, do you know what happened to Hank?"

He just shook his head. "I take care of the flowers. Hank's flowers."

I sighed. If Bernard did know something, it was buried deep inside his mind. He missed Hank. That seemed obvious, even if he didn't show it in an ordinary way, but I couldn't help him understand that Hank was gone. I did not want to be the one to break that news to him. "They're beautiful flowers," I said as we slowly made our way back inside.

He started in immediately. "I take care of the flowers. Only I. Everyone, get out. Get out!"

Janice was on her feet in an instant, rushing to Bernard's side. She put her arm around him, patting his shoulder. "Shhh, Bernard. It's okay. Of course, you take care of the flowers. Hank knew you would." Her voice was calm. Soothing. Bernard's eyes had been wide, like he was disconnected to the here and the now, but as Janice talked, he relaxed. His face smoothed out. His shoulders hunched forward.

"Come on, buddy," Richie said, leading the way into the kitchen. Bernard went, shuffling along, his body language defeated.

My gaze lingered on him, but my worry about him slipped away. Janice had calmed him, Richie was with him, and now Bernard was noisily crunching an apple. Mental illness, if that was Bernard's situation, was a beating. I felt for him. He probably didn't realize he was not functioning in reality, which made it all the more heartbreaking.

I steadied my nerves as I switched lenses to a different wide-angle to optimize the light in the house. My goal was to use the ambient light that filtered in from outside, rather than the artificial light from my light kit. My Canon had a fast lens, plenty capable of capturing the details I wanted for the interior shots.

I slung my bag with my lenses over my shoulder, just in case, and went from room to room, shooting from different positions. I hadn't done this type of photography before, so I wanted as many options as I could manage. I'd cull through the photos tonight, choosing the best ones to show Janice and Richie.

Richie rejoined me as I walked down the hallway downstairs away from the community rooms and toward the bedrooms. The first was unoccupied. Several collapsed cardboard boxes were leaning up against the wall, several square wooden boxes — one of them overflowing with books and magazines — in front of them. "My mother can't seem to part with her books, but she doesn't have room for them in her own house," he said. "She's packing them in these crates to keep them in the shed."

I gave a low whistle. "That's a lot of books."

"Yep. She won't switch to an e-reader, but she won't stop buying them. I wish she would."

I wandered to the opposite side of the room, glancing out the window to the backyard. It was a work in progress. A little outbuilding sat in the back corner of the yard — the shed Richie had just mentioned — the double doors wide open and swinging in the breeze. A few boxes like the ones in this room were visible, as well as a pile of long-handled gardening equipment. I closed my eyes for a moment, picturing Hank holding a shovel, digging in the yard, planting the flowers Bernard tended to.

Richie was preoccupied with the lid of one

of the wooden boxes, so I turned from the window and walked over to an antique desk, stopping to take a picture. Its back sat against the wall. Hanging above the desk was an antique letter cubby. It reminded me of something from an old hotel, room keys hanging below. Two rows of vertical slats held envelopes and magazines and catalogs, the openings large enough to see what each space held. It was an interesting setup.

The bottom of each slat was marked with a tag, several layered with new tags on top of old ones. I scanned them, wondering if Hank had had one, and if so, what it held. I read the tags on each slot and noted what was held in each slot: *Leonard.* A stack of letters. The pile was neat, so I could only see the top letter. It was addressed to an *L. Chester* and was from Social Security; *David.* An investment letter of some sort; *Chase.* An AARP letter. Chase's tag was curled on one end. An older one was underneath, the paper peeling, but the visible letters were hard to make out. An O, maybe, or a G. And an L? I leaned in to get a closer look. No, an E. A bank statement from a local credit union lay flat inside, along with a *Garden & Gun* magazine and a prescription bottle. I never did understand the combination of those two disparate ideas.

The next box belonged to Collin. There were no envelopes or magazines, but there was a check from Social Security. My eyes continued to scan the boxes. After Collin's was a cubby marked *Dixie.* A magazine — no, I corrected — a catalog for vintage clothing was the sole piece of mail.

The second to last on the top row was Bernard's. I wanted to understand him better and I wondered what mail he had tucked away for his perusal, and if he even understood whatever he received. The contents inside were staggered enough for me to see. A seed catalog, which seemed apropos, a medical or — no, an insurance statement, something from another local bank, a letter with a seal I couldn't quite make out. Government, I thought, or maybe military? But I couldn't be sure. A postcard mailer for a local hardware store was next, and on top of it all was a prescription bottle. I liked that Richie took care of all the tenants' needs.

My gaze skipped to the last box. Finally, the space I'd hoped to find. It had been Hank's box, but it was empty. I was disappointed, but not surprised. The bottom row of mail slots were marked differently. They were marked with abbreviations in no particular order: *Mags; Pers; Bnk; Bill; Gov; Rich; Soc; Com; Jan.* They stopped there and I supposed the rest of the boxes would eventually be tagged for the rest of the months. Each held a hefty pile of mail that looked like it still needed to be sorted and distributed to the tenants' boxes. I imagined it was a weekly task, and I was impressed with the organization. It had to be challenging to manage so many things for so many people.

"We should move on."

I jumped, straightening up to see Richie suddenly beside me. I had been so engrossed in the mail slots that I hadn't heard him approach.

"This is great," I said. "It looks like it belongs in an old movie." Truthfully, I wanted one for my house, albeit on a smaller scale.

"It's handy," he said.

I floated my hand out, palm up. "That's a lot to manage, with all the tenants you have."

"Our occupancy is low at the moment. At their age, and in their mental capacity . . ." He trailed off. "They pass on, or move."

"Where would they move to?" I asked, and then I answered my own question. "Oh, to a place like Rusty Gates."

339

"Or a nursing home if they became unable to care for themselves."

I looked back at the name tags. "Leonard and Chase?"

He nodded.

"Collin?"

"A few months ago."

"Dixie?" She was the only female tenant.

"She's here."

I was glad somebody was left. "I'm sorry," I said. It had to be hard to care for the elderly or the indigent and to know that you'd lose them eventually.

"It goes with the territory," he said, but I could hear the melancholy in his voice.

"How do you find the time for the paperwork?" I asked, genuinely interested. Staying on top of the few bills and incoming mail I had was a chore I didn't relish.

"I'm not great with numbers," Richie said, "but it's a necessary evil." He picked up a small pile of envelopes and a magazine, quickly riffling through them and sorting them into the general boxes on the bottom row. He slid bills into the appropriate slot, and quickly slid the remaining into the January space.

"I bet."

"My mother usually takes care of the bills, utilities, banking, things like that, and I do

340

the medical stuff, the appointments, et cetera. Divide and conquer."

I admired that they had a strong and collaborative mother-son relationship and business. My dad was the city manager and oversaw the historic district. That was not my passion, nor was it something I could be part of even if I wanted to. A father-daughter enterprise was not in the cards for my dad and me, but we connected in other ways. Lately, that meant over the bread that I baked and took over to him.

Richie closed up that room and we moved down the hall. He knocked lightly on the next door and a female voice said, "Come in." He swung the door open. Inside, a woman stood in front of a mirror in a silky, lightweight, cream-colored slip. She reminded me of an aging pinup girl from the thirties, complete with her side-swept, finger-curled hair and ruby-red lips. She reminded me of Jessica Lange in *Cat on a Hot Tin Roof*. Sultry and raw.

She turned, a slow smile spreading on her face when she saw Richie. An old Mae West quote came to mind: *When I'm good I'm very, very good, but when I'm bad, I'm better.*

"I knew you'd come back," she said to him with a subtle wink. "I've been waiting for you, Georgie."

Richie glanced back at me before smiling awkwardly at the woman, but played along. "You're looking beautiful, Dixie," he said.

She tilted her head coquettishly. "That's what all the men say."

In the corner, the arm of an old record player bounced, the LP on the turntable spinning and spinning and spinning. "Should I fix your record album?"

She looked over his shoulder with clouded eyes, but they cleared a moment later. "Of course. Come in, George. You can take care of me."

Richie didn't correct her. He strode across the room and popped the arm up, gently placing the needle on the edge of the black vinyl. The speakers crackled for a few seconds until the sultry voice of Billie Holiday filled the room. I stood, transfixed, watching her move slightly, her hips swaying to music. "Can I take your picture?" I asked after a moment, waiting in the doorway.

She turned, gracing me with a sublime smile. "Of course," she said as she struck a pose. She put one hand on her hip, leaned her body so her other hip curved seductively. "Where will you put it?" she asked.

I didn't quite know how to answer that. First Bernard, and now this woman, Dixie.

Both lived in an alternate reality. I had to give it to Richie: Providing stability and having the patience to deal with people who had such day-to-day, maybe minute-to-minute, challenges was no small feat.

"It'll be everywhere, Dixie," he said, jumping in to answer for me. "Posters, playbills, you name it."

Instead of her smile widening, it grew more subtle and more satisfied. "I'll be famous," she said, "and then she'll set me free, won't she?"

"You'll be free as a bird," Richie said.

She looked at me and fluttered her hand, which I took as a sign to go forth and photograph. I changed my lens quickly; I didn't want Dixie to change her mind. She truly looked as if she belonged to another era and I wanted to stop time for a moment. I took several shots of her posed. When I lowered my camera, she turned to the full-length mirror, patting her hair. That moment, that gesture — that's when I was able to really capture her image in a way that was unique and unplanned and uncensored. She didn't notice as I raised my camera again, shooting her from the back, but seeing her expression in the mirror. It was confident. Poised. Beautiful, but at the same time, her face held a measure of loneliness.

I placed her in her midfifties, but she carried herself in a timeless manner.

She turned to the turntable and bent over it, moving the needle forward to another song. Snap, snap, snap. I took photo after photo, glancing quickly at the images on my display screen to make sure the lighting was good. I shot a few more before thanking her.

"For what?" she asked, and then her gaze dropped to my camera. "Do you want to take my picture?" And then she struck her pose again, smiling and hand on hip.

"Dementia," Richie said softly. "She has really good days sometimes, but other times, like now, it's hit-and-miss. I have to keep an eye on her, but I couldn't turn her away."

We left Dixie to her Billie Holiday record album. "Who's Georgie?" I asked when we were in the hallway again.

"A former tenant. They had a little May-December romance going. He's about eighty."

"Where is he now?" I asked.

He took a beat before he answered. "We don't know, actually. He up and walked out. We searched for him, the police searched, but we could never find him."

I thought about our conversation from a few minutes ago. People passed on, went into a home, or simply vanished. Alzheimer's, I imagined. It could lead to a tragic ending. I didn't know this man, George, but I was sad for him.

Richie pointed down the hall. "These are more tenant rooms. Like I said, most of them are empty right now, but we're looking for new people to take in."

"Their families pay the rent?" I asked, curious how Richie was able to cover his expenses.

"Usually. Some collect disability or Social Security." He moved on down the hallway. "There are more bedrooms upstairs," he said. "We had one room redone so it's ready to be photographed. The others have tenants. I knew Dixie would welcome the company, but the others I'm not so sure." He took me upstairs to the second floor and showed me the three bedrooms there. The one he'd referred to looked straight out of a movie. It was tastefully done, but minimal. A queen-sized bed with an off-white down comforter, a tall, dark-wood dresser, and side table with a little lamp, and pale sheers on either side of the window. "This is lovely," I said. "*I'd* stay here."

"My mom has a knack," he said. "She's been redoing the rooms one by one. It's been kind of slow, but we're picking up the pace now. Several rooms are empty, so we're going to get them spruced up before re-renting."

"Good idea," I said, admiring Janice's talent. "I should have her over to my house. Get some decorating advice."

"She'd love that," he said. "Spending money is one of her favorite pastimes."

I laughed. "It would be one of mine, too, if I had the money." Janice and I had agreed on a price for my time and the finished photos. With her approval, I'd put them together in a book to commemorate the house and the renovations. It would be a good memory. The photos of Dixie and Bernard, however, I'd keep for my own collection.

The third floor consisted of just two rooms, one a converted attic and the other a mini-suite complete with a full bathroom. It was darker on the top floor. "I might need my light kit for up here," I said after taking a few test shots.

"Should I get it?" he asked, turning toward the door.

I looked at the digital screen of my DSLR camera. "No, wait," I said. "They might be okay." The lighting wasn't great, but if I opened the blinds . . . . I walked to the window, my camera lifted and ready to shoot. I twisted the slats open, directing the light inside. "This could be enough," I said.

I quickly took a few shots through the blinds. As I lowered the camera, it slipped and my finger depressed the shutter button. I heard the *click-click-click* as a series of pictures were taken. They'd be lovely shots of the wall and floor. I held on tight, quickly slipping the strap around my neck. The strap was a safety precaution. I scolded myself. With an expensive camera, I knew better than to take chances. I'd delete the rogue pictures later, for the moment redirecting my attention to the room, moving to the entrance to get the space from all angles. "Done," I said after a couple more shots. "I should have proofs for you to look at in a day or two."

"Just send them to my mother," he said. "She's in charge."

I could completely relate. My mother had been the same way. Multiple scrapbooks for both Billy and me. A box full of trinkets that represented important moments in our childhoods. A small wooden jewelry box with a delicate strand of pearls my dad had given me, a tiny signet ring that had been my mother's, a woven friendship bracelet from Emmaline. "Moms are like that."

A few minutes later we were back downstairs, and a few minutes after that Mrs.

Branford, Olaya, and I were back in my car and heading into town. I hadn't seen any evidence of a computer anywhere in the house, which made sense to me. Bernard and Dixie didn't strike me as people who would do well with them. It seemed safer to not have them around. I'd already eliminated the idea that Hank had met someone online. If that had been the case, why would his body have ended up in Brenda's garbage can? It just didn't make sense to me.

As I drove, we each fell into our own thoughts. I suspected that Olaya and Mrs. Branford were thinking about Hank. For my part, I was thinking about an uneasy feeling I'd gotten at the boardinghouse. Specifically, I was uneasy about Bernard. His demeanor and his agitation had both been concerning. I replayed the conversation I'd had with him in the garden. He said he didn't know anything about what had happened to Hank, but I wasn't so sure. I couldn't put my finger on it, but buried in his head somewhere, I thought Bernard knew something about Hank's disappearance. Maybe even about his murder.

CHAPTER 22

After leaving the boarding house, we went straight to Yeast of Eden. I parked in front and turned in my seat to face both Olaya and Mrs. Branford. I'd filed away the idea that Bernard knew something and turned my attention to my other working theory. "Alice and Michael Ryder."

They both stared at me. Mrs. Branford was the one who spoke first. "What about them?"

"Hank borrowed money from Alice."

"You think Alice, she could have killed Hank?" Olaya said, her voice incredulous. "I do not think that could be possible."

Mrs. Branford jumped in from shotgun, notching her thumb toward Olaya. "I hate to admit it, but she's right. I spoke with Alice last night and early this morning. She is utterly distraught. She cared for Hank."

"Maybe," I said, but it was without conviction. Alice acted as if she cared for Hank, but did she really? She'd lent him the money he'd asked for, had tried to get it back, and none of us knew what had happened after that.

But Mrs. Branford was having none of it. She lifted her chin, full of indignation. "I would be more inclined to think Michael was capable of murder."

I raised my eyebrows at her. Was she just trying to divert my attention away from Alice, or did she really believe Michael could have killed Hank and put him in Brenda's garbage can? "Do you really think so?"

Mrs. Branford was going with it full throttle. "Anyone is capable of anything," she said. "You know that."

She was right. I'd learned that right here in Santa Sofia not so long ago. I went with it. "What if Michael found out and confronted Hank? And what if it went bad and Michael —"

We fell silent, each of us contemplating that scenario. "Hank is dead," Olaya said, as if realizing it again for the first time.

I continued the thought in my head. Hank was dead and someone was responsible. "Does Michael have — I don't know — a dark side?"

Mrs. Branford scoffed, which was something I had not seen her do before. The idea that her friend's husband was on our radar was sending her into a tizzy. "A dark side? This is not a Marvel movie."

I snuck a glance at her. I shouldn't have been surprised by her cultural reference, but I was. Surprised and impressed. "*Whoever* killed Hank has a dark side," I said.

She came right back at me. "But that doesn't mean it was Michael."

I stopped my jaw from dropping. "You're the one who just suggested that he was capable of it."

She looked out the passenger window, turning back to me a minute later. "Maybe he is," she said. "I just don't know, anymore. I just don't know."

I took Olaya back to Yeast of Eden, dropped Mrs. Branford at home, and took Agatha to the beach for a walk. The day had finally warmed up enough that all I needed was a sweatshirt, but beneath it, I shivered anyway. With a murderer on the loose, Santa Sofia wasn't the town I wanted it to be.

Agatha trotted along beside me, kicking up the dampened sand along the way. We walked and walked and walked, and I thought all the while, trying to sort out what I knew, which wasn't near enough. I kept coming back to two things. Make it three things: Bernard, Michael, and the money. Why had Hank borrowed that money and what happened to it? Did Michael try to get it back? Could that money really be at the core of Hank's death? It made the most sense, but what did Bernard have to do with any of it?

"Nothing," I muttered. "He had nothing to do with it." Bernard was not stable, and I'd just read too much into his behavior, that's all.

I kept walking. Death. It seemed to be everywhere. Seaweed washing up on the sand. The limp body of a black-feathered bird. Driftwood. I peered out toward the horizon, trying to push away the reality that Hank was now among the dead.

I drew in a few bolstering breaths. There was nothing I could do. I couldn't unearth the killer if I didn't know what had happened to Hank in the first place. All I had was a very loose theory that centered on the money Alice had lent Hank. Money had the potential to drive people to distraction. Whether it was Michael Ryder or someone else, whoever was behind Hank's death, I felt quite certain that the money was at the center of it.

My dad's voice rang in my ears, telling me that it wasn't my responsibility. I should leave it to Emmaline and her officers, but maybe I really did have some latent need to crime-solve. I couldn't get it all out of my head.

After another ten minutes of walking, Agatha and I trudged up the beach. I shook off my shoes, wiped her skinny little legs off, and we drove back home. I had the photos of the boarding house to review, and it dawned on me that I hadn't ever gotten back to take photos of Baptista's. It felt like he'd asked me eons ago, but it had only been a matter of days. Did he even want me to take them anymore?

So much had happened in the last few days: Hank going missing, the Winter Wonderland Festival, the Blackbird Ladies, Miguel's revelation that he didn't want to see me, and now Hank's death.

I could only control so much, and right now understanding what had happened to Hank wasn't possible. Instead, I went with what I *could* control and what I could be productive with: Photographs. I transferred the pictures I'd taken earlier in the day to my computer by inserting the memory card into the port. The transfer started immediately, a little image icon showing up and moving pictures from one file to another. Once the transfer was done, I replaced the memory card in my camera, snapped the little battery flap shut, and turned my attention to the uploaded files.

I labeled the folder *Thompson Victorian* and opened the first photo. It was a time-consuming process to rename each photo so they'd be easily identifiable, but it was the smart thing to do. I'd been lazy in the past, not taking the time to do this tedious task, and I'd regretted it. It was better, I'd discovered, to just bite the bullet and do things the right way.

I opened the pictures one by one. It took time, but I analyzed whether each one was worth keeping or discarding, dragged the rejects to the trash, and named the ones worth keeping. The exterior shots from the front had turned out pretty well, given the lack of vegetation. These photos were only for the Thompsons' personal documentation, so even if there were a few things I wished were better, I could live with them. I did think it would be worth reshooting in the spring, though, when all the flowers were in bloom.

The backyard shots weren't as good. The lighting wasn't as even, and the patches of dirt throughout the yard were distracting. We'd definitely need to redo them whenever the landscaping was finished. The shots of the flower petals and the crocuses close up were nice. Good detail, but Bernard had been right; the dead branches scattered here and there were another distraction. I wanted to show Bernard the flowers, though, so I kept them. I'd print them and make him a collage, or something. Maybe they could have a calming effect on him. And maybe, if he was calm, I could convince him to tell me if he knew anything.

I spent an hour or more sorting through every photo, culling the collection until I had the best. I finally opened the last set, the pictures from the third-floor bedroom — and that's when my hand froze. My heart nearly stopped. My jaw dropped.

Surely not . . . Was I really seeing what I thought I was?

It took me three minutes to call — and leave a message — for the cavalry and a total of twenty-five minutes for that cavalry to arrive. Emmaline came first, bursting in through the front door with nary a knock. She hollered from the entryway. "I'm here!"

"Kitchen!" I yelled.

The *clackity-clack* of her heels against the tile floor grew louder, but a second set of footsteps, this one heavier, came alongside it. "Hey, sis." I looked up. Billy's heavy footsteps. Billy's voice. The two of them appeared at the archway to the kitchen, and I looked them up and down. My brother was dressed in khakis and a navy pullover sweater. He was the spitting image of our father — tall and lean at five-feet-eleven inches with a wave and a hint of red in his brown hair. His arm was around Em, his hand on her slim waist. Emmaline had on a red knit dress that hugged her curvy figure and three-inch knee-high black boots. The red of the dress was gorgeous against her perfect mocha skin, her hair loose and untamed in wiry strands of black spiral curls. She was devastatingly sexy, and from the way Billy looked at her, even in the aftermath of my phone call, it was clear he was never leaving her side.

No wonder they hadn't answered the phone. I laid my hands flat on the table, one on either side of my laptop. "You're on a date?" I said.

"Your deductive reasoning skills are beyond compare," she said as she held a large envelope, tapping it with the pads of her fingers. "The crime scene," she said.

My heart raced and I had to stop myself from grabbing the envelope right out of her hand. "I'm allowed to see them?"

"I can't seem to stop you from digging

around, so I figured, why not? Maybe you'll notice something I missed. Look at them first, then show me whatever it is you found."

She sat, Billy standing behind her chair, and slid the photos from the envelope. I inched forward in my chair to get a better look. TV and the movies were one thing, but I had never seen crime-scene photos in real life. I hadn't expected the impact it had on me. I recognized Brenda Rivera's house in the first one. It looked completely ordinary. But the next picture, this one of the garbage cans on the driveway, was more ominous. Crime-scene tape, just like on TV, spanned the width of the driveway, secured with two stakes the police had presumably driven into the ground on either side. There were photos of the ground, little areas marked with numbered tags: The forensic evidence Em and her team would process as they tried to solve the crime.

It was the next photo, though, that gave me pause. One of the garbage-can lids was open, and there, shoved heartlessly inside, was a body partially wrapped in what looked like a large, black plastic garbage bag. I slapped my hand over my mouth, my heart in my throat. The image made it horrifyingly real. Hank Rivera really was dead.

The next picture was a close-up of the body in the can. I gasped at the matted hair, caked with blood. I quickly stuck it to the back of the pile to look at the next picture. It was a collection of items spread out on a tarp of some sort. Number tags sat beside each item. I held the picture up to look more closely. "The next few are of each item," Em said.

I slid the one I'd been looking at to the back of the stack. Each photo in the next set featured one of the items from the selection on the tarp, including the number demarking the find. I looked at them one at a time: A worn, brown wallet with a broken zipper closure. A crumpled brochure, which I recognized. "That's for Rusty Gates," I said, holding up the photograph. "That's where Hank's father lives."

Emmaline nodded as I turned to the next several images: A chunk of splintered wood. A muddy work boot. A wad of tissue. I stopped at the last one. "Is that a bank receipt?"

"It's for a deposit," Em said. "I have someone looking into it."

At that moment, Miguel appeared in the archway, broad-shouldered and filling the space in a way only a former marine can. "Looking into what?" he said, avoiding meeting my eyes.

Seeing him, I instantly regretted my phone call to him. I'd phoned Emmaline and Billy first, but had gotten no answer. Mrs. Branford had been exhausted by the end of the day. She'd probably chew me out for not calling, but I didn't have the heart to prevent her from a good night's sleep. Olaya had to be at the bread shop before it was even light outside the next morning, so I couldn't ask her to give up her sleep, either. I'd thought about calling my dad, but in the end, Miguel seemed like the best choice. He'd initiated this investigation, so he had to be the one to help finish it.

Billy answered, his voice revealing his torn-up emotions. "A bank receipt found at the crime scene."

"All of this was found on his person," Emmaline specified.

Miguel's face looked ragged, his jaw tight. "I can't believe he's gone," he said. He pressed his thumb and forefinger against his eyes and gave his head a slight shake. "That he was killed." Finally, he looked at me. "We were too late."

As Emmaline slid the photos back into the envelope, I felt my eyes prick with emotion. Blinking to clear them, I pushed my open laptop across the table. The picture

I'd taken at Richie Thompson's boarding house was open on the screen.

The three of them stared at it, as speechless as I had been. I'd wondered if I'd been seeing things, but their reactions proved that I was, in fact, sane.

I remembered the shot with my camera almost as if I were experiencing it again. The third-floor bedroom. I'd opened the blinds, shooting through them to capture the light in the sky. And then lowering the camera, accidentally depressing the button, the camera snapping a series of pictures. I hadn't looked at them, not until I'd downloaded all the pictures from the shoot.

Two of the resulting photographs had been of the wall and floor, but the first one in the series . . . that was the money shot.

When I'd been in the yard, the patches of flowers seemed more present, while the mounds of dirt had been less noticeable. In the picture, it was the opposite. The dirt was most prominent, while the flowers were more clustered than I'd originally thought. But it was more than that. From a bird's-eye view, albeit a blurry one, the backyard looked . . . disturbing.

The thing that drew my immediate attention was the mound of dirt. It was big. Oddly shaped. Sort of rectangular.

Emmaline drew in a sharp breath. "Seriously?"

Billy took a step back and dragged his hand through his hair. "Dude."

Miguel looked more closely, his arms propped on the table. He gave a low whistle and then murmured, "Holy shit. Do you think that's a grave?"

CHAPTER 23

We looked at the picture, none of us sure what to say next or how to voice our thoughts. My voice was low. Hushed. As if I might raise the dead if I spoke too loudly.

Billy shook his head, his mouth agape. "It can't be. Can it?"

In my head, I reordered my theories, taking Michael and Alice off of my list for the moment. I came back to Bernard. I'd thought he knew something, but I hadn't really thought he was behind Hank's death. That impression was starting to shift. What if he wasn't quite as feebleminded as he seemed?

I shared the possibility with Emmaline, Billy, and Miguel. "You think this guy killed Hank?" Miguel asked.

Good question. *Was* that what I thought? Before I could answer, Em shook her head. She was always the first to play devil's advocate. "You having a feeling about someone based on their behavior — especially someone like this guy, Bernard — does not give him a motive."

I ignored her, continuing with my theory, though. "But it makes sense, doesn't it? The way Bernard is obsessed with the garden and how he keeps talking about Hank. He can't let the flowers die." I remembered how he'd picked up the dead branch, how adamant he was that it not be there. Was that his way of subconsciously trying to reclaim his yard?

"I don't know," Em said, but I could see her thinking. Processing.

I didn't necessarily consider myself a keen observer of human nature, but I had my intuition. "Bernard loves that yard. Think about it. Hank moves in and takes over, pushing Bernard out of the way. Not literally, of course, but, you know, he makes the yard his domain. Plants flowers and all that. From everything I've learned about Hank in the last few days, I don't think he'd have done it maliciously, but if it happened, Bernard might have snapped."

Emmaline hesitated. "I don't know if that's motive enough to kill."

She might be right, but I was not willing to abandon the idea. "For someone with Bernard's mental deficiencies, it could be."

Em seemed to consider my argument. "I suppose it could be possible, but how *would* he have done it? We know that Hank was killed somewhere else and moved to the Rivera residence. This Bernard, he can't drive, can he?"

"No," I said slowly, remembering that Mrs. Branford had told me that Richie took his tenants to the doctor, the store, to wherever they needed to go.

My skin pricked with anxiety. I didn't know the scope of Bernard's issues. To assign blame to him or accuse him of killing Hank based on the circumstantial evidence I'd presented suddenly didn't feel right. It didn't seem as plausible as it had sounded in my head. Maybe I was trying to settle on the easiest answer, or the first one that had presented itself.

Billy still stood, his arms folded over his chest. "Bernard's not the only person who lives there, is he?"

"No, there are others," I said, thinking about Richie, who ran the place, Mason Caldwell, and Dixie. There were also other tenants who I hadn't met. We talked through the list, trying to think of possible motives. I went with Richie first. "He runs the place, is the caretaker for the people there. It seems like a good gig. Why would he kill Hank?"

Miguel stood, his hands on the back of a chair as he leaned over the table. "The money."

The money. I considered that. "How would he know about the money? How would anybody know about it?"

"Which discounts the other tenants," Em said. "Unless Hank told people about it, that can't be the motive."

"Hank was trying to get Mason to move to the senior community," I said, my mind going back to the brochure for Rusty Gates that had been in Hank's pocket at the crime scene. "It's an expensive place. If that's why he borrowed the money from Alice in the first place, maybe he explained to Mason how they could make it happen." I hated the mere thought that Mason could be involved, if only because it would crush Mrs. Branford. But I had to keep an open mind. The truth was that anyone could have killed Hank, and without knowing the motive, how could we ever know the truth?

"We don't know it's a grave," Miguel said, and he was right. We were jumping to conclusions. Shifting gears, I looked again at the photograph still up on my computer screen and touched my finger to the screen.

"Maybe we're looking for something sinister when it's totally innocent. Maybe they have an irrigation problem, or something?"

Billy picked up the laptop to look closer at the picture. "Could have been a leak."

"Maybe a burst pipe," Miguel said.

"Maybe this has nothing at all to do with Hank's death." I shifted gears, going back to the other theory I had and the bank-deposit slip found on Hank's body. "Alice Ryder lent Hank fifty-thousand dollars."

Billy grunted. "What the . . . ?"

"Right," Miguel said, giving a low whistle. "That's a good chunk of change. Maybe enough for someone to kill over."

Emmaline laced her hands in front of her face, pressing her thumbs against her lips. "Definitely enough for someone to kill over," she said.

"When Alice found out Hank was missing, she had a breakdown." I told them about her reaction with the Blackbird Ladies at Yeast of Eden. "She was worried Hank had run off with the money and that he'd never pay it back. And she was worried about her husband's reaction when he found out."

"So maybe he *did* find out," Miguel said, looking at Emmaline instead of me. "He didn't exactly look like a killer to me, but then again, does anybody?"

We tossed around ideas for a while longer and then, with Emmaline as the point person, we made a plan. She was going to look into Hank's bank account, she was going to have Alice and Michael Ryder questioned, and she was going to do background checks on everyone Hank had been involved with.

"What are we going to do?" I asked her, but I already knew what her answer would be.

As expected, she tilted her head; with her expression firm, the look she gave me left no room for argument. "You're going to bake some bread, walk Agatha, see your dad, take some pictures. Et cetera, et cetera, et cetera."

I heaved a resigned sigh. I'd given her things to work with — now I needed to let her do her job. A short time later, she and Billy left, his hand on the small of her back as they walked down the front walkway to their car. He opened the passenger door for her and she slid in. Emmaline was a tough woman, full of strength and confidence and intelligence. But she was also a woman in love, and clearly, my brother was mad for her, too.

I stood at the door, Agatha by my feet.

Miguel gave me an innocuous good-bye and started to walk out, but then he stopped and stood at the threshold. Slowly, he turned around to face me. "I never should have gotten you involved in this, Ivy."

Did I wish I hadn't been involved? I didn't think so. Hank had been a Santa Sofia icon, and I'd gotten to know him vicariously. I was mourning his death as much as everyone else. "You didn't know it would turn into a murder."

"No, I didn't," he said, and then he lifted his hand in a slight wave, gave me a faint smile, and left me standing there, one hand still on the doorknob, wondering where we'd gone wrong.

Left on my own, my mind worked, processing what I knew. My instincts were telling me that Michael Ryder should be the focus of Emmaline's investigation. I knew she was tackling that angle and if he was, in fact, a murderer, I didn't want to be the one to confront him. After considering my options, I decided to go to the boarding house. Honing in on the money Alice had lent Hank, and Michael's reaction to it, was the logical decision. But I still wanted to eliminate Hank's short-lived roommates as suspects. It was 8:00 and dark out, but I couldn't just sit here and twiddle my thumbs.

I took Agatha out to the yard for a few minutes, changed into sneakers, grabbed a sweater, and headed to the garage. A minute later, I was driving across town to the old Victorian. I parked across the street, left my wallet tucked under the front seat, locked the car, and crossed the street. As I reached the curb, a truck pulled up, its lights blinding me. It parked, the lights turned off, and a door slammed. My vision cleared and Miguel appeared.

I stared at him as he came toward me and for a fleeting moment, I thought, Oh my God, did he kill Hank? But then I blinked and the ridiculous idea vanished into thin air. "What are you doing here?"

"I should be asking you that, shouldn't I?"

I drew my head back, feeling indignant. "No. You made it pretty clear how you felt. You should be off at the restaurant, telling your sister that I'm out of your life. What, did you follow me?"

"If I did?"

I grumbled under my breath. "What is going on, Miguel?"

Under the street lamp, I could see the grim expression he wore. He came right back at me, his voice low and tight. "What are you doing here, Ivy?"

I balked, irritated. I knew it was due to self-preservation, but I didn't care. "Why are you answering all my questions with questions?"

Before he could answer, headlights speared through the darkness, coming in our direction. Miguel grabbed my arm and pulled me off the street and onto the sidewalk. I was sure it was instinct, but I yanked my arm free. "I can take care of myself."

The car zoomed by, the red taillights fading away before he answered. "Things have changed, Ivy. Hank isn't missing anymore, he's dead. Emmaline is right: You need to stay out of it."

I'd put my hair up into a messy bun and the hairs on the back of my neck pricked against my skin. "I want to meet the other tenants. There's nothing wrong with that."

"You have no fear, do you?"

"Of course I do," I said — there was that indignance again. "Look, I didn't know Hank, but everyone who did, loved him. How can I sit around idly when whoever killed him is out there?"

"I know the way you think, Ivy —"

My mouth gaped. "You don't know me at all. I'm not the same person I was in high school."

He grimaced. "I would hope not."

Once again, I balked. "What is that supposed to mean?" I thought about what his mother had said about what Laura saw, and Laura's warning to stay away from her brother. She'd said I'd driven him away, but that was the opposite of what had happened. "Why did you leave Santa Sofia?" I asked suddenly.

He shoved his hands into the pockets of his jeans, his eyes growing dark in the dim light. "Let's not go back there, Ivy. Water under the bridge."

I threw my hands up. "But it's not. Your sister told me to stay away from you. You've been friendly. You called me to help with your brochures or menus, or whatever it is you need. So why exactly are you conflicted about me being back in Santa Sophia?"

He cursed under his breath. I didn't catch it all, but he muttered something about Laura keeping her mouth shut.

"Just tell me," I said, my patience all but gone. "I want to know why your sister thinks I'm the devil incarnate, because that's certainly how she made me feel."

He hesitated, his lips drawn into a thin line, and I could feel the heat emanating from him. Finally, he shook his head with either exasperation or disdain, I couldn't tell which. "Well, Ivy, it probably has to do with the fact that I was in love with you, and you didn't give a shit. Granted, it was teenage love, but it still hurt like hell."

I stared at him, slack-jawed. "What are you talking about? I *was* in love with you." Part of me still was. Would always be.

"I thought you were, but apparently I was wrong." He turned and took a few steps before wheeling back around. "You asked why I'm conflicted about you being here? Because as much as I tried, I never stopped loving you, Ivy. I get that we were teenagers and it's stupid, but you broke my heart."

My heart was beating out of my chest. I took a step toward him. "No, you broke mine. You left without saying good-bye."

"What else could I do? You cheated on me. Laura heard all about it at school. She *saw* you."

"Saw me what?"

He sighed, looking tired and drawn. "She heard about the guys you were seeing behind my back. She saw you with somebody else. I didn't believe her at first. I told her you would never do that." He ran his hand through his hair, shaking his head. Even after all these years, it was clear that the memory was still fresh in his mind. "But she gave me details. Names. You lied to me.

Played me." He shrugged. "I thought I was long over it, but seeing you again brought it all back."

My mind reeled, my thoughts going a million directions. I remembered Laura as a jealous little sister. "Laura is the one who lied," I said. "I never cheated on you."

He shrugged again. "Like I said, water under the bridge."

Before I could reply, the front door of the Victorian flew open. Bernard stood there in his bathrobe, beckoning to us. "Come. Come."

I couldn't look at Miguel, so I turned and walked down the sidewalk to the walkway, marching up to the front porch. I'd hoped Miguel would just leave, but I felt him behind me.

"Hey, Bernard," I said, pushing everything else out of my mind.

He didn't say anything. He stood back, opening the door wide to let us in, and then he walked to the back of the house, straight to the French door leading to the backyard. He yanked it open and practically hurled himself outside.

Instinctively, I wanted to glance at Miguel, but I resisted, instead following Bernard. There was something about the dim light that made the yard look different. Sinister.

Or maybe that was just my imagination.

Bernard stopped in the middle of the yard, bent to pick something up — maybe a rock or a hunk of wood — and chucked it aside. He did it again, crouching low, gathering the debris scattered around him in the dim light, cleaning up the little patch of yard where he stood. A moment later he stood and snapped his gaze up at us. "No, never mind. No. No. You should go. Go now."

"Are any of your roommates here?" I asked. I'd come here to talk to them, so I had to at least try.

"Go now," he repeated as if he hadn't heard me at all.

"Let's go, Ivy." Miguel's voice was cool. Collected. As if we hadn't just had the heated conversation we did.

I turned to go back to the house, feeling like a thief in the night, when Miguel muttered harshly under his breath.

I stopped, my curiosity getting the better of me. "What?"

He pointed. About two yards to our left was a freshly dug hole in the ground.

"That was not there earlier," I said.

"You sure?"

I'd been kicking myself at how woefully

unobservant I'd been during my photography session here. I might have missed the odd plot of dirt, but there was no way I would have missed a gaping hole in the ground.

"One-hundred percent positive." I stepped over chunks of wood piled into a mound in order to get a closer look. Miguel was right behind me, never more than a few feet away. I was entirely focused on the mission of finding out more about the hole.

Before I got to it, Bernard hurled himself through the air, careening into me. I yelped, losing my balance, tripping over a rock, and landing on my knees. Bernard landed with a thud beside me.

"Go!" His eyes were wild. "Go now. Go now. Go now!"

But the impact of the hit had pushed me right onto another hard object. It dug into my knee. I shifted my body, grabbing whatever it was to move it aside, but as my hand touched the rough surface, one of the pictures Emmaline had shown me popped into my head. One of the items found on Hank had been a piece of splintered wood. I pulled the object in my hand up, but in the dark, I couldn't see it. I clambered up, but the ground was damp, the dirt sticky, gripping my sneaker. As if he could read my mind, Miguel stretched out one arm, reaching to help me up. He gripped his phone in his other hand, the flashlight on. I held up my hand, letting the light fall onto it. I gasped. The chunk of wood was rough and splintered. Its jagged edge had dug straight into my knee.

I tried to ignore the staggering pain as Miguel shone the light right into the hole. A wooden box sat cockeyed in the uneven space. Without thinking, I reached for the lid. If I could lift the lip of it, we'd be able to see inside the box.

But Bernard had other ideas. He'd finally managed to stand, and now he held a shovel, pointing it toward us like it was a sword. "Go go go go go go!"

But I had already touched the edge. My fingers pressed against the rough grain. It was cheap wood, full of hairy splinters that drove into my skin, but I didn't let go. I shoved, lifting the lid enough to slide it out of place and immediately lurched back. It was as if a gust of air had burst from the box, coming at me and forcing me back.

The stench was immediate and overwhelming. I stumbled back, covering my mouth and nose with my hand.

Bernard stumbled backward, dropped the shovel, and ran.

Miguel let out a gruff, indistinguishable sound, bent, and dragged the lid to the box back into place. He grabbed my hand and pulled me up and away. "Call Emmaline," he snapped, and then he took off after Bernard.

My thought exactly. I dug my phone from the back pocket of my jeans, pressed the *home* button, and dialed. She answered on the second ring. Emmaline didn't give me a chance to speak. "Hank deposited a huge amount of money into his account a few weeks ago. Fifty-thousand dollars. And get this. Three days ago, he made a direct payment."

"To who?" I asked, almost afraid to find out.

"Bernard Washington."

So my first instinct had been right. "He has a bank account?" I asked, trying to make sense of what was happening. Why would Hank give $50,000 to Bernard?

My brain felt as if it were ready to explode. "Em, I need you to come —"

She cut me off. "Oh my God, Ivy, please don't tell me —"

"We're at the boarding house. Bernard is here and we found something," I said, this time cutting her off. "It's a grave. With a wooden casket." I paused, swallowing my nausea. "And a dead body."

She cursed under her breath, surprised and angry and scared for me, all rolled into a few choice words. To me she said, "Be careful, Ivy. I'm on my way."

CHAPTER 24

I kept my cell phone in hand as relief flowed through me and air once again filled my lungs as Miguel prisoner-marched Bernard back to where I stood. Bernard's dark skin blended into the night, the whites of his eyes practically glowing in the light.

"I am in trouble," he murmured. Looking to the ground, he swung his head back and forth, frenzied and spastic. His gaze skittered around — at the house, at the yard, over his shoulder to the hole in the ground. "I have to take care of the garden. The flowers. Oh no, I am in trouble."

"It's okay, Bernard," I said, wanting him to stay calm until Emmaline and her people arrived. "Why are you in trouble?"

He kept his mouth shut, and then, from the direction of the house, we heard a door slam. "Bernard!" Mason's voice bellowed. "You got a party going on out here? Where's my invitation?"

Mason pushed his walker across the patio, stopping at the edge.

"No. No! Bernard . . . Bernard . . . Bernard get in trouble. No!" He tried to break free, but Miguel held him tightly.

Mason looked at me. "What in the devil is happening here, Ms. Culpepper?" he asked, but he didn't wait for my response, instead looking at Bernard. "Bernard," he said evenly. He was calm and rational. "It's okay. You'll be fine. The flowers will be just fine."

I didn't have a chance to tell him that this was not about the flowers, but another voice yelled, this time Richie's. "Bernard!"

He appeared at the backlit French door and flipped on a light switch that illuminated the yard. "What the — ?" His gaze landed on Mason first, then Bernard — being held by Miguel — and finally me. He charged forward. "Let him go!" His gaze swept over the yard. When he saw the hole, his eyes grew wide. "What is that? What the hell is going on here?"

From somewhere in the back of my consciousness, I heard a gate close. Long shadows stretched along the ground. Emmaline, flanked by two uniformed officers, came into the yard from a side gate, weapons drawn. I could see her eyes flash and survey the entire space in a matter of seconds.

Richie staggered back. "Have you all lost your mind? This is my property. Get the hell out!"

Everything seemed to slow and I took it all in. Mason leaned heavily on his walker. Miguel, grim, a vein surfacing in his forehead, held tight to Bernard. Emmaline directed her pistol at Bernard. Bernard looked terrified. And Richie had full, unadulterated rage on his face.

A barrage of information cascaded over me, all the little bits of information I'd unwittingly tucked away, suddenly blending together like one of Olaya's long-rise bread doughs. It all came back to this yard. The freshly dug hole with the body in the box. The body, which by the smell of it, had been decaying for some time.

What if Hank really had discovered something sinister here? What if he'd seen Bernard digging a hole and burying someone? Who was it? A tenant? I remembered someone telling me that one had recently left. A chill ran over my skin. Could Bernard have killed him, too?

If Hank had discovered the body, it would certainly explain why he would have tried to talk Mason into leaving. He would have feared for his former teacher, that Bernard could turn on him. But the leasing fees at Rusty Gates was a lot more money than Mason happened to have. So he'd borrowed the money from Alice to get Mason out of harm's way. But now that money was in Bernard's bank account, which didn't make sense. And where had Hank gone when Richie had seen him get into his truck and drive away?

What had happened between that moment, when Hank was still alive, and yesterday, when his body was found?

Emmaline had pulled her mass of black hair into a fluffy mound on top of her head, changed from her date clothes into jeans and a Santa Sofia sheriff's-department jacket, and now she stood with her hands on her hips. She motioned for one of the officers to go check out the hole in the ground while the other took Bernard from Miguel's hold, took each of his wrists, and handcuffed him. He was read his Miranda rights, and then Emmaline asked him, "Do you understand these rights as they've been read to you, Mr. Washington?"

"Jesus Christ," Richie ranted, surging toward Bernard. "No, he does not understand the rights as they've been read to him!"

The officer at the edge of the hole lunged toward Richie, holding him back, but Richie fought him. "Don't say anything, Bernard. I'll get a lawyer. I'm going to help you!"

And with that, Bernard was hauled away, sobbing and muttering, "Hank's flowers. No, no. I'm taking care of Hank's flowers."

CHAPTER 25

Emmaline had gone into full deputy-sheriff mode, speaking on her cell phone after Bernard was safely ensconced in the back of one of the police SUVs. "John Doe. Deceased. Age unknown. Dead about three days." She'd waited as whoever she spoke with said something. "Right."

Again, there was a pause, and then she nodded her head and said, "We have a suspect in custody."

After the call, she turned back to Miguel and me. "We're getting a warrant so the county's forensic team can excavate the yard."

My blood ran cold. "You think there are others?"

Em looked shaken, too. "I don't know, but we have to look."

I looked at the house and saw Dixie standing at one of the windows, gazing out at us. Was I imagining it, or did she look sad?

Something she said came back to me. "Georgie," I whispered.

Em looked at me. "What?"

"There was a tenant here not too long ago. George. He wandered off." I turned to Richie. "Right?"

The strain of the last hour was taking its toll on Richie. He was pale and looked like he might collapse. He gave half a nod.

"You searched for him, but he was never found."

Em stared at me. "Hank's the only missing person we've had," she said.

"No, his name is George." I pointed to the window where Dixie still stood. "They were friends. He just wandered off."

Em's gaze swept over Dixie, then refocused on me. "Ivy, there's no missing person named George."

"But . . ." I looked back at Richie, but he wasn't where he'd been standing a moment ago. He was walking quickly toward the side gate Emmaline and her officers had come in through.

"Richie!" I called, worried about his state of mind, but then another barrage of buried information came crashing into my consciousness. The empty mail slots at the desk area, the empty rooms. Tenants who'd left suddenly, or, as Richie had said, passed on.

Hank so determined to get Mason Caldwell out of here and the money he'd borrowed. George, who apparently was nowhere.

A complete idea hadn't formed in my mind, but I turned to Em. "Stop him," I said. My voice was forceful. Urgent. I grabbed her arm. "Stop Richie."

Emmaline didn't hesitate. She ordered an officer to go after Richie, but Miguel was quicker. The second I'd spoken, he'd taken off after Richie. Richie had started to run, but Miguel caught up, grabbing him by the arm. Richie tried to pull free, but by then the other officer was there. It took some doing, but together, he and Miguel restrained Richie and dragged him back. Richie bucked, the color back in his face, his cheeks blotchy and red.

"What, Ivy?" Em said, searching my face. "Tell me."

I didn't think before speaking, my words tumbling out, so many little facts circling in my mind, straining to come out. "The wood." I pointed to the chunks of wood on the ground, to the box in the grave. "It's the same wood you found on Hank. He was wrapped in plastic. He was here. He was buried here."

"Right," Emmaline said. "We figured that. But Bernard —"

"No, not Bernard," I said, suddenly sure. He was a victim as much as whoever was in that box. Was it Leonard? Chase? George? I pointed to the hole. "That box. There are more like it in the shed," I said, gesturing to the outbuilding in the corner of the yard. It seemed clear that Richie had taken a few from the house to the shed for his own use.

This time, no one said anything. "Richie gave me a tour. There's a room with a million books and boxes. Crates made out of this same wood —" The mail cubbies came back to me then. The letters in each slot. If the tenants were gone — if they were reported as deceased — they wouldn't have mail. Yet, each of the boxes had held something.

The bank statements. The Social Security checks. I let out the breath I'd been holding, trying to calm my racing heart. I didn't know how he did it, but I knew with a certainty that he had. I stared at Richie, horrified. "It was fraud, wasn't it? You killed all of them for the money."

Richie didn't speak. But he bent his head, his knees buckling. And he broke down sobbing.

CHAPTER 26

"I'll call you in later for a statement," Emmaline said to Miguel and me, and then she offered a wan smile. The fact that we'd discovered another body and had identified Richie Thompson as the man who'd killed Hank diffused any residual anger she might have had that I'd ignored her directive to stay out of it.

I thought about Bernard and his part in this, coming to the only logical conclusion: He'd been the unwitting gravedigger. A victim of a serial killer. But then I thought of his warnings to go, the way he'd cared for the flowers Hank grew, and changed my mind. Maybe he did know the truth; he just didn't know how to stop it.

My heart broke for Bernard, but I knew that Emmaline would do everything she could to take care of him.

With nothing left to do at the boarding house, I headed to my car.

Miguel stopped me at the curb. "Are you okay?"

I was spent. Beyond that, I wasn't sure. I'd thought Richie was such a good guy, taking care of such sad souls like Bernard and Dixie. How could I have been so wrong?

But we'd found Hank's killer. And we'd stopped a madman. "I will be," I said.

"Where are you going?"

It seemed that we were brushing everything from our earlier conversation under the rug, at least for now, which was fine with me. I didn't have the energy to revisit more of the past, but his forced concern irked me. "The bread shop."

His expression was a cross between fresh concern and long-buried anger. The concern seemed to win out. "I can come with you. Make sure you get there safely."

Emmaline had the bad guy in custody. There was nothing to fear. I didn't need him to be my guard, but was too tired to argue, so I just sighed. "I can't stop you," I said.

A minute later, we were a little caravan of two, driving through Santa Sofia to Beach Road and the quaint street where Yeast of Eden resided. I parked, waving Miguel on, and climbed out of the car. The lights inside were on, which wasn't unusual. Olaya typically left a low light on behind the display cases, but it looked like the overhead bakery lights were blazing.

I tensed. Olaya had given me a key, but I still hesitated before inserting it into the lock. Then I kicked myself. Richie had been arrested. There was nothing to be concerned about. I unlocked the door and walked in.

I stopped short. Olaya was bent over the table, placing a plate of sliced loaf of cranberry-orange bread in the middle of the table. All four of the Blackbird Ladies were gathered around one of the tables, each with a cup of coffee and tears in their eyes. They would be mourning Hank for a long time to come. And when they learned the truth about what had happened to him, their grief would be compounded.

I forced a smile, my mind racing, my gaze settling on Janice. I'd completely forgotten about her. It wasn't my job to tell her that her son had been arrested for multiple murders, and worse, that one of the victims had been their friend.

Footsteps sounded behind me and Miguel spoke. "Ladies," he said with a wave and a charming smile. To me he said, "I'm going to call the restaurant to check in with Em."

I nodded, suddenly glad he was here to help navigate the grief that was sure to come. He'd call Emmaline and she'd be able to break the news to Janice. I imagined that she'd need to interview Janice, too, to see if she'd had any inkling of what her son was up to.

Olaya poured me a cup of coffee. I wanted to ask her how and why the women were all here. I'd thought she and Mrs. Branford went to sleep early, yet here they were. Mrs. Branford answered my unspoken question before I could think of a way to ask it. "We are forgoing our weekly gin and tonics at my house for decaf coffee and pastries." She laughed, trying to make light, but I could tell it was forced. There was no levity in the room.

The door *dinged* as Miguel came back in. "All's good," he said, meeting my eyes, and I knew Emmaline was on her way.

My stomach grumbled, and I realized that I hadn't eaten since lunch. "Any bread left?" I asked, sniffing to see if I could detect the scent of any residual baking, but my voice betrayed my stress.

Mrs. Branford pushed the plate of cranberry-orange bread toward the edge of the table, but her gaze stayed glued to me. We were so connected that she knew something heavy was on my mind. She also seemed to know that asking me what was wrong was not a good idea.

Janice wasn't so intuitive. "You look pale as a ghost, Ivy," she said. "What's going on?"

"Nothing," I said quickly. Maybe *too* quickly, because all five women turned their concerned, but curious, eyes to me.

Alice didn't buy it, either. "Something is definitely amiss."

I tried to keep my expression even, to wait for Emmaline, but I second-guessed myself. How could I withhold the truth from them? From Janice?

Mabel was the most perceptive of the bunch. She brushed her bright hair out of her face as she considered me. She stood, pulling her chair out. "Sit down before you collapse, Ivy."

I didn't move, wishing I could turn on my heel and walk back out. But Miguel put his hand on the small of my back and gently guided me to the chair. I sat, swallowing, trying to think of some small talk I could make. Some excuse for my distraction until Emmaline arrived.

But my effort was short-lived. The color had drained from Alice's face. "It's about Hank, isn't it? Did they find who killed him?"

I couldn't bring myself to say it, but my body reacted. My head inclined, maybe by only a fraction of an inch, but it was enough.

Alice sobbed quietly, pressing her hand against her mouth. I could see it in her eyes. She was experiencing the loss of her friend over again.

Mabel was the one who asked the obvious question. "Who?"

I hesitated. Part of me wanted to spill everything, but I stopped myself. Where was Emmaline?

Mrs. Branford came to stand behind me, a show of support. Janice stood, too, going to stand next to Miguel. She whispered something to him, completely calm. I watched them. Miguel responded to whatever she had said. She was so calm. She walked to the door. It seemed odd. She was calm. Too calm, I thought. And then suddenly the hairs on the back of my neck pricked. I studied her back as she pulled the door handle.

So much had happened in the last several hours. Something jogged in my memory. I thought about Dixie's reaction when Richie had told her she'd be famous from my photographs. Her eyes had lit up and she'd said something I'd taken to be innocuous. "Maybe she'll set me free," she'd said. I thought it was just part of her delusion, but looking back, maybe it hadn't been so innocent. Maybe she wasn't actually allowed to leave the house.

My mind shifted to the desk area in the room next to Dixie's, and the mail slots. I'd come to the conclusion that Richie had been killing his tenants to steal their Social Security. There had been investment and bank-statement envelopes, too. The bottom row of the cubbies materialized in my mind. All the labels marking the slots. I visualized the last one. *Jan.* I'd assumed it mean January. The month we were in. But I'd seen it wrong. It was Janice. Richie said he wasn't a numbers person and that his mother did the banking.

Fifty-thousand dollars had been transferred into Bernard's bank account. But what about the other tenants? Richie must have been cashing Bernard's disability checks. Social Security, too. Which meant it was very possible he had access to the tenants' bank accounts?

But Janice did the banking.

And then there were the boxes. The boxes that Richie had connected to his mother. The boxes supposedly filled with books. The boxes that were exactly like the box Miguel and I had found the body in.

My eyes had blurred, but now they refocused on Janice. She stood, watching me, her eyes revealing what was going on beneath the surface. She looked like a caged animal.

I didn't need to wait for Emmaline anymore. She had helped Richie. She'd known. My throat tightened, my stomach roiling, but I swallowed and stared her down. I was not going to let her leave.

Janice turned her back on me and reached for the door handle.

"Richie was arrested," I said, my voice even.

She froze.

Behind me, Olaya and the Blackbird Ladies drew in audible breaths. I knew it would be hard for them to hear the awful details, but I had no choice. "The police found a dead body in the backyard," I continued. "They think Richie did it."

As I spoke, Miguel seemed to understand what I was saying. What I'd realized. He moved as stealthy as a cat on the prowl, stalking its prey. Janice didn't seem to register his movement or presence. She stared at me, drawing her lips in until they disappeared, panic on her face, but she tried to pull off indignation. "My Richie? That is a mistake. He couldn't have done that!"

"Oh, but he did," I said. "And they think he killed Hank."

This time the Blackbird Ladies gasped in unison, each with their own expression of shock. I kept going, wanting to keep Janice off-balance. I recounted all that had happened since Miguel and I had arrived at what I now thought of as the Victorian murder house, holding nothing back.

"I need to go see him," she said, reaching again for the door handle. But Miguel was there, blocking the way. "Would you please move?" she asked, her voice terse. She said it more as a command than a request.

Miguel narrowed his eyes at her. "Don't think so," he said.

She tried to push past him, but he side-stepped, again blocking her.

"You," I said, blatant accusation in my voice. "You did this with him. You killed Hank. You killed the others. George. David. Collin —"

I broke off, suddenly remembering where I'd heard that name before. He'd been the handyman she said she'd wanted to refer to Alice. He'd moved away, she'd said. "You're a liar." My voice cracked with the realization that Richie hadn't worked alone. She'd known about all of it. She'd been part of it. "You're a killer."

Suddenly, as if they'd choreographed it, the Blackbird Ladies were on their feet.

They rushed toward Janice, circling around her. Through the window, an SUV pulled up to the curb. Emmaline stepped out from the driver's side and came around the front of the car. Richie was in custody. She had no reason to suspect anyone else, just like I hadn't. But she saw us through the window. In a matter of seconds, there was a shift in her posture, and I knew she was evaluating what she was seeing and making a determination on how to react.

She withdrew her gun from its holster, moved to the door, pulling it open. For the first time, I was glad the bell was broken. She edged in, her gun now clasped in both hands, held steady in front of her. "Janice Thompson," she said.

Janice whirled around to face Emmaline's gun. She balked, stumbling back, but the Blackbird Ladies were there, blocking her retreat. She tried to move around them, but Miguel was in her way. She headed in the other direction, but I moved to fill in the open space. She was closed in with no place to go.

"Why'd you do it, Janice?" I asked, confronting her. More than anything, I wanted her to confess. To admit to her friends what she had done to Mustache Hank and the other dead tenants. I suspected, and was fairly confident now, that the backyard of the Victorian was littered with the bodies of people she and her son had killed.

But where Richie had broken down, Janice was stony-faced and suddenly it hit me: Richie wasn't the mastermind behind their deeds. Janice hadn't been helping *him*. It was the other way around. Richie had been helping *her*.

Mrs. Branford confronted the woman she'd thought was her friend. "Why Hank?" Her voice trembled with a combination of rage and sorrow. "Why Hank, Janice?" she repeated.

It took Janice a moment, and her expression never melted into remorse, but she answered. "The damn garden. He and Bernard found —" She stopped, surely realizing that she had to measure her words. "They figured out —" she started, but then she stopped again and clamped her mouth shut, refusing to say any more.

She didn't need to. The blanks were easy to fill in. Hank had discovered something in the backyard. A body. A box. Something that revealed what Janice and Richie were doing. That explained why he wanted to get Mason out of there. The most likely reason he'd borrowed the money from Alice. He'd had no choice. He wanted to help his friend.

I wondered why Hank hadn't gone to the authorities, but then I remembered something Bernard had said. Hank had watched out for him. If Richie or Janice had threatened to hurt Bernard, Hank would have done anything to protect him. I'd learned enough about him to know he was that kind of man.

Another memory forced itself to the forefront of my mind. The first time I'd met Hank, he'd sat with the Blackbird Ladies at the bread shop. Janice had said something to him, and he'd looked away uncomfortably. I'd chalked it up to him not liking attention, but what if it was more than that? He had to already have known what the boarding house's backyard held, and if Janice was holding Bernard's safety over him until she could get ahold of the $50,000, which she surely knew about by then, then his reaction made sense. He was worried for Bernard and for himself.

Emmaline took over, forcing Janice away from the door, telling her to put both hands on the wall in front of her. Janice seemed to understand that she had nowhere to go, and even if she tried, she'd never outrun Emmaline. Or Miguel. Or me.

It took only a few seconds for Em to withdraw her handcuffs and shackle Janice's wrists. She read Janice her Miranda rights and hauled her away. She'd be held accountable for her crimes and for Mustache Hank's death.

CHAPTER 27

After a long night at the sheriff's station, I finally drove home. Miguel followed, once again wanting to make sure I didn't veer off the road from exhaustion or fall asleep at the wheel. I was worn out, and frankly, still in shock, and I knew he was, too.

The good news, if there could be a silver lining, was that Alice would get her money back; Bernard and Dixie — and any other tenants at the boarding house — would get the care and treatment they needed, and no one else would die.

"Ten victims over three years," Miguel said once we were both standing in my kitchen. He gave a low, disbelieving whistle. "I can't even get my head around that."

I couldn't, either. It hadn't taken long for Emmaline to turn Richie and Janice against each other. Before long, she'd pieced together the story. It had started by accident. A dead tenant. An uncashed Social Security check. And a plot had been born. Janice had cashed the check and no one was the wiser. They never reported the tenant as dead, so for all intents and purposes, she wasn't. The checks kept coming and Janice kept cashing them.

She directed Richie to take in people with no family, or those who were mentally ill. She took over their finances and reaped the monthly income, parceling out just what the tenants needed to live. And occasionally, when someone began to suspect what was going on, she killed. She was like Miss Hannigan from *Annie*, except instead of poor, unloved orphans, Janice Thompson and her son preyed on poor, unloved adults.

Poor Bernard had been the lackey, digging holes and burying boxes. "He knew on some level," I said to Miguel. He'd known, but had been powerless to stop it.

And then Hank figured it out. "Those flowers," Miguel said. "Hank's flowers."

Yes, Hank's flowers. Ultimately, it was Hank's flowers and the garden that led us to the truth.

A short while later, our conversation about the night was exhausted. I leaned back against the kitchen counter, arms folded. Miguel stood next to me, his hip against the counter. "Ivy," he said after a minute. "I need to know what happened."

I knew he wasn't talking about Hank or Janice or Richie or anything else from the present. He was referring to our history and to whatever he thought had happened between us.

I turned, mirroring him by leaning my hip against the counter and facing him. "There was never anybody but you."

"Laura heard . . . she saw . . ."

"It didn't happen."

He hesitated, and for the first time since he'd revealed what had driven him away, he looked unsure. "She gave me details."

I released a shaky breath. "You didn't trust me. You never *asked* me. You just left."

"She kept pushing and pushing," he said. "I believed her."

I looked up and into his eyes. "In her mind, I'd probably stolen her big brother away from her. She was, what? Thirteen? Fourteen? Whatever she told you, it wasn't true."

The muscles in his jaw tightened, moving with the tension. "It's festered all these years."

I knew the feeling. He'd driven away without a word. From that moment, what I'd thought my life would be had changed, and the unfinished relationship we'd been in had grown into some tragic myth for both of us.

"I loved you," I said.

He looked at me and I thought he was deciding if he believed this alternate reality, so different than what he'd believed all these years. Finally, he spoke. "We were kids back then, Ivy, and I was stupid for leaving. But we're all grown up now." His hands found my hips and he pulled me close, wrapping me up in his arms. "That wasn't our time."

My breath caught, his hands on me like bolts of lightning against my skin. His lips grazed mine, one of his hands leaving my hip and wending up my back, his fingers splaying through my hair. "Maybe this is," I said.

And then his hands left my body, settling instead on either side of my face. He tilted it up, gently, until I was looking into his eyes. "I know what I want," he said softly. "It's always been you."

Surely he could hear my heart beating, feel it nearly pounding out of my chest. "I don't want to get hurt. I don't want something temporary."

What I wanted were his arms around me, his lips on mine. "I'm all in, Ivy," he murmured.

In that moment, after so much death, I felt a ray of hope and I knew that once again what I thought my life would be had changed, this time for the better. I relaxed into him. I was all in, too.

ABOUT THE AUTHOR

The indefatigable **Winnie Archer** is a middle school teacher by day and a writer by night. Born in a beach town in California, she now lives in an inspiring century-old house in North Texas and loves being surrounded by real-life history. She fantasizes about spending summers writing in quaint, cozy locales, has a love/hate relationshiboth yoga and chocolate, adores pumpkin spice lattes, is devoted to her five kids and husband, and can't believe she's lucky enough to be living the life of her dreams. Visit her online at WinnieArcher .com.

DATE DUE

PRINTED IN U.S.A.